ACT OF TRUST

THE SECOND CHANCES SERIES
BOOK 2

by

Marsha R. West

ACT OF TRUST
THE SECOND CHANCES SERIES, BOOK 2
©2016 by Marsha R. West

Cover Art© by Charlotte Volnek

Edited by Joy Clintsman, Big Sister Edits LLC

Formatting by www.Top-ePublishingServices.com

Print and eBook version published by MRW Press LLC
Released January 2016.

ISBN for print version: 978-0-9961475-4-5

ISBN for eBook version: 978-0-9961475-3-8

ACKNOWLEDGEMENTS

The number of people it takes to bring a book to publication still amazes me. The small and large tweaks that happen with the passing of each new gaze upon the pages continually shape the manuscript. Many writer friends over the years have looked at my writing and given me feedback. Thanks to my daughter Laura West Strawser for the idea for the Second Chances Series.

Thanks to my editor Joy Clintsman, my cover artist Charlotte Volnek, and the wonderful folks at Top-ePublishing Services for formatting. I could not manage without them. Special thanks to my three Beta Readers for this book: Jane Sisolak, Kim Hightower, and Paula Whitmore. Thanks to Ken Hicks for help with a New York City hospital. Thanks to Susan H. Vaughn for helping with what flowers my heroine might smell in September in Maine.

While Margie Lawson hasn't looked at any of this book, what I learned from her led to publication of my first book and thus to this my fourth book. Thanks, Margie.

None of this would be possible without the support of my wonderful husband Bob West, who shares his time so generously to edit my books, talk plot points, and make suggestions to improve the story, not to mention helping with the business end of things.

Any errors, however, are my own. I hope you enjoy The Second Chances Series, Book 2.

AUTHOR'S PERSONAL NOTE

If you're of a certain age, 9/11 resonates with you in the way Pearl Harbor did with the Greatest Generation.

We all know where we were when the planes hit the towers. Many lost loved ones or acquaintances, and we all have our stories.

My younger daughter and her husband moved to New York City on Sunday 9/9. On Tuesday morning, September 11, as the principal in an elementary school, I'd arrived at my regular time, around 7:15 to get a jump-start on the day. My husband normally left later for his downtown high-rise to miss the traffic. He never went in that day after receiving a call from a good friend telling him to turn on the TV.

It was three that afternoon before I knew my daughter and her husband were okay. Trying to keep staff, kids, and parents calm in the face of what we didn't know took my focus. Parents flocked to the school to take their children home. Making sure students went with the right person took the full attention of my staff and me. I was one of the very lucky ones. My family was okay.

So ACT OF TRUST is a personal story to me. I admire those who've gone on after losing a loved one in this tragic experience. I can't imagine it, though, as a writer, that's my job. My intent was to honor their loss and commend their courage. I hope people find comfort in the happily ever after ending of this story.

I will send a portion of the sale of each book to the 9/11 Memorial Gardens and Museum. If you care to donate directly, as well, here's the link: http://www.911memorial.org/

CHAPTER ONE

Sunday, August 18

"Who do you know in Maine?" Kate Thompson's friend Devon Moore fanned the two legal size envelopes she held in her hands. They made a snapping sound, punctuating the quiet of the evening.

Kate glanced at her friend, who'd driven to Fort Worth from her home in Dallas, but she didn't respond.

"You haven't opened either one, Kate. The return label reads, James Donovan, Esq., Griffin Harbor, Maine. You keeping secrets, my friend?"

"Oh, foot. I've been busy with house showings and just forgot. I got one last week and then the other letter arrived today." She nibbled at a cuticle on her thumb.

"You realize the Esq. means he's a lawyer, right?" Devon said.

"You're going to make me open them, right?"

"Of course." Devon flipped the envelopes against her

thigh.

Kate's puff of frustration sounded louder than she'd intended. Dealing with a lawyer in a real estate transaction was one thing, but otherwise she'd prefer to keep her distance from lawyers. Red bloomed on her thumb where she'd picked at the cuticle on her left hand again. She grabbed a tissue to stop the bleeding.

She'd had enough of lawyers when settling her husband's affairs. Time to change the subject. "Where do you want to go for dinner?"

"Anything's fine with me. You or Addie pick. You know the places here in Fort Worth better than I do. Too bad Kim couldn't get away from Wichita Falls for a quick visit."

"She had a family obligation." Kate couldn't stop the grin from forming. "You know I'll pick Italian if it's up to me."

Devon handed over an envelope. "Open. You'll have to stop picking then."

Despite all the products from her make-up company Devon had given her over the years, Kate still picked at her cuticles.

"Okay, okay," she lowered the drop leaf on the hall desk and lifted out an old letter opener handed down from her grandfather. She slid the long silver blade across the edge of the envelope, the ripping sound grating on her ears. Then she pulled out the one page missive and scanned the words. "Oh, my goodness."

"What's the matter?"

"John's Aunt Liddy died."

"I don't remember he had an aunt. Wait, do I hear a car?" Devon turned toward the front window and separated the edges of the drapes. "Addie's pulling into the driveway." A quick honk confirmed her words. "Bring those with you. We'll talk more at dinner."

Kate didn't know if there was anything to talk about, but she pushed the envelopes inside a purse large enough to carry her laptop when she needed to work away from the house or office. Tonight she left the computer at home. The lightness of the bag fit her mood because she and two of her best friends were having dinner together.

Addie drove them to a restaurant, serving Italian only three nights a week. Their favorite Italian restaurant had closed, but the people who owned that place also owned this German spot, so the two restaurants in effect merged.

"Does this seem odd to you?" Placing her napkin in her lap, Devon glanced around at the Bavarian decor, waiters in lederhosen and waitresses with round-necked puffed sleeve, white blouses.

"Yeah, but I want to be supportive of the Rudolfo family." Addie said. She sipped her Sauvignon Blanc. "Tell me more about this business with the Maine lawyer, Kate."

Drat Devon for bringing up the issue on the ride to the restaurant. Kate reluctantly pulled the letters from her purse, her fingers trembling ever so slightly. John's aunt had stopped sending Christmas cards, which had been their main way of communicating.

"Liddy must've been in her 90's. She had a nice long life. Right after John and I got engaged, he took me to Griffin Harbor. I recall the location being the back of beyond. I flew from Fort Worth. He met me in Boston, and still we had an all-afternoon-drive. The house sat on a ridge of land overlooking a waterway. I don't recall which one now, but it ran into the Atlantic and had a lovely view. No other houses around made it God awful remote." She shivered.

"I'm sorry for your loss, Kate." Addie reached across and squeezed Kate's hand. Kate squeezed back.

"Doesn't sound like a place I'd like to be." Devon agreed.

Kate smiled at her gorgeous redheaded friend. The consummate city girl drew attention anywhere she went. When they were teenagers at camp, Devon was the only one of the four of them to wear make-up. Camp wasn't her favorite place, but both her parents worked and needed to safely stash her away. They'd gone to college with the owners and knew she'd be okay there.

Addie hadn't been wild about the place either. She

returned each summer to be with her three friends. The outdoors stuff challenged her, but she loved the skits. Not surprising Addie had gone into theatre.

"I don't know, Devon." Addie sipped her clear white wine. "Maine is a beautiful state. I made a quick visit there when I was in New York before marrying the kids' father."

Kate's middle clenched with memories of the mess Addie had gone through with her first husband. How he'd nearly destroyed their daughter. The new gold band sparkling on the ring finger of Addie's left hand a testament to how people got a happily ever after.

Not for Kate though. Or rather, she'd already experienced her happily ever after. The *ever after* part had just been very short and ended in grisly abruptness.

"Have you ladies decided what you'd like to have this evening? Would you like me to repeat the specials?" The young server smiled at the three women.

Kate shook off her malaise and straightened in her chair. "I'll have the spinach cannelloni and the house salad."

"Do you want separate checks?"

"Please," Devon spoke before the others.

Kate cut her gaze toward her always perfectly put together friend. Frequently they asked for one check and split the cost between them, not worrying who paid more than their fair share. In the long run, they figured it worked out. This was the third time in recent months Devon had asked for separate checks.

She hadn't ordered her usual champagne, settling for the house Sauvignon Blanc that Addie drank. Devon's cosmetics company was successful and had been from the beginning. Her husband handled all of the company's accounting as well as running his own CPA firm. She couldn't be having financial problems, could she? No, but something odd was going on.

The server moved off after promising to bring their salads soon. Apparently, the other two women had ordered while Kate woolgathered.

"Well, the lawyer was kind to let you know about John's aunt." Devon dipped her piece of bread into the seasoned oil in the center of the table.

Kate sipped her Merlot then set down the glass. "Guess I'd better read the rest of the letter." She lifted the most recent envelope from her purse, removed the sheet, and read. Sounds from the other dinners and wait staff swirled around the words. She dropped the letter on the table and looked at Addie and then Devon. "Aunt Liddy left the old house and surrounding land to me."

"Oh, fun. A cabin in the Maine woods." Devon's eyebrows shot up and her eyes rolled to match the sarcastic tone in her voice.

Kate suppressed a chuckle at her friend's reaction. Clearly not an inheritance Devon would appreciate.

The waiter set their salads before them, and Kate picked up her fork and dug in. "Hmm. Scrumptious." This land business had nothing to do with her.

"When are you going to go look?" Addie doused her salad in pepper before she pulled off a piece of bread from the loaf in the center of the table. "Maybe one of us can arrange to go with you." She glanced at Devon who shrugged.

Kate dropped her fork, coughing on a bite of tangy tomato. Finally, she found her voice. "I don't have to look at the property again. I'm going to sell. It's out in the boonies. The house wasn't in good shape when John and I went there all those years ago. It must be a wreck now." She lifted her fork. "Let's focus on our meal and enjoy our salads. Tell us how rehearsals are going, Addie."

Kate sighed with relief when the discussion moved to Addie's challenges with the current show. No point continuing the discussion about the old house. An old house in Maine.

They finished their salads before the server approached and placed their orders at each plate. "Can I get you anything else?" He smiled at each of the women in turn, as if he wanted to pay tribute to their beauty. Addie, a longhaired brunette, Devon, a redhead and when Kim, also brunette but with a shorter style, joined them, they'd been known to turn heads.

Each was striking in her own way, but Kate always considered herself the lesser of the lights she hung with. Her dishwater blonde hair and brown eyes faded in comparison to her friends' more dramatic looks.

"Oh, bring more of this yummy bread, please." Devon spoke before the others. "I like this odd little place. We can't come often, though this yummy bread is going right to my hips." They all laughed.

Kate cut off a small bite of her steaming pasta stuffed with spinach and three types of cheese then blew a couple of times before putting the fork in her mouth. Bubbling cheese scalding the roof of your mouth was the worst and spoiled your enjoyment of the rest of meal. Unfortunately, she'd done that several times before learning her lesson.

"You know, Kate, you haven't taken any kind of a vacation since you lost your parents. Maybe this would be a good opportunity." Addie paused to sip her wine. "I know you don't like to fly, but how about we give you a couple of pills to knock you out. You'd be there before you know it."

"What?" Kate frowned at Addie. Had she gone back to the idea of Kate going to Maine? What in the world was her friend thinking? Kate's breathing hitched at the mere idea of getting on a plane.

"But if that's not an option, what about driving up there?" Addie continued, ignoring Kate's outburst. "Take a couple of weeks and drive for four or five hours a day and then stop. Check out the local historical sites and eat at places the locals say are awesome. You'd see beautiful scenery, learn interesting tidbits, and eat great seafood."

"Well, I—"

"You may not want to hear this, Kate, but Addie's right." Devon stopped eating and leaned across the table. "While I'm not at all sure you need a house in the woods of Maine, I am sure you need a break. You've worked constantly since you moved back to Fort Worth after John's death. Except for our get-togethers, have you made any big trips?"

"No, but I was busy working, raising Blair, and later taking care of Mom and Dad, which didn't leave much time for fun and games."

"That's our point, hon." Addie squeezed Kate's hand again. "You need a little, to use your phrase, fun and games in your life. At least consider the possibility, okay?"

* * * *

Monday, August 26

Kate dragged up the stairs to her house after her brisk morning walk. Her feet and calf muscles burned. She'd gone farther than her usual three miles, making up for a large supper the night before. Her hand trembled with the effort to unlock the door. Sweat dripped from every pore. Catching her breath was a challenge. She stepped into the living room and the jangling noise of the landline from the kitchen greeted her. Would she be able to get there before the answering machine kicked in? Be okay if she didn't. Talking with anyone would require more energy than she had right now. The heat always did a number on her. She picked up the phone.

"Hello." Kate grabbed a kitchen towel to blot the sweat from her face.

"Ms. Thompson?"

"Yes?" August in Texas. Mind searing heat. A friend suggested going to walk in the mall. She needed to consider the idea.

"Ms. Thompson, my name is Jim Donovan."

Kate stuck a glass under the appropriate spouts on her refrigerator, desperate for ice water. She found the clinking sounds themselves comforting. Why'd the name sound familiar? She swallowed a couple of gulps of the cooling liquid.

"Ms. Thompson, are you still there?"

The person spoke with a deep voice and something of what she'd call a Yankee accent.

"Yes, sorry. Got in from a long walk and I'm winded. What's your name again and why are you calling?" Kate snapped off a dry leaf from the violet sitting in the window. Past time to water the plants. She leaned against the kitchen counter, giving her trembling legs a break.

"Ms. Thompson, I'm Jim Donovan. Did you get my letters telling you about the death of your aunt Liddy Oliver Thompson? I'm executor of Liddy's will."

Oh, that Jim Donovan. He sounded impatient.

"Yes, I got the letters. Mr. Donovan. I mailed a response. I assume you haven't received anything from me, yet." She dipped her finger into the ice water and trailed it across her forehead, her heart rate slowing.

"No, I haven't received your letter. Can you tell me when you're coming up here to claim the property?"

"I'm not coming up there, Mr. Donovan. I'm going to sell the property to the highest bidder. I can't imagine its being worth much, but I don't need or want to own property in Maine."

"Your aunt's house, your house, sits on a valuable strip of land, Ms. Thompson."

"Can you recommend a good real estate agent? I'm not licensed in Maine or I'd handle the process myself."

"Ms. Thompson, I represented Liddy for many years and especially where this property was concerned. She didn't want the property to fall into the hands of a developer, especially one with a history of concreting over our beautiful Maine forests."

His tone indicated what he'd like to do to one of those developers, and it wasn't pretty. Well, not her problem. "I'm sorry. I'm not interested. If you can't recommend an agent, I'll find one myself. I need to let you go now, or I'm going to be late to work. Thanks for getting in touch." Kate hung up the receiver and let out a long breath.

Goodness, but the man was persistent. She'd talk with Pam and Jerry at work. They'd have ideas of someone to represent her interests, her interests, which didn't include owning a piece of Maine.

* * * *

"Damned, Texan." Jim Donovan resisted the urge to throw his cell across the room. "Aren't they supposed to be big on land down there?"

A quick knock and then Tom Jenson stuck his head around the door before he stepped into the room Jim used for a home office when he was in Griffin Harbor.

"Is that a sack of muffins from the Center Café in your hand?"

"Ahyah." A big smile spread across Tom's wrinkled face.

"Well, get in here then. I'll trade you a cup of coffee." Jim rose and strode to the sideboard where he kept a pot on all day long. "Did you bring one of those carrot muffins?"

"Of course." Tom pulled out a napkin and laid the cake-like pastry on it. "What has you so bent out of shape? Just now, your voice coming through the door sounded like you'd like to beat someone over the head." He slouched into the chair in front of the desk.

"Liddy Thompson's niece wants to sell the family land." Jim set a cup of coffee in front of his friend then ran a hand through his hair overdue for a cut. He'd considered yanking it back and wrapping a leather cord around, but that wasn't his style. Guess it was time he got to the barbershop.

"Not to the Conservancy, I take it."

"No she specifically said the highest bidder, and that won't be the Maine Coast Conservancy Trust."

"That's lousy. Hard to find a prettier view than Liddy's. What have you done to convince the niece to change her mind?"

"Sent two letters. When I never heard from her, I called."

"And?"

"She was adamant she's selling. Said the house was too far out in the," Jim finger quoted, "the *boonies* is the word I believe she used."

"Well, it's not in town, but it's not out in the wilds either. Sounds like she doesn't know what she's talking about." Tom sipped his coffee.

"The woman asked if I'd recommend a real estate agent." Jim slumped into the chair behind his desk and proceeded to crumble the muffin into pieces. "As if I'd do anything to help her sell. Liddy loved the land. I've got to find a way to get through to the niece."

Tom glanced at his watch swallowed the last half of his muffin. "Well, I gotta get outa here. Need to check on the catch of the day. I'm sure you'll come up with something. You usually get what you want."

"Not always." He hadn't been able to stop his ex from giving the chunk of Donovan land she'd received in the divorce to the developer she'd had an affair with. The damn developer who'd plowed up the trees and made a parking lot for his condo units. Jim's stomach churned at how he'd let down his family. Oh, they still had considerable property but nothing with the incredible timber the jerk had destroyed.

He glanced at Tom. "You ever miss those early morning trips checking your lobster traps?"

"What?" Tom swallowed the last of the coffee, washing down the muffin. "Nah. Why would I miss such back-breaking hard work, freezing my balls off?" He headed toward the door, then paused and looked over his shoulder. "Sometimes. Crazy, huh? See you later."

Had his friend since birth found solace in running his family's restaurant, The Lobster Pot? Everyone said it was one of the best in Maine. After the injury he'd received in the bar fight with a lobsterman from another town who got drunk and assaulted one of the diners—well, he had to be glad he was able to get around without using a cane or limping.

Jim dusted the crumbs from his fingers into a napkin and threw it into the trash. Now he had to figure out what to do about Katherine Thompson. Tom had faith he'd pull out a solution. He damn sure wasn't letting the woman sell Liddy's land to Ray Holland Development. At least not without a hell of a fight.

* * * *

Monday, September 2

Blair Thompson's cell chirped the distinctive sound she'd selected for her mother. Blair worried about her more than she liked to let on. One of the reasons she'd set up the separate sound. Blair didn't want to take a chance on missing a call from her.

"Hey, Mom."

"Happy Labor Day, Blair." Her mother's soft Texas twang came through in a nice reminder of what she'd once considered home. Blair had lived most of her life in Fort Worth, but she'd been born in New York City, and now the Big Apple was more home to her than Fort Worth. Probably best not to share that with her mother, who'd never gotten past the tragic events of 9/11.

"How are you celebrating? Lying around reading a good book?" Her mother shared Blair's love of reading and for them there was no better way to spend a holiday.

"No. While everyone at work has the day off, most of us aren't taking it. There's still much to be done before the memorial service on the 11th, and we also are continuing to push on the preparations for the opening of the museum."

Blair paused giving her mother a chance to deal with the emotions her words would dredge up. Generally, she tried to avoid talking about her job. Awkward, but less painful for her mother. "What are you doing today, Mom?"

"I'm working. We're having specials for Labor Day. I'm holding two open houses. I finally convinced the owners to lower the asking price. We sure weren't having any luck with the numbers they wanted."

Her voice had squeaked at the beginning but grew stronger as she talked about her work, which she loved. "I'm going to Addie's for a barbeque cookout later on."

"Should be fun. I love her husband's small ranch. I'll probably take a minute to grab a hot dog from one of the street vendors and then crash early with that book you mentioned."

Laughter twinkled across the airways. Everyone said what a contagious laugh her mother had. They also said no one heard it enough. Blair clamped her fingers around her cell, and drew in a deep breath before plunging in. "I want you to think about coming up for the memorial service, Mom. It would mean a lot to me for you to be here."

Silence greeted Blair's request. Not surprising. The trip they made when she'd been seventeen nearly destroyed her mother. She'd returned to visiting her counselor for a time afterwards.

"I won't say no right now, Blair."

"Thanks." That was better than usual when her mother out and out refused. Blair sighed. She'd lost her father. Her mother lost her husband. And in a way, Blair lost her mother, too. She was never the fun loving, willing-to-try-anything parent she'd been before. Everyone had to deal with that dreadful loss the best way he or she could in whatever time possible. She sighed. "Good luck with your houses, Mom, and eat some barbecue for me."

"Thanks, sweetie. You can count on that."

Blair disconnected and prayed again for something or someone to blast her mother out of the cocoon of work in which she'd wrapped herself.

* * * *

Tuesday, September 3

Kate parked in the garage, entered the kitchen, and straightaway kicked off her heels. Only a bit after four in the afternoon, but she made straight for the wine rack. Definitely time to celebrate. The 1.5 million dollar sale had closed at long last. She'd almost given up on finding a buyer. She filled her glass with Merlot, and tipped it for a long slow sip. Ah, yes, she'd earned her money on this one. She raised her glass and the sun streaming in the kitchen window heightened the ruby glow. Another swallow slid down her throat like silk, followed by a sigh.

The family selling the house consisted of two sisters and a brother. None had ever married, and none of them had any kids. They'd finally found a retirement home fancy enough to please them. Kate swore they were all nuts, but she got their house sold. She wandered into the living room and sank into her favorite chair, propping her feet on the small ottoman.

The Labor Day holiday had been fun with a cookout at Mike and Addie's ranch. His brother, sister-in-law and their kids, both of Addie's kids, several of her friends from the theatre, and Mike's friends from the Fort Worth Police Department rounded out the crew. They barbecued brisket and corn on the cob. Kate and a couple of other folks provided salad. Addie had baked two chocolate sheath cakes that everyone swore were sinfully delicious and thoroughly devoured.

The deep bonging of the doorbell startled her, making her slosh her wine. She jumped from the chair and peeked through the side window. A tall man she didn't recognize stood on the front porch. One hand was in the pocket of his sport jacket. She gulped convulsively. Damn, she should've put the alarm system back on, which she normally did as soon as she entered her house.

Her fingers fumbled at the numbers and before she finally got it set, the chime sounded again.

Feeling safe with the alarm on, Kate drew in a quick breath before speaking. "Who is it?" She hated the timidity she heard in her tone.

"My name is Jim Donovan. I'd like to talk to Katherine Thompson." The deep voice with a Yankee accent she recognized from the phone rumbled through the door.

"Are you the lawyer from Maine?" Why in the world would he come down here?

"Yes."

Kate shut off the alarm and swung open the door, and her thoughts jumped straight from her brain and out her mouth. "What are you doing here?"

"So much for that Texas hospitality I've always heard about." He held a briefcase in one hand.

"I'm sorry. You've taken me by surprise. Come in." She stepped back for him to enter and headed for the living room in bare feet, wishing for her shoes. The Yankee was tall. Over six feet, and her five feet four inches, which technically was average, seemed dreadfully short. "Can I offer you something? Normally, I wouldn't have a drink this early, but I'm celebrating a big closing." She sipped and then self-consciously set the glass on the coffee table and settled on the sofa. She waved her hand toward the large leather chair. What was the matter with her, babbling? She didn't owe him any explanations.

"Congratulations." He sat in the chair, setting the case at his feet.

His tone implied he didn't mean it. What was his deal anyway?

"Did you sell land for a strip shopping center?"

His emphasis on the word "strip" made Kate uncomfortable. She rose and clasped her hands in front of her. "You know, I don't believe we have anything to say to one another."

Donovan stood also. "I'm sorry." He raised his hands in a stopping motion. "Let's start again. I apologize. I've had a long day. Delays at airports," he spit through gritted teeth. "I planned to get here much earlier."

"All right, Mr. Donovan. I accept your apology, but I still don't believe we have anything to say to each other." She sat down again, and after a moment, he settled back on the chair.

He reached into his case and drew out a laptop. "I won't say anything. Let me show you a few pictures instead."

"Pictures of what?"

"Your aunt's property. May I?" He rose and gestured to the place next to her on the sofa.

Kate nodded. When he sat next to her, she caught a

pleasant aroma. Despite his being a captive in an airplane all day—she managed not to cringe at the idea—he brought to mind the outdoors and forests. Unexpected and odd she'd noticed.

Donovan flipped open the laptop and then touched the screen a couple of times. "Look at these. I only need you to give me a few minutes."

She sat silently while he flipped through pictures of forests, fields, and several amazing vistas, which looked out over vast expanses of water.

"These were all taken on your Aunt Liddy's land."

"Actually she was my late husband's aunt."

"You were family to her." Kate didn't miss the hint of censure in his voice.

"I can't deny the pictures are beautiful, Mr. Donovan, but I'm a city gal who has no interest in your northeastern woods."

"There are several small towns nearby."

"What's nearby? And how small is small?"

"Oh, ten to fifteen minutes. And about 2500 excluding the tourist season, when we grow to over 5000."

"I didn't notice any other houses nearby in these pictures of Aunt Liddy's."

"None right next door. Liddy's house sits on the crest of a hill overlooking the mouth of the Damariscotta River. The nearest house is a mile in either direction."

"Well, Mr. Donovan. I grant you the views are amazing, but I don't want the land. I want to sell."

"Listen, Ms. Thompson—Kate—that's how Liddy spoke of you. The land was important to her. It is to me, but not to everyone. A group of us, including your aunt set up a conservancy."

"What is that, Mr. Donovan?"

"Our website explains that we're *an organization dedicated to the conservation of wildlife and wildlife habitats along the Central Coast of Maine*. We're nongovernmental and non-profit. There are several in our state and other states as well as around the world."

"That's lovely, but what does it have to do with me?" Her fingers tapped on the arm of the sofa.

"Our conservancy is called the Maine Coast Conservancy Trust. Many people don't value the land the way we do. Your aunt wouldn't want one of the unscrupulous companies to be able to concrete over it all with condos or worse, hotels."

"Mr. Donovan, I appreciate your sentiments, but there's no reason for me to own land in Maine."

Donovan rose and paced back in forth in front of her. Kate reached for her wine and the short gulp resulted in a coughing fit. The energy radiating off the man made her nervous. After all, what did she really know about him? He claimed to be Aunt Liddy's lawyer, but did she know that? She'd been stupid to let him in without checking any identification. She must've taken leave of her senses.

He jerked around and crossed toward her, his lips clamped in a straight line. "Come with me to look at it."

"What?" Kate leaned away from him. His intensity bombarded her, making her feel like a wave on the beach had caught her up and was about to smash her against the bottom. He must be nuts. The beginning of her victim's flush crawled up her neck.

"Come with me to look at Liddy's property."

"I don't fly, Mr. Donovan." Her hands clenched at the mere idea.

"I know, Kate. Liddy told me how you lost your husband, her nephew. There are no words to express how sorry I am for you. I can't begin to imagine how difficult that had to be. I do know how hard it hit Liddy." He paused, then in two steps was next to her on the sofa. He sank down so close his leg brushed hers. His large hand folded over hers resting in her lap.

Her heart jerked at his touch. Was the man crazy? By now, the flush had grown to full-blown across her cheeks. She was helpless to stop it. Her heart beat at an ever-increasing rate.

"This land has been in John's family for generations.

Wouldn't he want it to stay that way?"

Her eyes filled with moisture. Damn if she'd cry in front of this man. She blinked several times and dug for composure. "How dare you?" She yanked her hand away and leapt from the sofa. Distance from Jim Donovan a must. "You presume to know what my husband would or wouldn't want?" The words tumbled out vibrating with the pain rising from her middle. Despite many years of counseling, the devastating events of September 11, 2001 still clamped her in a vice.

Her husband's voice on the phone came through loud and clear in her head, when he told her how much he loved her. When he told her how much he loved Blair. When he told her, he hoped she'd get on with her life without him. "Ahhhh." She folded in on herself, sinking to the floor with loss engulfing her, shocking her in its intensity. The pain hadn't hit her like this in many years.

"Ah, Kate. I'm sorry." He knelt. His arms came around her, and he rocked her back and forth, as if she were a child. "I'm sorry I hurt you, but I have to get you to come to Maine. We can't let Ray Holland get his hands on those acres."

Finally the sobs stopped. Only small little gasps racked her body.

"Don't you owe John? Owe Aunt Liddy to at least come look at the land before you decide to sell?"

Donovan was relentless, wiping out all opposition in his

path, regardless of whom he hurt in the process. Kate pushed herself to stand. His arms still held her, supporting with a surprisingly tender touch. When was the last time a man had held her this way? Other than her father? Over fourteen years.

He brushed a tear from her cheek. "Kate, sleep on this. I'll give you some time, and then we'll talk more."

* * * *

Wednesday, September 4

"Thanks for coming over, Addie. I hated to bother you, but I had to talk with you." Kate paced her living room about the same place her visitor Jim Donovan had yesterday.

"You're never a bother. Kate. You know that. I have about twenty minutes before I have to get back to the theatre." Addie wore her usual rehearsal clothes, dark tights with a turquoise skirt thrown over her leotard.

"Gosh you've started on your next show. Sorry. I forgot. You don't have to stay."

"No, you've offered me a glass of wine. I'll take one and thank you." Addie sank gracefully onto the sofa. "Mike was supposed to take me out to lunch during the rehearsal break, but he got called into work, so I'm yours."

"The news carried a breaking story about a shooting behind a high school." Kate got a bottle from the wine fridge and poured Addie a glass.

"Pretty certain that was it. Don't know when he'll be home."

"How do you handle the uncertainty, Addie? Don't you just about go nuts?" She set Addie's Sauvignon Blanc on the coffee table. "I mean he goes out and then maybe doesn't come back." Kate filled her own glass with her favorite Merlot. Her finger circled the top of the glass, stopping just before it sang.

"True, anything is possible. The reality for the most part is the homicide detective is there after the danger is over, unlike beat cops who get caught in tight spots all the time."

"I don't know how you deal with the fear." Kate drank a large gulp from her glass.

Addie's raised eyebrows and the cock of her head caught Kate's attention and she put down the glass.

"So what's going on with you? You seem hyped up—like you'd taken one of those diet pills we used to pop when we were young and not terribly smart."

"Jim Donovan came to the house yesterday." She raised the glass again for another sip of wine, but this one more controlled.

Addie's eyebrows drew together clearly confused by the direction of Kate's words. Then the blank look cleared. "Oh. The Maine lawyer? He showed up here?" She leaned back, one long leg over the other in a gentle swing.

Kate nodded, afraid to say much and give a clue about her odd reaction to the man.

"Well he's persistent, isn't he?"

Again, all Kate managed was a nod. This wasn't going to work. At some point, she had to give voice to her fears. If she couldn't tell Addie, who then? "He asked me to go up there and look at the property. Told me I owed it to John."

"Oh, my dear." Addie set her glass on the table, scooted next to Kate, and slipped an arm around her shoulder. "He's more than persistent. He's brutal."

"I told him I don't fly. He said Liddy told him."

"So he knows about John."

It was a statement, but Kate nodded.

"Well, hon, what would be so bad about taking a look at the property?" She picked up her glass and sipped her wine. "Then you'd feel like you were honoring John's family. My artistic director is down with the flu, so I'm handling rehearsals or I'd go with you. Maybe Devon or Kim can get away."

"But I don't want him to come here again." Kate swallowed another large gulp of wine, which brought on a coughing fit.

Again, Addie cocked her head the way a puppy does when it can't figure out his master. "I don't understand."

"He made me feel…" Kate couldn't stop her voice from trembling.

"How did he make you feel, sweetie?"

"He made me *feel*. He put his arms around me and rocked me. He made me feel...cherished." Then despite her best efforts, the tears spilled over and ran down her cheeks.

Addie pulled Kate into her arms. "Oh, sweetie. That's the place we've all hoped for you to reach. All the men we've introduced you to over the years only to have you shut them off after the first or second date. You've been frozen in time, raising Blair, selling houses, caring for and burying your parents, but never moving on past the tragedy of 9/11."

Finally, Kate got herself together and pulled a tissue from a box sitting on the end table. She blew her nose and finished her wine, then rose. "You want a refill?"

"Better not. I won't know stage right from stage left. Makes giving directions tough." She glanced at her watch. "Sweetie, I hate to leave you like this, but I have to get back."

"Bong. Bong."

"I'll always be glad you let me record that. It's been great for several shows."

Unexpectedly, Kate laughed. "I'm sure there aren't many people who have friends who've recorded their door chime."

"*Bong. Bong."*

Addie joined her laughter to Kate's. "Well, I've got to leave, and you need to check on whoever's sitting on your wonderful doorbell."

Kate peeked out the side window. "Oh, dear."

"What's the matter? Someone with a gun?"

Addie's overly dramatic question brought a smile to Kate's face. "No. It's Jim Donovan."

"Great. Open the door. I want to meet him."

"*Bong.*"

Kate jerked open the door. "Hello."

"Thank God. I was afraid you weren't home. When no one answered I feared your office must've been mistaken."

"Well, you found me." She pushed her hair off her face. No telling what she looked like after the crying jag. Odd, she never considered her appearance, especially not in connection to a man.

"I'm Kate's friend, Addie, and I understand you want her to go to Maine to look at a piece of property."

"That's right." His eyebrows drew down. "I know she doesn't fly. My solution to that problem is to suggest we drive up there."

Addie smiled. "What a super idea." She hugged Kate who couldn't put two words together. What was the matter with her best friend? Had she gone in with the enemy?

The man had the audacity to shake hands with Addie as if they were collaborators, taking her hand in both of his.

"Anything you can say to convince her, I'd appreciate.

The Maine Coast Conservancy Trust would also."

Addie looked him up and down. After a moment, she nodded. "Good luck, Mr. Donovan. I wish you well then with blasting our girl out of her comfort zone." She turned to Kate. "Love you. Listen to what the man has to say. I'm off." Addie slipped by Donovan and down the stairs to her car.

Kate shifted from one foot to the other as Addie drove away. What was she thinking to desert her that way?

"May I come in, Kate?"

She let out a long sigh. She'd get through this somehow. "Come in, Mr. Donovan."

"Call me Jim, please."

CHAPTER TWO

Sunday, September 8

All of his life people had told him "stubborn" must be his middle name. He preferred to use the term "persistent" to describe himself. When he saw something he wanted, he went after it. He wanted Kate Thompson to hand over the Thompson family land to the Maine Coast Conservancy Trust. He wanted to protect that gorgeous property for generations of future people to enjoy and to find solace in.

In addition, much to his amazement, he found he wanted Kate for herself. He cast a glance in her direction, a shapely blonde with medium length, thick hair. Hair that made a man want to run his hands through the strands. Her soulful brown eyes, like those of an abused puppy, made a man want to pull her into his arms and hold her close. When he'd done that on Wednesday, something bubbled up in the vicinity of his heart. The one people said he didn't have. He ached for what Kate had experienced.

Jim clenched his hands on the steering wheel, fighting that intense desire she aroused. They'd left Fort Worth two mornings ago. While he'd never doubted he'd win her over, still surprise and anticipation hit Jim in the gut when late Thursday afternoon Kate agreed to drive with him to Maine. Now, more than halfway through the trip, she hadn't been forthcoming.

Maybe he'd draw her out when they ate lunch. "I'm getting hungry. About time we stop. What would you like?"

"Anything is fine."

She seemed to be afraid to express any desire for what she wanted because then she set herself up for pain and loss if it fell through. Huh. That was exactly what this was. Jim determined he'd get her past that. His secret weapon was Liddy's gorgeous land, now Kate's. She wouldn't be able to resist its beauty.

They'd stayed in the Suites Hotels both nights and gotten on the road early, grabbing a bite of the complimentary breakfast His stomach growling had reminded him to leave I-95 and head for the coast and the small diner in Branford, Connecticut he wanted to share with Kate. She'd love the quaintness.

He pulled into an open space along the street down from the restaurant. The aroma of wood smoking, beer, and seafood greeted them. A waitperson settled them at a table, wrote their orders, and with little delay she served the generous portions.

"How're you doing, Kate? You've been pretty quiet." He bit into the crab burger garnished with spicy tartar sauce. Other than lobster, this was his favorite meal.

"I'm still befuddled to find myself on a trip with a man I've known for only a few days." A rueful grin tugged at the corner of her mouth.

Jim hadn't seen that barely-there-smile often. Warmth grew in his gut, making him want to see the smile more. "What was the turning point? What tipped the scale in favor of this trip?" He didn't say in favor of him, better to stay impersonal, fearing to scare her.

"All my friends and my daughter Blair ganged up on me. Addie's husband checked you out. Blair used her non-profit contacts to check out the Maine Coast Conservancy Trust. She said everyone on the Conservancy Trust board had contributed lands and served without pay. I was impressed, so you passed their inspections."

"I'll be sure to thank your friends and daughter."

"The deciding factor was the opportunity to visit with Blair. She has a hard time getting away from her work, especially this time of year."

Damn. Her voice sounded tight. She swallowed a few extra times. Grabbed her glass of iced tea, he'd learned she was seldom without. She glanced up at him and then out the window that provided a beautiful beach scene with the waves lapping gently on the sand. If they had time, he'd drag her out to walk there, but they didn't, not if he wanted to get her to the Maine coast as soon as possible. Once she saw it, she'd fall in love and understand what he and her Aunt Liddy felt about the land.

"She works in the PR department of the 9/11 Museum." Kate volunteered.

"Good for her. You must be proud of her."

"Proud of her? Absolutely, but I don't know how she does that. How can she work every day with the constant reminder of how her father died?" Her finger worried a cuticle. She stopped but then returned to the task.

"Maybe she feels closer to him there."

She leaned back in her chair. Her other hand twirled the tea glass around and around on its coaster. "That's perceptive of you because that's what she's told me."

Kate scooted forward and sipped the iced tea in which she'd put an excessive number of lemon wedges. "Blair can't come home for Thanksgiving, and I haven't seen her since last December. I figure after I check out the land, I can rent a car or take the train to NYC."

"That will work." They ate in silence for a while.

"Thanks." Kate bit into the burger she'd ordered.

He'd noticed she ate a lot of beef. That and pasta. Not that her eating habits affected her figure because the day at her house when he'd held her, he found her to be fit and trim. "Sure. What for?"

"For forcing me to come. I couldn't have made the trip by myself, and I wouldn't want to impose on my friends to get them to drive with me. I'm excited about the opportunity to see Blair."

Jim nodded, and inhaled a few more French-fries. "How are you managing to leave your real estate business?"

"Jerry and Pam Baker have been friends for years. I worked for them before John and I married, and I moved to NYC. When I returned, they let me come back to the company. They're making sure my clients are covered. And many issues can be handled on-line and with my cell."

"What did Addie mean when she said you haven't been anywhere but what she called your girls' trips?"

The smile he loved spread across her face. "Addie and Devon and Kim, who you haven't met, and I connected at summer camp. We've been best buds ever since that year after second grade. We're there for each other through whatever. Do you have friends like that?"

Kate never used his name. Jim wanted to hear her say his name. She'd stopped calling him Mr. Donovan the third day they'd talked, but she still hesitated to use his name. What was that about?

"Yes. I'm lucky. One person I've known since before we were born."

She raised her eyebrows at his statement.

"My best friend Tom's mother and my mother were pregnant at the same time. Our families were close, so, we've always known each other. Then there's my older brother, an architect, and his family who live in Boston. We get together pretty often."

"Is Tom also a lawyer?"

"No, he isn't. Tom owns one of the best restaurants in Maine, The Lobster Pot. We'll get a couple of meals there, I can promise."

"Do they have anything besides lobster?"

"Well, yeah, but why would you need anything else?"

"I've never actually eaten lobster."

"What?" He pushed back his empty plate. "How is that possible?"

"I don't like the way the thing looks?" She glanced at him from under her eyelashes, as if she were embarrassed to tell him.

"What the hell! We'll have to do something about that."

"No, please, leave me be." Her hands rose to ward off the sea creature.

"We'll see. If you're finished, we need to get back on

the road." He held her chair and she rose.

"I need to use the restroom before we head out again. I've learned you don't stop often."

"Good God, woman. If you need or want to stop, sing out. We don't have a schedule."

She nodded and scooted back to the rear of the restaurant. Why doesn't she ask for what she needs? He couldn't imagine what she'd gone through after 9/11. Maybe after such a traumatic loss you never expected to get anything for yourself again. Jim finished his business and waited for her at the front door. When she appeared, his hand settled quite naturally at the small of her back to usher toward the car. Clearly, he was losing it with this complicated woman who didn't like lobster. He couldn't wait to get her up to Maine. His state would win her over, even if his words couldn't.

* * * *

Monday, September 9

"Oh, my goodness. Of course, it's been many years, but the cottage doesn't look at all the way I remembered."

He ushered her through the front door then stepped aside, letting her get the full effect of the view through the wall of windows. A grin spread across Jim's face, which must match the one on hers that she couldn't stop if she'd wanted to. "Amazing!"

"Liddy had the cottage redone about eight years ago when she decided to move in to town. A caretaker looks after the property whether someone is staying here or not. She leased it out for a pretty good income."

"But who wants to come? There is nothing else near."

"People come for the hiking, kayaking and fishing. Hunting and snowshoeing in the winter are big draws. And this view."

She stared at him. None of those things held the slightest interest to her. In fairness, she admitted the view was something else. "Where are the closest neighbors?"

"A little more than a ten minute walk along the road you'll find Josiah Barton's house. He spends the summer and part of the fall here. The town of Griffin Harbor is a mere twelve-minute drive. A fifteen-minute walk on up the road in the other direction several houses are built around a beautiful small cove. A great little neighborhood runs around the edge of the water."

"Through forests?"

"Well, there's a road, but yes that is the point. The trees and this magnificent view." He opened the slider.

Kate followed him out onto the balcony. The land dropped away below to that ubiquitous rocky coast of Maine she'd heard about in songs. The breeze from off the water countered with the warmth of the sun. Birds chirped and flitted through the trees nearby. The waves splashed gently against the rocks below. A couple of lobster boats putted to and fro while the men checked their traps.

"Well, I…this view…well, it's spectacular." She shot a quick glance at Jim and then back to the water. Why in the world was she the least bit attracted to this hard-boiled Yankee with his hint of Maine drawl. She'd fought with herself about her reactions ever sense she'd opened the door to find him standing on her front porch not a whole week ago.

"No argument from me."

Jim looked at her rather than the water. Her heart stuttered and then kicked back into a regular rhythm. Surely, he didn't mean her. By most people's standards, she was pretty ordinary. Her hair with a mind of its own decided this moment was perfect to fly across her face. She shoved a strand behind her ear. If she had a friend here, she'd run and ask if Jim liked her. Whatever was wrong with her? She wasn't back in middle school.

"Let's sit here and talk."

She lowered herself into the comfortable Adirondack chair, leaned her head back, and sighed. "This is restful."

"That's why people come here, Kate. It's restful. Peaceful is another word people use. Liddy loved hearing people's reactions to her cottage. She experienced great pleasure in sharing the site with others. A book on the sofa table holds their comments."

"Well, why wouldn't she want lots of others to get to enjoy this then?" She gestured toward the water view.

He leaned forward, emphasizing that the words he was about to speak were important to him.

"Two to four people here don't have a negative impact on the environment. If this cottage is torn down and condos—or God forbid a hotel—are built, the numbers of people coming and going, tramping through the woods, and adding their trash...well, the environment can't manage more."

"Driving here I saw other condo units in the area."

"Yes, absolutely, you did. During the high season, they are full, and we are happy to have those tourists come, to walk and camp our lands or to kayak and canoe our waters. Problem is now we're at a critical mass, and one more condo development will be one too many. That's why a group, which Liddy was a big part of, wants to stop any more expansion. The last development the Griffin Harbor Town Administration approved was with the agreement that no more would be granted."

Kate rose and leaned her back against the rail studying this earnest man who obviously believed in his cause. "So, I don't get what the problem is."

"You're the problem Kate. No one knows what you'll decide. When I probated Liddy's will, the land and this cottage became yours free and clear to do whatever you want."

"Didn't you say the town had agreed to not have any more development?"

"I did, but there's been a recent turnover in the Town Planning Board, and the development group is waving a lot of money around to get members to change their mind."

Kate didn't see how she'd make any kind of decision with the 9/11 anniversary looming. Frankly, she was amazed she was doing as well as she was. Many years she became ill around this time.

"Kate, would you like to stay here instead of going to the Inn?"

"What? Oh, that's not a good idea. The cottage is charming and warm, but oh my goodness, so isolated."

"But it's your house. Wouldn't you enjoy staying here for a few days? People had booked for this week and next, but had to cancel due to illness. Because of Liddy's death, we just didn't try to rebook it."

"I don't know. It's so remote." For Kate the deciding issue.

"Try it. You'll find the quiet comforting."

"I'll think about it." The man was persistent.

"Good." Jim slid his hand under her elbow. "Come on. We'll get you checked into the Inn and then we're going to get you your first real lobster." He led her inside, locked the sliding door, scooped up her purse, and herded her out to his 4-wheel drive truck, quite different from the luxurious SUV they'd driven across country in. He'd turned in the rental in Portland and picked up his own vehicle there. The man was like a tornado with a mind of his own, determined to go wherever he chose.

A quick, less than fifteen-minute drive got them into town. He hauled her bags into the Inn and up to her not overly large room, but with a great view of the harbor.

"Do you want to take time to unpack?" Jim paced. Was he that impatient to get to the restaurant and start eating the lobster?

"If you don't mind."

"Sure. I'll wait downstairs, and then we'll run over to The Lobster Pot."

Kate nodded. What had she gotten herself into with this man? He was what you might call "driven." She closed the door behind him and quickly unpacked. After using the restroom and freshening up, she left her room. Jim met her at the foot of the stairs. She hadn't kept him waiting a long time, but again he paced.

"Now you're in for a real treat." He ushered her from the Inn to his truck and the five-minute drive to his friend's restaurant. The Lobster Pot, all weathered gray wood, sat on the wharf with a wrap-around-deck with tables and umbrellas.

They settled into a booth and perused the menus on the table.

She breathed a sigh of relief. "They've got steak. I'll have that. I can look the other way while you eat your lobster."

Jim laughed at her. Kate frowned at him. "I'm serious." Then he waved to a man making his way toward their table. He looked older than Jim. Was he the friend Jim had talked about?

"You've brought the little Texas lady in. I'd heard you'd convinced her to come for a visit." His accent was much more traditionally Maine with that broad "A" sound.

He extended his hand. Kate met his rough grasp.

"Kate, this is my best friend Tom Jenson, former lobsterman, and now owner of his family's restaurant, one of the best in Maine."

"One of?" Jenson raised one eyebrow at his friend.

"Okay, okay. The best." Jim corrected.

"Nice to meet you, Mr. Jenson."

"Tom, please. You're Liddy's niece, Kate. Practically family."

The rough weather the man had faced most of his life hadn't completely ruined his good looks, even though his ruddy complexion displayed way more lines than Jim's face did. From Jim's earlier story, she knew them to be the same age, but you'd never think that to look at the two men. Jim had mentioned he was nearing 50, but Tom's 49 was weather scarred from his years on the lobster boats. Still there was a solidness there, a trustworthiness Kate liked. Jim was lucky to have such a good friend.

"So two lobster dinners coming up. I'll get the salads out to you first."

"Wait." Kate's voice squeaked. Maybe she was being silly, but she didn't want a giant red bug sitting on her plate. It would be bad enough to face it from across the table.

Tom crossed back to their table. "What's the matter, Kate? Would you rather have chowder than the salad?"

She straightened in her chair. To handle this, she needed to pull on her big girl panties. "I'd rather have the six once fillet I saw on the menu." Her voice came out softer than she'd intended.

"What?" Tom looked scandalized.

"Cooked medium please and a baked potato with butter and nothing else." She sent Jim's friend a direct look to go along with her firm voice.

"You gotta be joking."

"No, I'm not." She shook her head. He looked confused and hurt. Made her almost wish she'd ordered the lobster. That wasn't happening.

Tom looked at Jim and then back to her. Others in the

restaurant turned at the loud huff he expelled walking away. Jim reached across and gathered her hand into his larger one. Electricity zinged up her arm. Her gaze locked on his. Her breath hitched.

"It's okay, Kate. We'll take small steps." Was he talking about the lobster or something else? He squeezed her hand and then released it, leaving cold behind where warmth had been. Was she nuts? This was only the second time she'd felt anything for a man since John's death, and it was this strange Mainer committed to convincing her to give Aunt Liddy's land to him. He must be a magician to have gotten her to come up here in the first place.

The salad was crisp and fresh tasting, the dressing tangy. She looked out the window when Tom deposited the giant red bug in front of Jim. If she kept her head turned down and concentrated on her steak and potato, she'd be fine.

Not even when Jim asked if she wanted a bite of the lobster meat, did she look up. The tenderness and taste of the steak kept her focus. Cooked to perfection, moist with a light pink center. Who knew the people of Maine—or at least Tom— understood how to cook a steak? The potato had a crunchy peeling, which was her favorite.

* * * *

After dinner, Jim followed her in to the Griffin Harbor

Inn. "I wish you'd decide to stay at the cottage. I know Liddy would be pleased."

"Maybe later." Should she ask him up? The room had two chairs, but seemed an intimate area. She wanted to stay in a public place when she was with Jim Donovan. Safer for her emotions.

"Glad you're at least considering making the move. Come and sit here, Kate." He led her to the large Queen Anne style chairs sitting in the bay window of the Inn's front parlor. "We need to talk about Liddy's services. We waited to have a memorial because everyone hoped I'd succeed in getting you to come up here."

"Does everyone know who I am?"

"Ahyah," Jim said then he laughed. "We're a small tightknit community. Liddy played an important role, and then she came from a family with a long history in Maine."

"Did she worship at a particular church?" One of the many things she didn't know about John's Aunt Liddy.

"She and her family were long time members of the Congregational Church on Church Street. You can also find a Baptist and a Catholic church all practically next to each other on that street."

"Very ecumenical." She nodded. "I guess we should have something at the church."

"I'll introduce you to Carter Fitsimon, Liddy's minister,

tomorrow and you can get something planned. I'm certain Liddy left her wishes about her service with him."

"Too bad she didn't take care of the land then I wouldn't have had to come up here." The words left her mouth sending the victim's blush flooding across her chest and spreading up her face. "I'm sorry, Jim. I didn't mean that to sound ungrateful. This time of year is difficult for me, and you've pushed me way out of my comfort zone."

He nodded once, his lips in a straight line then he seemed physically to force his mouth to relax. "It's all right, Kate. We'll work through it all. I'll check with you in the morning and take you to meet Carter. We'll get the memorial scheduled and planned."

"Thank you." She rose and followed him to the front door of the Inn. "Tomorrow then."

"Tomorrow." He bounded down the steps two at a time to the sidewalk.

Kate wandered back into the sitting room. A plate held cheese and crackers next to two wine bottles and glasses. She liked the amenities here. Why in the world would Jim suggest she should stay at the cottage where there were no people around? He clearly had bewitched her to get her to make the trip to Maine in the first place. Yes, she'd get to see Blair, but to stay out there in that isolated spot? No thanks. Even Liddy in the end had moved into town.

* * * *

Tuesday, September 10

The Inn's small restaurant offered strong coffee, fruit, and muffins for a lite breakfast. Exactly what Kate preferred, even if not the healthiest choice. Well, she'd get back to her stricter diet when she got home. She'd started on her third cup when Jim Donovan marched in and pulled out the chair across from her and sat with nary a by-your-leave.

"Morning. Glad to see you're up. I've set up an appointment for us at ten with Liddy's minister. Carter was pleased you wanted to meet with him."

Kate was blown away by the man's take-charge attitude. Of course, she had to deal with these matters, but she wished she'd pushed it off. Of course, tomorrow wasn't an option.

"Kate. You don't have other plans, do you?"

"No, of course not. Thanks for setting that up."

"No thanks," he said to the server who stopped by to check if he wanted anything. "We'll be leaving soon anyway."

He turned his attention back to her. "Have you finished? My car is outside. We can get to the church in about five minutes."

The man swept her up with his energy and drive. "Sure. Of course." Seemed the only thing to do was go with the flow of the strong current of Jim's plans.

In a short time, they'd reached the white clapboard Congregational Church and were sitting in the minister's study. The medium height man with salt and pepper hair and lines on his face like Tom's suggested he'd spent his fair share of time out in the sun and maybe on the water. He gestured toward a short sofa in his office then pulled up a chair and sat across from them.

"I'm pleased to meet you, Kate. I hope I may call you that. Liddy always referred to you that way."

Kate swallowed the guilt piling up in the back of her throat threatening to suffocate her. She should've kept in better touch with Liddy, but Kate didn't travel. The phone system was iffy, and Liddy didn't do the internet. What other options did she have? Letters. She should have sent letters, but when Liddy stopped sending Christmas cards…

"Of course. Thank you for seeing us, Pastor Fitsimon."

"Call me, Carter. We're pretty informal around here. We all loved Liddy and miss her."

She smiled and nodded her thanks. "Jim mentioned that Liddy had left a few instructions for the service?"

Carson rose and crossed to his large oak desk and lifted a file folder. "We did a six-week study on death and dying a few years back, and all of those attending made a list of their wishes, regardless of their age at the time. We none know when our time will be up. Better to be prepared."

Kate swallowed and blinked against the sudden flood of moisture to her eyes. Nobody knew that better than she did. In fact, she'd already made her own plans, hoping to make that time easier for Blair.

The folder Liddy left with her wishes did make the arrangements easier for them. All that remained was to pick a date.

"The church and I are available for a service on Wednesday, the 11th, if that will be okay with you."

Kate's victim's flush started its slow steady rise. What kind of minister was this who was so insensitive? Of course, the anniversary wasn't as big to everyone else as to her.

"What about Friday?" She'd be able to handle it by then, wouldn't she?

"Well, if that's what's best…I know her friends have been eager to have the service. Are you sure you can't have the service on Wednesday?"

Her hands locked in her lap, and she barely opened her mouth enough to force out the words. "It's 9/11. I don't do anything on that date."

"Even after all these years?" Carter cut his glaze at Jim and then came back to her. "I'm sorry, Kate."

"Thank you."

"I'll pray for you." Without waiting for her response, he went on. "We'll set the service for 10:30 on Friday morning.

Will that do?"

"Yes. Thank you." She seemed to have no other words.

He rose and extended his hand. "I'll get the word out. I expect a full house. The women's circles will handle all the food for the reception."

Kate shook his hand. "Considerate of them. Thanks for doing all this."

"It's what we do here. Take care of each other. Wouldn't you say, Jim?"

"Yes, absolutely. See you Friday, Carter."

Jim placed his hand on Kate's back and escorted her out. She hated how much she liked the feeling flowing through her body from that light touch.

"I have a case I need to work on at my office. Will you be all right on your own?"

"Of course. Thanks for setting up today's meeting and taking me."

"Do you want me to drop you back at the Inn?"

"No, you go on. I can walk back to the main part of town and explore. The exercise will be good for me."

"You sure?" Jim studied her. Was he afraid she'd fall apart? Well, he wasn't much wrong, but she wanted to fall apart by herself.

She nodded. "I'm okay. Go on." Clearly, she needed to work on controlling her reactions to the Yankee, but she needed to be by herself. Right before the anniversary wasn't a good time.

He nodded once, "I'll be in touch," and strode toward his truck.

Kate headed into the main part of town. The church was only a few blocks from the Inn. She wasn't sure why Jim hadn't insisted on walking there in the first place.

She meandered through the streets. People smiled and nodded. She had to admit, Griffin Harbor was a charming little town. Lunch was a cup of clam chowder at one of the quaint restaurants in town. She knew no one but Jim, but Kate felt safe here.

Her wanderings led her to the harbor and then back up into the town where she stopped at many small, original stores. Finally, she stepped up on the Inn's front porch. The soft breezes caressed her skin. She sank into a whicker rocker and let her gaze take in the harbor, the view nice, but not up to the standards set by the one from the cottage.

"Ms. Thompson?" A middle-aged man with graying hair, dressed in a suit stopped in front of her chair.

"Yes. I'm Kate Thompson." Jim must be right in what he'd said. Everyone in town knew who she was.

"Ms. Thompson, I'm Ray Holland owner of Holland Development Corporation. I'd love to talk with you about your aunt's property."

Sitting put Kate at a distinct disadvantage, and not knowing exactly what to expect, she rose.

"Mr. Holland, I don't want to talk with you about this now. I...have personal business to attend to." She moved toward the door. Holland stepped in front of her.

"You don't want to miss out on hearing my offer. I only need a few minutes of your time."

"I'm sorry. Before I do anything I want my daughter to come up and check out the property." Where did that idea come from? Would Blair want to come? Would she have time to come?

"I see. And when do you expect your daughter to arrive?"

"Blair lives in New York City. I'm not sure when she can get away." She didn't have to tell him that, but the man was pushy and made her feel uncomfortable. "If you'll excuse me, I'm going in now." Would he continue to block her or let her proceed?

"All right, Ms. Thompson. How about if we visit more on Thursday, the 12th?"

Good grief he was persistent, just like Jim Donovan. "All right, Mr. Holland." Anything to get him to leave her alone now. If she wasn't up for it, she'd cancel. "We can meet at The Lobster House at 11:30."

"Here's my card, and I'll meet with you then." He turned

and strode from the porch.

Her shoulders slumped; a sigh slipped between her lips. She dropped the card into her purse, straightened up, and hurried through the door. The wine sitting out on the serving table called to her. She grabbed a glass of red and headed for her room.

She let herself into her room and set the wine on the small table where two wingback chairs flanked the window. She pulled out her cell and called Blair. Despite living in New York City, she'd love the quaintness of this town.

Voice mail. Blair probably didn't have time to chat what with taking care of last minute details for the commemoration ceremony tomorrow. She must be swamped. She'd asked Kate to come, but that wasn't happening. Not since that one time when Blair had been seventeen and begged to attend the ceremony. They'd driven to New York. Her daughter loved it. She connected with other teens who'd lost a parent or family member and still kept up with a few of them.

Kate had found no comfort at all. Someone might just as well have reached in and torn off another hunk of her heart. Only being there with Blair kept Kate in her chair, but she had to dig deep for the strength not to run screaming before completion of the two-hour service.

Of all times for Holland to show up. She was barely keeping herself together and still had tomorrow to get through.

Since the first year after 9/11, Kate had spent every anniversary, but the one when Blair was seventeen, in her home in Fort Worth.

She rose and paced the room. Odd to be away. Odder still not to have anyone near who understood her situation. She shouldn't depend on Jim. Tragedy wouldn't get the man down. He was strong.

Well, she was strong. She'd raised Blair on her own with her parents' assistance, and, of course, her friends. She had a great career. Why couldn't she get past this date every year?

CHAPTER THREE

Tuesday, September 10

A knock on the door sent her heart to thudding. Had Holland come back? Maybe she'd pretend she wasn't here. She tiptoed closer then put her ear against the door. Two more deafening thumps made her jump back.

"Kate?"

Jim. She sucked in a deep breath, turned the lock, and swung open the door. Her heartbeat tripped up for a reason she didn't want to inspect.

"What are you doing here?"

"Where's that Texas hospitality we're always hearing about? You've opened the door twice now and asked me that." A smile tipped up one corner of his mouth. He leaned against the door jam, two boxes in his hands and a six-pack at his feet.

"I'm sorry."

"I've brought supper. Sandwiches, chips, cookies, and,

of course, the beer. Can you grab it?" He nodded toward the floor and whizzed by her. Glancing around, he turned toward the small table in front of the window. "This will do."

"I... I..." She sighed. He was such a whirlwind of energy. She scooped up the beer. She started in, stopped in the entryway. Should she leave the door open? Get a grip, woman. She used her hip and pushed it closed.

"Let me open one of those for you."

"Jim, I don't drink beer."

"I like the sound of my name when you say it. You haven't much."

Before she found a response, he went on. "You don't ever drink beer?"

"No. I prefer wine with everything." She lifted a glass with her choice of merlot.

He laughed a loud guffaw. "Well, I'll be damned. I've never met anyone who didn't drink beer at all." He popped the top and took a long pull.

Her gaze followed the path of the gold liquid as he swallowed making the muscles in his throat work. She'd never noticed how sexy a handsome man drinking beer could be. Clearly, she was out of her mind here.

He set down his bottle and held her chair. "I got you a chicken salad on croissant. Somehow, it seemed like something you'd like. I've got a lobster roll."

"Thank you, and of course you do." He scooted her in then settled in across from her. She smiled at him, shook her head once and then bit into the sandwich. "Um yummy!"

"Glad you like it. How'd you entertain yourself this afternoon?"

"I wandered around town. It's quite charming." She followed another bite of the sandwich with a nibble of the dill pickle and potato chips that accompanied the sandwich. "This was thoughtful of you. Thanks."

"You're welcome." He smiled but went back to his meal. The man must be ravenous. He was inhaling the lobster roll.

If she ever had to eat lobster, maybe she'd put it on a bun. It didn't look a lot different from her chicken salad. All of a sudden, Jim glanced up at her.

"Would you care for a sample, Kate? I'm sure you'd like this. It looks a lot like your sandwich, but without all the celery. It's just plain lobster."

Good heavens. The man must be reading her mind. Kate nodded. "Okay, a small one." Jim speared a piece of the white meat tinged with a coral pinkish color on the edge. He held the fork across the table for her. Her diaphragm froze and finding a breath became difficult. How was she going to swallow?

"Please, Kate. It's a small bite."

He was so earnest and wanted to please her, she hated

to disappoint him. Leaning toward him, she took the bite from his fork, somehow making it seem intimate. He kept his gaze on her while she chewed and swallowed.

"Well, did you like the taste?"

She nodded. "It was good. I didn't realize there'd be all that butter." She smiled. "Everything is better with butter." Kate sipped her wine.

He laughed and went back to his beer. "You were telling me what you did this afternoon."

"I hadn't been back at the Inn for long when I had a visitor."

"Oh? Who was it?" He got up and grabbed another beer. "Sure I can't tempt you? Since the lobster was okay?" He sat.

"No, I'll stick with this." She twisted her wine glass. "He said his name was Ray Holland."

Jim choked on a bite of sandwich and grabbed for the bottle.

"We talked on the porch."

"Did he say what he wanted?" His tone held a sharpness she wasn't used to hearing.

"To talk about buying the land."

"Damn. Well, I'm not surprised. I figured it wouldn't be long before word got around to him you were here. He has several people in town on his side in this because of the jobs his project would create. Did you tell him no way?"

"I told him I'd meet with him for lunch on Thursday."

"What? Why would you do that?"

"It seemed like the thing to do."

"Humph. I'll take you. Where are you going to meet?"

"The Lobster Pot. I wanted a public place, since I don't know him."

"That was smart. What time is the meeting?"

"11:30." Kate ate more of the sandwich. She couldn't get over how tender the chicken and how tangy the dressing was.

"Why didn't you meet with him tomorrow?"

"It's 9/11. I don't do anything on the anniversary."

"Oh. That's right." They ate in silence for a few moments. The dill pickle tingled Kate's tongue. She'd have to monitor herself with food this good around. Easy to over-indulge.

"Why don't I pick you up in the morning, and we can drive into Gerard for a rental car for you. That will give you more freedom to come and go."

"I-don't-do-anything-on-the-anniversary." She met his gaze square on.

"You mean nothing at all?" He tipped his head and studied her.

"That's right. Nothing at all." She'd stopped planning

anything for the date because her reactions were unpredictable. The least thing could set her off, and she'd dissolve in tears. Over the years, she'd found staying home to be the best option. If she cried, she didn't disturb anyone else.

He stared at her for a moment, chewed the last bite of his lobster roll followed by a swallow of beer. Finally, he said, "Well, Kate, I don't know how any of you managed to come through that tragedy. Whatever you have to do, whatever works for you, I'm good with."

Kate slipped her hand across the table and clasped his. "Thank you so much, Jim. Many people don't understand, and they try to pull me out of my cave. I'm grateful to you."

He covered their grasp with his other hand. "You're welcome. Anything you need, I'm there for you."

Kate blinked at the tears threatening to spill over at his kindness and sensitivity. Warmth smoldered in the area of her heart. An unusual but not altogether unwelcome feeling.

"We'll leave early Thursday morning to drive to Gerard to get you a car and be back in time for your meeting with Holland."

"That should work." He was such a take-charge man.

"I can go to the meeting with you, if you'd like."

Kate realized they were still holding hands. What was the matter with her? She released her grip and made to remove her hand. Jim squeezed one more time before releasing her. Always the one in charge.

"Thank you, but I can handle the meeting on my own. Over the years, I've met with many powerful men who thought they knew what was best."

"Do you include me in that group?" He glanced at her over the top of the bottle.

"I haven't decided yet. You're being comfortable with me spending tomorrow on my own is a point in your favor."

* * * *

Wednesday, September 11

Kate flipped one way then the other. Her cell said three o'clock. From the bed, the moon painted its white image across the harbor. Beautiful. Peaceful. But she didn't feel peaceful. She'd been afraid to go to sleep. Nightmares were common around the 9/11 anniversary.

In Fort Worth, she was alone—Blair had been at school for 4 years and in New York for a year–but neighbors who knew her were nearby. Even the mournful sound of the train going by in the middle of the night and barking dogs comforted her.

Here in Maine, sounds were limited to the swish of a wave against the docks and the hoot from an owl. While she was in the Inn with other people, she didn't know anyone staying here. She struggled out of bed, yanked on her robe, and moved toward the fireplace; the fire snapped on with a switch. Wasn't that a genius invention?

After Jim left, she'd gone downstairs and gotten another glass of wine before returning to her room where she set it on the bureau. For hours, she'd sat curled up on the loveseat and studied the fire flickering in the grate until the wee hours of the morning before she went to bed to toss and turn.

* * * *

Around ten in the morning, Kate made herself get dressed and go downstairs in time to get a muffin and coffee before the staff cleared away the breakfast goodies. She ate in her room, sitting in one of the chairs overlooking the harbor.

About three her phoned chirped. Blair. Kate smiled.

"Hey, sweetie."

"You catch any of the ceremony?" Blair's voice held the same note that a kid's did, hoping for a birthday cake every year. One that never arrived. Somehow, Blair clung to the hope her mom would come around.

"No. Sorry. Were you pleased?"

"Yes. I believe you would've been also."

Silence. Kate couldn't find words to make a difference. Her daughter wanted actions, but Kate couldn't give her what she wanted.

"So how are things up there?" Blair filled the void.

"Griffin Harbor is a quaint little town. On Monday, I visited Aunt Liddy's quite charming cottage. Jim said she completely redid the place about ten years ago because she wanted to rent the property. He told me she's had a caretaker ever since, and she updated it again five years ago. It's beautifully decorated."

"Jim?"

Kate heard the questions running around in her daughter's head. "Yes, dear. You remember. Jim Donovan is the attorney who worked for your Aunt Liddy. You checked out the Conservancy Trust."

"Of course. What have you decided to do with the property?"

Kate's answer about Jim must've satisfied her curious daughter. "I'd like you to look at it, Blair. After all, it's been in your father's family for generations. I don't feel right making a decision without input from you. Is there any possibility of you getting away to come up here?"

"I'd like to, Mom, but I can't manage a trip this weekend. Many loose ends to tie up after the ceremony today. How about next Friday? I can stay over that weekend. How would that be?"

Disappointment filled Kate's soul that she had to wait to see her only child. Then her practical side took over. "I only planned to be here a few days, Blair. I don't have enough clothes for a longer stay."

Blair's laugh rang through the cell. "Go shopping, Mom. What better excuse do you need?"

Kate joined her daughter's laugh. "Well, you do have a point. There must be a few shops here in Griffin Harbor. If I can't find something, I'll drive in to Gerard later, and if nothing there, Portland's only two hours away."

"Great, Mom. Let me check the schedules. I should be able to catch a flight from New York to Portland. Can you pick me up? That will give us more time to visit."

"Yes, Jim's taking me to Gerard to pick up a car tomorrow."

"I see. Well, don't decide anything until I get there to help figure out what to do with Aunt Liddy's property."

"Great, Blair. I appreciate you coming. When we finish up here, I'd like to visit with you for a time in New York before taking the train home. Would that be okay?"

"Of course. I'd love that. What if we take in a show and visit a museum or two?"

The excitement bubbling from her daughter sent pain to Kate's middle. She was such a bad mom. She dragged in a quick breath. "Let me know your travel arrangements."

"Will do. Love you, Mom."

"Me to you." Kate disconnected and sat for a few moments. Blair was such a blessing, and there'd only been the two of them, especially after Kate's parents died. They were good friends and talked a couple of times a week, though Kate had never visited her daughter in NYC. After that one dreadful trip when Blair was in high school, Kate had never returned. Her heart tripped up considering the upcoming visit. She was proud of herself for pushing through that fear to agree. She'd handle it if Blair didn't make her go to the Memorial site.

Jim's idea of her getting a car had been smart. When he'd mentioned it, she didn't think it was necessary since she wouldn't be in Griffin Harbor but a few days. Staying at the Inn, she easily walked to every place in the town. She hadn't made the 1000 foot walk across the footbridge yet to the side of the harbor where Jim's house was. Griffin Harbor was vastly different from Fort Worth, where she didn't go anywhere unless she drove.

She flipped through pictures of her daughter on her cell. Guilt that she hadn't watched the ceremony clogged her throat. Blair had worked on this one and had asked her to come or at least watch. Kate should've been able to push through her personal pain for her daughter's sake. What kind of mother was that selfish?

The whoosh of the water hitting the pier soothed her spirits, but not enough to get past the guilt. The guilt for not being able to make herself watch the ceremony for her daughter. The guilt for not crying as much as she usually did on this day. The guilt over her attraction for Jim Donovan.

Guilt gnawed at her gut. The lite lunch she'd eaten came right up and burned the back of her throat. Maybe she could grab a nap on the sofa.

No. No relief anywhere. Not today. She was looking forward to seeing Blair and showing her the property. First, she needed to get past this day.

* * * *

Jim pulled out his cell at four in the afternoon and looked at Kate's number for the tenth time. So far, he hadn't called her, but each time he found the temptation more difficult to resist. He ached for the suffering of the beautiful woman who was Liddy Thompson's niece, and he had no idea how to help her. If her daughter Blair came, maybe she'd give him a clue of what, if anything, he needed to do to help Kate move on with her life. Until she did that, she'd never have a place in her life for someone else. He was very much afraid that he'd like to be that someone else.

What a crock. He'd only just met her. He clenched his hands on the arms of his desk chair at his inability to fix the problem. Since splitting with his ex and losing part of the family land, no other woman had caught his attention the way Kate did. She filled his mind and his dreams. Unfortunately, for all intents and purposes, she still hadn't moved past her husband's tragic death.

Jim made a colossal error asking her to come up here. Now he'd pay for that mistake when she left. If he convinced her to turn her property over to the Conservancy Trust, she'd have no reason to stay. If she decided to sell to Holland, she'd have no reason to stay or ever return. Either way he was screwed.

At the least, he had to get her to turn the property over to the Trust. After her lunch with Holland, Jim would take her around to visit other lands they'd preserved. Once she realized what a good job they were doing, and how beautiful the lands were, she'd have to understand the rightness of keeping the property out of the damned developers' hands.

* * * *

Thursday, September 12

Kate parked the small, 4-wheel drive SUV Jim had insisted she get. The blue color pleased her. She walked toward The Lobster Pot at precisely 11:30, pushed open the door, and looked around. Would he already be there? A man rose when she approached. Ah, yes.

"Ms. Thompson."

"Mr. Holland." She didn't hold out her hand and he didn't either.

He nodded and led her to a booth. "Let's sit down, shall we?"

Kate settled onto the hard bench.

"Thanks for agreeing to meet with me. I've brought plans I'd like you to look at. When you understand what we'd like to do with the property, you'll be happy to sell your land to my company."

Holland opened his briefcase, removed a large envelope, and unfolded several very large papers.

She shook her head. "I'm sorry, Mr. Holland. I'm not familiar with the area. Your drawings are not helpful."

"Bear with me. I'll help you understand."

Thirty minutes later, Jill put her hand up to stop Holland. "You've done a good job explaining the project, Mr. Holland. In fact, I'm sure I'd enjoy living in a community like you've planned here."

"I'm glad to hear that, Ms. Thompson. You'll be proud of what we can do with the land."

"I'm sorry, Mr. Holland. I didn't mean to mislead you." The rush of her victims' flush began its movement from her chest to flood upward toward her cheeks. She plowed ahead. "As I said Tuesday, I haven't decided what to do with the land yet. I want my daughter to come look before I decide one way or the other."

"How soon is she coming up here? What kind of delay

are you talking about?"

"I'm not sure." She wasn't telling the man it would be more than a week. None of his business. "But she deserves to see the property before I decide anything final."

"Well, I'll be in touch then." He refolded the papers and slid them back into his briefcase, rose from the booth, and stalked from the restaurant.

Kate closed her eyes and rested her head against the back of the booth. She hated confrontations. She was surprised she'd gotten through this one.

"Kate, are you all right?"

Kate straightened up. "Oh, hey, Tom. Yes. Just need a moment to recover from Mr. Holland's displeasure. I told him I hadn't decided what to do with the land. He seemed surprised, as if he'd expected me to sign over the property today. He wasn't happy."

"Can I get you anything?"

"A glass of Merlot and a shrimp salad please."

"Sure. Be right back with the wine."

She did her deep breathing all the psychologists suggested she use when she grew tense.

"Here's your wine, Kate. Salad will be out shortly."

"Thanks, Tom." She took a healthy sip and relaxed against the bench. She could hardly wait to see Blair. Getting her prospective on selling would be helpful, but mainly she just wanted to see her daughter.

Kate palmed her phone and clicked on Addie's name, better touch-base with her friend, who'd be worried she hadn't heard from her in a while. No luck there, Kate got Addie's voice mail, so she left a message. *Tell me when I can call.* Maybe she'd have better luck reaching Devon. Unless she was doing a presentation or in a meeting, Kate should be able to find her friend at work.

"Hey, Devon. Do you have a few minutes?"

"Sure for you, girl. How'd you do yesterday? Did you stay by yourself?"

"Thanks for asking, Devon. Yes, I spent the day alone. You know that's what I always do."

"Well, we're all kind of hoping something will come up between you and the Maine Yankee. Addie told me about the sparks flying between you two that afternoon at your house."

Kate drew in a deep breath. "Devon, you and Addie are reaching. Nothing's going on there." Did she want something to be going on? Well, that was perhaps a different question. "I wanted to bring you guys up on how things were going here."

"Well, that's what I'm talking about. How are things between you and the handsome Yankee lawyer?"

"Devon, there's nothing between the handsome Yankee lawyer and me. I've told you that."

"Ahem."

Kate looked up expecting Tom to be standing there with her salad, but the handsome Yankee lawyer himself stood next to the booth. Damn. A flush inexorably pushed up from her chest. He gestured to the place across from her and mouthed, "May I?"

Good grief. Had he heard her description of him? She nodded and waved him to the chair. "Listen, Devon, I've got to let you go. I'll call back another time."

After disconnecting, she glanced up at the man sitting across from her who, if she wasn't mistaken, had an extra bit of red in his cheeks.

"I'm sorry. I didn't mean to interrupt anything."

"It's okay. Devon and I were only chatting."

"Here you go, Kate. Shrimp salad." Tom set the shell-shaped bowl in front of her. "Jim, what can I get for you?"

"Fried fish sandwich, fries, and a beer. Thanks, Tom."

"Back with the beer right away and the sandwich pretty quick thereafter." He strode away toward the kitchen.

"I love that he chopped up the shrimp for the salad. I've never liked them lying around on top of a bed of lettuce. It's not a shrimp salad, just a salad with shrimp on it." She raised her fork. "Um. Good. Did Tom call you and tell you I was here?"

"Why do you ask?"

"Answering a question with a question, Mr. Donovan?

Makes me suspicious."

"And if he did?" He raised the bottle to his lips and swallowed. "He knew I was worried about how you did yesterday and how your meeting with Holland went. He told me you seemed upset after Holland left. I needed to see for myself how you were holding up." He picked up her hand lying on the table; his thumb traced a slow circular caress.

Kate's breath hitched. She should pull her hand away, but the motion caused unexpected heat to spiral through to her core.

"How are you holding up, Kate?" His gaze never left hers.

"I… I'm fine. I got upset with Mr. Holland."

* * * *

Jim tightened his grip her hand. "Did he do or say anything to scare you?" If the bastard threatened Kate, Jim would make him sorry.

"No, no nothing like that. I don't do confrontation well. Hate to tell people something I'm sure they don't want to hear. That's been a pain when a real estate deal goes sour."

Jim filed that piece of information away for when he might need it. Before he commented, Tom showed up with Jim's lunch. He dropped Kate's hand, and noted she hadn't pulled away earlier.

"Thanks. This smells great." Jim swallowed a gulp of beer, glad his friend hadn't interrupted them to deliver the food earlier.

"How's the salad?" Tom glanced at Kate's plate.

"It's excellent, just the way I like, with the shrimp chopped and mixed with celery and a bit of onion. Do you use mayo or remoulade sauce?" She picked up her fork.

"It's remoulade. I make it myself. Well, I'll leave and let you enjoy. Signal me if you need anything."

They ate in silence for a few minutes. Jim dunked his fries in copious amounts of catsup. His friends teased him about his love of the red sauce, but he ignored them. He shoved a couple in his mouth.

Kate put down her fork and leaned forward. "Don't you want to know what I told Mr. Holland?"

"Sure, but I figure when you're ready you'll tell me." He raised his bottle, took a swig, and then set it on the table.

"I told him I hadn't decided what to do yet. I want Blair to come up here and look at the property. Get her take on selling to Holland or the Conservancy Trust." She picked up her fork and ate more of her salad.

He nodded. "That seems like a good plan. Do you know when she can come?"

"She'll be here on Friday the 20th and stay the weekend."

"That's good news." He leaned against the high wood back of the booth with his arms stretched out in front and his palms resting on the table. He couldn't keep a big smile from spreading across his face. She hadn't immediately handed over the property to Holland, and she'd be here longer.

"Well, you needn't look pleased. I haven't decided in favor of the Conservancy Trust either."

"I know. If you don't sell to Holland or us, what are you going to do?"

"Maybe Blair will want to keep the land in the family."

Had Kate said they might keep the land? Jim could hardly believe it. This was beyond what he'd hoped. Kate wouldn't be returning to Texas right away. He possibly had more time than two weeks with a woman who had begun to mean a great deal to him in much too short a time.

"That's not a bad idea." Years of trial work helped him keep his voice calm and from leaning over and kissing her. The first was good, the second maybe not. Maybe that's exactly what he should do. Kiss the living daylights out of her. The lower parts of his anatomy found that an intriguing idea. Guess he'd need to sit here for a while before getting up and embarrassing them both.

They ate in silence except for the noises of the other diners.

"Jim, I have a favor to ask you."

"Sure anything." And that was the God's honest truth.

She toyed with her fork, pushing around the half-eaten salad. Couldn't she make up her mind to ask now she'd brought it up? He didn't push.

"Well, I wondered if you'd take me back to the cottage. I was exhausted, when we stopped by when we got here, and we didn't stay long. I'm wondering how remote it is. Sometimes memories play tricks on us."

"Of course, we can go whenever you like. You may change your mind about staying out there and that's the best way to let the land speak to you."

"Actually," she glanced down and then up. "I'm giving that more thought. The Inn is delightful, but having more room would be nice if I'm going to be here longer. Not to mention, the cottage is free."

"I'm proud of you for reconsidering." She hit him with that smile that did things to his insides. "Why don't I take you out there later this afternoon and afterwards you can have supper at my house. I'll grill you a steak."

"I'm surprised, counselor, that you'd stoop to bribery."

He chuckled. "Then you don't know me well. Listen, I'll pick you up from the Inn at four and we'll go out to the cottage. Afterwards, we'll eat steak and beer—" Her eyebrows rose—"Okay, I promise a good wine for you. What do you say?"

"Okay, the wine clenched the deal for me. The offer of steak was tempting in and of itself. Guess, I should ask if you know how to grill a steak."

"You wound me, woman."

Kate's laughter bubbled out at the dramatically placed hand over his heart, and the sound filled him with hope and expectation for an awesome ending to their dinner.

* * * *

Thursday, September 12

"Is Ray in?" It was almost four-thirty when Kenny Gouge flipped his lighter in the air while he perched on the edge of the desk in the outer office. Ray's secretary hated for him to sit there. Kenny loved to annoy her, but he knew where to draw the line. If he ran off his boss's secretary, there'd be hell to pay.

"Only if you have a death wish." She waved her hand at him to get him off her desk. He complied. "He came in mad like one of those bulls in Spain. I don't know who waved the red material at the boss, but he was steaming."

Ken nodded, hopped of the desk. "I'll do what I can to protect you and the rest of the staff." He tapped on Ray's door, opened it a crack.

"Damn, damn, damn."

Ken glanced over his shoulder at Ray's secretary.

Shrugged and stuck his head in. "Boss, you okay?"

"Hell, no I'm not okay." He stomped around his desk and then started another loop.

Kenny shoved the door closed.

"That damn bitch put me off with an excuse about wanting her daughter to look at the property! I keep running into delays!"

"That's tough."

"Damn, I need this project to work out."

"Is there anything I can do?"

"Yeah, sure." Ray dropped into the chair behind his desk. "Make the broad change her mind." He leaned back and closed his eyes.

"I'll do my best, boss." Kenny turned and ambled toward the door. "I'll be out of the office tomorrow." Ray waved a hand without looking up. Kenny nodded to the secretary, left the building, and headed to the parking lot. He climbed into his truck and turned the ignition. Time to check out the woman who was causing his boss so much heartache. He made the two-hour trip from Portland to Griffin Harbor, a piss-poor little village. Kenny couldn't figure why anyone chose to live out in the back of beyond.

According to what he'd heard, the only good thing the town had going for it was The Lobster Pot. Kenny sauntered in for supper and to pick up whatever info he could.

"What can I get you?" The man behind the bar swiped a damp cloth over the surface.

Kenny eyed the chalkboard menu. "Draft beer and a fried fish basket. Can I eat here?"

"Sure can."

Kenny settled on to the stool.

"Let me put in your order, and I'll grab your beer."

"Thanks." Kenny swiveled around to check out the place. At seven fifteen in the evening, people filled more than half the booths and tables. He was surprised. Focusing on the people, he found a real mix of old and young, professional, and what looked like fishermen.

"Here you go." The barkeep put an icy mug of frothy golden brew in front of Kenny.

"Thanks. You the owner?"

He nodded. "The restaurant's been in the family for about 60 years. My granddad, my father, and now me."

Kenny nodded. "You must know everyone in town." He didn't make it a question, but hoped he'd get an answer.

"Pretty much except when the tourists hit in large numbers." He polished a glass and set it on a shelf.

"So these folks here now, locals or tourists?"

The bartender looked around. He smiled. "These are all old timers. We always have a few tourists and visitors, but more in the summer and fall. It's still too early for the large crowds of leaf peepers to arrive."

"If a person wanted to hang around for a few days, where would you recommend staying?"

"The Inn on Main Street has rooms. Melba was in here for lunch today and mentioned they had a couple of vacancies."

"Okay, I'll check it out."

"You staying for a while or just passing through? You don't strike me to be a kayaker."

"Hah. You got that right. Looking for time away from the rat race."

"What business you in, if you don't mind my asking?"

"You know when a deal's about to fall through? I fix things to make the deal work out."

The bartender nodded. "Everybody needs someone like that. I bet your food's ready." He turned toward the kitchen and returned in a moment with Kenny's fish basket. "Here you go. Tartar or red sauce?"

"Tartar and vinegar."

The barkeep set down the requested condiments. "Let me know if you need anything else."

Kenny sprinkled the vinegar on his fish and dipped a French fry into the tartar sauce. He'd been to the property several times before and was certain he wouldn't have any trouble finding it even in the in the dark. He'd chow down fast, get a room at the Inn, and then drive out to the cottage.

* * * *

At almost 7:30 on Thursday, Kenny drove past the Thompson house and pulled off the road into a place used by snowplows about a hundred feet farther on. A small SUV and a truck were parked in front of the cottage. What's that about? No one was supposed to be here. He got out and walked toward the house.

A tall man pushed open the front door followed by an attractive blonde woman. Kenny crouched behind a large boulder. The woman had a sweater over one arm and a purse slung over her shoulder. Could that be Kate Thompson? The man was Jim Donovan. Kenny had seen the lawyer in a number of town meetings when he and Ray had been checking out the possibility of buying the land.

"Thanks for walking me around and introducing me to the neighbors. I wasn't expecting that, mostly I wanted to get a handle on what all is here."

"We may be more spread out over the land and we may not have the numbers of people you're used to, but we keep up with each other. You can always count on Josiah Barton up toward town. He stays longer than most of our short termers do."

"Nice to know. Jenny at the small store up at the V in

the road is fun. She has all kinds of things in there."

"That's where I got the wine for supper. Speaking of which, we need to get a move on. I set the potatoes to be done at eight and have to grill those steaks."

He held the car door for her. "Now remember, go easy over that large boulder in the road. You don't want to bottom out on the dip."

She laughed. "Not good for the undercarriage of my rental. I'll be careful, and I'll wait for you to lead us out of here. Don't think I'm up to taking the twisty-turny roads in the dark yet."

"That's why I wanted you to drive, to help you get used to it." Donovan climbed into his truck.

The woman maneuvered out into the road and backed down the hill out of Donovan's way doing what she'd said she would. After following the same procedure, he headed up the hill with the woman following behind. Darkness settled on the land, except for the porch light on the cottage.

Interesting. He'd heard Thompson was staying at the Inn. He planned to check her out there tomorrow. Were they playing house out here? He'd get in and look for anything he could use to help him convince her to sell to the boss. Kenny worked his way toward the back of the cottage, stopped. Not getting up that way.

The cottage sat on a piece of land that dropped away to

the sea blocking access to the balcony from below. The basement looked to offer access. Kenny went down the couple of steps. The locked door proved no problem to him. He slipped inside, greeted by the musty smell of a cellar. He pulled the small, but powerful, flashlight from his pocket. The light revealed a small packed room. Old furniture, canned goods on shelves, sleds, and junk. He picked his way across the room toward another flight of stairs.

Kenny nodded to himself, had to be the way into the cottage itself. At the top, he found the door locked, but again he had no trouble jimmying it with a credit card. When he opened the door, he found himself in a bathroom. Huh. Seemed odd. He walked through and out into the front entry hall. Two closets to his right. Opening doors revealed a rack for hanging coats and in the other, a vacuum, mop, broom, extra toilet paper and towels, and sheets.

A bedroom a few steps past the closets on the right had three closets, two for clothes, and one with a stacked washer dryer. He moved back into the hallway. The kitchen to his left seemed stocked with the necessities, coffee, tea, oatmeal, salt and pepper. The refrigerator was empty. A coffee pot sat on the counter.

Small lights on the balcony rail broke the total darkness beyond the wall of windows. In the daylight, the view made this property valuable.

Too bad the woman hadn't stayed here. Kenny shook his head. He'd have to get into her room at the Inn, much more difficult. Whoa. What's this? His flashlight picked up something shiny in the corner of the sofa. A cell phone and look at that, not password protected. He scrolled through favorites. Blair Thompson. Maybe a daughter? He didn't remember hearing about a son. He put the number in his cell. Never knew when that might come in handy. A possible place to put pressure.

Texts indicated the mom and daughter talked often. Looked like Blair lived in NYC. He had contacts there if he needed access to her.

Kenny looked around a couple more times and then stepped out on the balcony. He was right. No access from there. Good thing the basement worked. Coming through the front door was harder to cover up.

"Okay, Texas bitch, I got what I came for." Ray would be happy if Kenny fixed this problem for him and Kenny was determined to do just that.

* * * *

Kate placed her fork and knife on her empty plate. "You earned points on this meal, Jim. The steak was tasty and perfectly cooked. Not overly red but not dried out either."

"Glad you enjoyed it."

"So this house was your grandparents?"

"Yes, they died five years ago, outlived my parents."

"I'm sorry for your losses." She sipped her merlot. "Did you move in then?"

"No, I moved in about five years before that. They needed help, but wanted to stay in their home. My brother and I discussed a retirement home in Gerard, but they wouldn't have been happy inland away from the water. Phil's family and his architect business are in Boston."

"So it was easier for you to move here than him?"

"Yeah. I had an old house I'd bought in Gerard I was remodeling, but this seemed more important. I sold the house and moved in with my grandparents."

"Is this how it looked when you moved in?" The white kitchen with stainless steel appliances impressed Kate.

"I did my share of redecorating after my grandparents died. Liddy was a big help. The remodeling bug had bitten her after redoing her cottage. She was hell bent on making sure everyone had the latest and greatest cooking gadget, but also that everything conformed looks-wise to historical integrity. Hence the large fireplace in the kitchen." He chuckled. "She had a good time helping me with the house."

"You've got lots of storage. I was surprised by the walk-in pantry."

"My favorite part is the tall water spigot for filling large pots."

"I noticed that. For pasta?"

"No." He laughed. "For boiling lobstahs."

"Ooooh. Let's change the subject. How often do you have to drive into Gerard? " Kate finished her glass of Merlot.

"Let me refill that." He rose, picked up the bottle, and poured the garnet red liquid into her glass. "It's unusual that I can't handle things from here with the internet, but sometimes if I'm in a trial, I'll go in every day. Generally, it's more like several times a week, and a trip of forty-five-minutes isn't much at all."

"It was a pretty drive."

"Yeah. Bring your wine into the living room. We can get more comfortable on the sofa. I'll light the fire."

"The definite chill in the air is lovely. It's still beastly hot in Fort Worth. The week before you arrived we hit 100 degrees."

"I remember being surprised at the heat. It was hard to imagine."

"One of the things I hadn't expected to enjoy about this trip was the delightfully pleasant daytime temps and the crisp evenings. I've lit the fire in my room every night partly because it's easy, a mere flip of the switch."

"That's the way the one in the cottage works."

"I can't get over how the look differs from my

memories." Kate settled into the middle of the sofa.

"Liddy knew if she wanted to rent it, she'd have to do the updates and redecorating." He sat on Kate's right, close but not touching. "Liddy had a ball doing it, I can tell you that. She became a fan of all the redecorating TV shows." He chuckled again. "I've seen enough of those to last me a long time."

"I find those shows can be addicting, and once you do one thing to the house you're hooked into three others."

Jim shifted, and his thigh brushed hers. Kate struggled to keep her breathing even.

He picked up her free hand with his left. His thumb rubbed her palm in slow circles. Kate gave up the fight to keep her breath even. She should remove her hand, but she liked the feel of his skin against hers. How could she let herself experience these feelings the day after the anniversary of the tragic loss of her husband? Wasn't she being disloyal?

Her friends' voices filtered into her head:

"Kate, you deserve to have a life of your own."

"Kate, he wouldn't want you to be alone this way."

"Kate, before long, Blair won't need you. She's moved on. You need to also."

They were right, but not now, not with someone from Maine. She reached for strength she didn't know if she had and then leaned away, withdrawing her hand from Jim

Donovan's grasp. She set her glass on the coffee table.

"This has been enjoyable. The meal everything I could hope, but I'd better go back to the Inn." She stood. "I have lots on my mind now. For one, deciding if I'm going to move out to the cottage."

He glanced at her, his eyebrows drawn down in what Kate concluded was disappointment.

"Of course. Let me get your sweater." He rose. The perfect host.

Kate stepped around the coffee table, and he helped her slide her arms into the sleeves. Did he hold her shoulders for a moment longer than necessary? Did she wish he had?

"I'll follow you back to the Inn."

Five minutes later, Kate pulled into the Inn's small lot in the rear of the building. Jim walked with her around to the front where a light spread a soft illumination. After holding her elbow to climb the stairs to the porch, he pushed open the Inn door.

She glanced up at his face reflected in the gas light on the porch.

"All the way to your room."

She nodded and climbed the stairs. His hand rested gently on her lower back until they got to her room. He took the key, unlocked the door, and pushed it open. He stayed outside. Should she ask him in? She wanted to, but that seemed like she'd be sending mixed signals. No. Better not to take a chance than risk either of them getting hurt.

"Thanks again for a wonderful evening, Jim, and for all your help with getting me transportation."

"Sure no problem. I'd like to set up a meeting for you with the officers for the Conservancy Trust. How would Monday be?"

"No plans. Anytime you set up would be fine for me."

"I'll walk with you tomorrow to Liddy's service."

"That's…" Kate had started to say it wasn't necessary, but having someone she knew near at the service would be helpful. Maybe he needed the companionship, too. Liddy clearly meant a lot to him. She nodded. "Thank you."

"Let me put the Conservancy Trust meeting on my calendar. There's nothing else there, but doing so gives me a small sense of control." Kate reached in her sweater pocket for her phone. "Gosh, I'm sure I had it at the cottage."

"Let's make sure it's not here, and then we can check that you didn't lose it at my house."

Jim pushed through the door, making her step back. So much for deciding whether she should ask him in. He wasn't the biggest man she'd ever met, but his personality filled up what was a large bedroom.

"I remember receiving a text from Blair, and I returned it while we were at the cottage. It must've fallen from my pocket then. How frustrating."

"We can run back out there and check. You'll sleep better knowing you've got your phone."

"Are you sure you don't mind?"

"Of course not. Come on."

Fifteen minutes later, they entered the cottage, flipped on lights, and looked around.

"Is this it?"

Jim held out her phone. "Yes. Where'd you find it?"

"On the dining table."

"Huh. I don't remember using the cell over there. Must be getting absent minded. Thanks." She pulled up her calendar and filled in the meeting with the Conservancy Trust, leaving the time vacant.

"Would you like to visit the Coastal Maine Botanical Gardens on Saturday? Spring is awesome, but this time of year offers its own special beauty."

"Don't feel like you need to entertain me, Jim. I'm sure you have other things you need to do."

"Nothing I'd like doing more than showing you the Gardens. With Liddy's service tomorrow, we don't have enough time to do them justice."

"Well, thank you. I'd enjoy that."

"Let me get you back to the Inn."

The drive passed in silence. Kate struggled with the

attraction she felt for the Yankee. They'd known each other a short time, but it seemed longer. Must be his connection to Liddy. If only Kate had kept in touch with the woman. But the pain of losing her husband had pushed everything from her focus except for Blair, her parents, and her job.

Again, Jim walked her into the Inn and to her room.

"I'll stop by here and we can walk to the church together."

"I keep saying thank you. It doesn't seem enough."

Jim leaned in and kissed her cheek. "For now, that will do."

* * * *

Jim clasped the steering wheel tightly. Why hadn't he kissed her properly instead of that sophomoric kiss on the cheek? Damn. He couldn't remember wanting a woman the way he did Kate, especially one he'd known for such a short time. Then again, he'd known of her for a long time. Maybe the drive across the country, which she handled in stride, forged a bond. Her vulnerability mixed with a strength that allowed her to carry on. The pain of the loss—he'd lost a lawyer friend on that tragic day—but that was nothing like losing a spouse.

He steered his SUV through the quiet, sleepy town. Stores were dark, lights swung from several of the boats in the harbor and illuminated the walking bridge which crossed to the other part of the peninsula, where his grandparents' house—guess he'd always refer to the house that way—stood. Could a big city woman like Kate settle down in such a small spot in the road?

Hopefully, her daughter would influence her to stay. She'd been successful in encouraging her to come up here. He parked in his two-car garage. The first change he'd made when he moved in with his grandparents was to build the garage. He wasn't about to spend half of every morning digging out his car during the winter. Fortunately, they had the land to expand. In the early years, he spent more time in Gerard than he did now. Gerard wasn't a big town either. Oh, it was larger than Griffin Harbor, but probably not big enough to convince Kate to stay. Why he thought that was even a remote possibility at this point, he didn't know. But that was what he wanted.

CHAPTER FOUR

Friday, September 13

Liddy's service had been beautiful. Several people spoke of her love for the town and their love for her. Mildred Steele talked about working closely with Liddy to keep the land safe from the developers. Seth Stigler, the Gerard County Sheriff and Brett Sutton, the probate judge, commented on her stubbornness to protect the land. They told of how ably she used the law to work in her favor.

People in the congregation who knew Liddy laughed at the stories told about her. A deep sense of regret engulfed Kate because she'd lost touch with the wonderful woman who'd been Liddy Oliver Thompson. A couple of folks commented that Liddy would've found having her memorial on Friday the 13th fitting. She was known for not having a superstitious bone in her body.

The stories raised Kate's curiosity about the history of the Thompson family and Griffin Harbor. After the ceremony at the cemetery and lunch at the church, Kate told Jim she wanted to be alone for a while. She wanted some time to herself, and she was sure he had work to do. He didn't need to entertain her every second of her visit.

Because she'd decided to research the area, Kate ambled up the curving walkway to the old library sitting on a hill. Leaves were beginning to turn, but none had fallen. The combination of the grass, the white-columned building, and the smattering of colorful leaves sprinkled amongst those still green painted quite a picture. Kate pulled her cell from her pocket and snapped away. Chances were good she'd never visit Griffin Harbor again. She couldn't deny the beauty of the place, but its remoteness made it less desirable.

The historic designation plaque on the wall stated a library had stood on the site since the 1700's, and the current building went up in 1787. A wonderful old-book-smell smacked Kate in the face when she pulled open the large black door and stepped inside. Wonderful.

"Good morning. May I help you?" A brunette middle-aged woman asked in a soft voice.

"Hey. Can you point me toward your history section?"

"Sure. It's on the far side of the building. I'll show you." The woman came from around the tall desk and gestured for Kate to walk beside her. "You're Kate Thompson, aren't you? I'm sorry for your loss and that I couldn't make Liddy's service.

She was a dear."

"Thank you. Since I've inherited Liddy's property, I decided to learn more about the area."

"She'd like that." The librarian stopped, held out her hand. "By the way, I'm Missy Talbot."

Kate shook hands with her. "Nice to meet you, Ms. Talbot."

"Call me Missy. Everyone does. We all loved Liddy. She'll be remembered for many good deeds, especially for her defense of our land. Between her and Mildred Steele, they were a formidable pair."

She stepped around a stack. "Here you'll find a variety of books about Griffin Harbor history. This one's about the earliest settlers, some of whom were an early branch of the Thompsons."

"Thank you Missy."

The bell over the front door tinkled. "I'll let you browse. Holler if you have questions. Mrs. Brown, good to see you today. I've got that book you requested."

The librarian hurried to check on the white-haired woman's needs. Kate lost herself in the history of Griffin Harbor. Sometime later, her cell rang pulling her from her research. Gosh, she'd been at her task two hours. She glanced at the ID. Her precious Blair's name appeared.

"Hi, sweetie. Is anything wrong?"

"No, of course not, but since we talked, I made my plane reservations and wanted to let you know when I'm getting in next Friday."

Kate waved to Missy before she hurried through the front door.

"Are you still there, Mom?"

Kate explained she'd been in the library and wanted to get outside to talk without disturbing anyone. "That's great, Blair. I'm pleased you found a way to take off." Kate settled on one of two wrought iron benches in the yard. When she decided to come, the main reason was getting to combine the trip with a visit with her daughter. She'd not expected that the land would have such an effect on her. The colors, scents, and sounds soothed her. What a perfect fall day. She drew in a breath and slowly let it out.

Kate noted the time of the flight and its number in her phone calendar. "You're going to love this small town. It's charming."

"Look forward to seeing it and you, Mom."

"Thanks again for rearranging your schedule to come, Blair."

"Of course. Don't forget to go shopping. We'll show that small town how to have fun." Her daughter's laughter was the last thing Kate heard as they rang off.

She'd need a few more clothes, and she wanted to find

out if and how to get a library card. Checking out a couple of books was in order. She loved her e-reader, but for the history stuff, she wanted "real" books for the touch and smell of those early years.

She pulled open the heavy black door of the library. "Missy, is there any way I can check out a few books? How long does it take to get a library card?"

"All of thirty minutes or less. Only depends on how many people walk in and need assistance."

Kate tipped her head in question. "What do the people coming in have to do with the length of time to get a card?"

Missy laughed. "Small staff. Only two of us and my assistant has taken off today. It won't take me long to type, print, and laminate if I'm not interrupted."

"Okay," Kate nodded. "I'm going to be here longer than anticipated, and I want to buy a couple of pieces of clothing. You have any suggestions of where to shop?"

"Sure do. Check out Sophie's which is straight down from us toward the harbor. Hook a right on Main Street. You'll find it about halfway down the block. She carries upscale clothing, beautiful colors, made locally."

"I'm guessing I need more casual wear, jeans, shirts, that sort of thing."

"We've got you covered there. Gerard's a local store owned by members of the Gerard family that settled this part of Maine. Lots of casual stuff there, but promise you'll stop by Sophie's to check out her beautiful outfits."

"I'll be sure to do that, and I'll check back with you later this afternoon for the library card. Can I leave my car parked here?"

"Not a problem. Gerard's sits between here and Main Street. When you get to Second Street, turn left. You'll see the big sign on your left. Hanson's is also a possibility if you're more into camping clothes."

"Well, no. The first two sound great. Thanks for your help, Missy. I'll be back later." Kate walked from the library armed with the locations of the two stores. She didn't need a lot, especially if she moved to the cottage with its washing machine. Was that a real possibility? Did she want to do that?

She walked down to Main Street and turned right to check out Sophie's. The lure of a small boutique dress shop called to her, especially if they carried pieces from local artisans.

Soaring music played in the background, the lovely smell of—what was that? Vanilla & maybe a hint of peach?—greeted her when she entered the shop, which was larger than it appeared from the outside. Items weren't crammed together, which made studying the selections easy.

"May I help you?" Again, that lovely not exactly twang, but definitely Maine sound coming from a more than middle-aged woman with gorgeous salt and pepper hair. Probably never has to do anything for that affect. Kate sighed, thinking of the trips to the beauty shop that streaked her dishwater blonde with highlights.

"I'm looking for a pair of good slacks. Color doesn't matter."

After a lovely interlude of trying on and purchasing slacks, matching shirt and jacket and with no one recognizing her, Kate headed back outside and walked up the hill toward the library and her car. She left her new purchases and then went in to claim her library card and check out a couple of books and brochures about the area. Then she steered the SUV into the street and made the short drive to the Inn. She sat in the parking area for a couple of minutes. Apparently, she'd unconsciously decided.

Inside her room at the Inn, she packed and then called the caretaker to say she was moving out to the cottage. He promised to meet her and give her a key. She checked out of the Inn and headed out of town, eager to look at the cottage through the eyes of Aunt Liddy, who'd picked out everything. Kate stopped at the corner grocery for a few supplies: salad fixings, chicken breasts, cheese, pasta, spaghetti sauce, garlic, bread, and wine. The staples of her life except for hamburgers. Those she'd get from a restaurant.

At last, she maneuvered into the odd parking space at

the cottage. A middle-aged man stood up from the porch, and stood up, and stood up some more. He made Jim Donovan look short. Kate stifled a chuckle.

"Ms. Thompson?" He came down the steps with his hand outstretched.

"Yes. Are you Stan Bennet?"

"Ahyah. I've unlocked the door. Can I help you carry those in?"

"That's kind. Thank you." Between them, they made short work of getting her bags and the groceries inside.

"It's quite a view, ain't it?"

Stan had caught her staring out the glass doors. She laughed. "That's for sure. What do I owe you?"

"Mr. Donovan makes sure I'm paid monthly. The money is always the same regardless of how much I do. I've been happy to look after Ms. Liddy's property for her. Be happy to keep on doing the work for you."

"That would be wonderful. I'm sure we can continue your arrangement at least until I figure out what to do with the property."

"You not gonna keep it?"

"Well, I don't know. I live far away and well...I just don't know."

"Ms. Liddy would be sorry to see it leave the family."

"I thought she wanted it to go the Maine Coast

Conservancy Trust?" Kate leaned against the kitchen counter.

"She did. But many a time she wondered about you and your daughter and what you'd think of the place if you saw it after the work she'd had done on the house."

"Oh." The only word to come to Kate's mind. If only Aunt Liddy had gotten hold of her or if they'd kept in touch some way.

"Here's your key and my cell number, though out here, it'd be better to text me. Enjoy your stay at Ms. Liddy's cottage." The tall man headed toward the door.

"Thanks, again, Mr. Bennet." She stood in the open door.

He stopped at the bottom of the stairs. "Stan's fine. Ahyah." He touched his finger to the tip of his cap, and then he walked up the hill to his gray truck, climbed in, and rumbled away.

Kate closed and locked the door. "Well, Liddy, I'm here now." Kate put away the groceries and poured a glass of wine. She slid open the glass doors and sank into one of the Adirondack chairs. Her head rested comfortably against the high back. The view, with sounds of the rushing of the wind and swishing of the ocean surrounded and comforted her. No problems for her on Friday, the 13th.

* * * *

Friday, September 13

Kenny settled back against the wrought iron chair outside his favorite fish restaurant, Anchors Away, which had started life as an old boat. He'd be happy to sit here all day with this view of the boats coming and going. He loved Portland and didn't understand the people who lived in these fire-ant sized towns barely deserving of the term. The wind had picked up and many of the customers had moved inside, but he wanted to handle his business in the privacy of the almost empty deck.

He punched in a number, disconnected, and waited. His cell rang in five minutes. Prompt. "Hello, Ed. Thanks for getting back with me."

"Never miss a chance for a score, and you always pay up. What can I do you for?"

Ray Holland's brother Ed was a dickhead, but he had a handle on the more unsavory parts of society. "I want you to keep an eye on someone for me. She lives in the Sunnyside part of Queens."

"Know it well. Have a few girls I run there."

"Name's Blair Thompson. She works at the 9/11 Museum. Find out what you can about her. You know the drill. Does she have any patterns in her life you can use to make it easy for you to grab her?"

"You want me to put her in the business?"

"No, but we may need her to give us an edge in a business deal. You give me a hand?"

"Sure. I still owe you for doing that nickel for me upstate."

"You bet your life you do." One damn sure thing, Kenny was never going back to jail. Once was enough. "I'll be in touch."

"Here's your beer, sir." The waitress, who could've been attractive if her blouse had been cut lower and her pants had hugged her rear more, set the ice-covered pilsner in front of Ken. "Are you ready to order?"

"Thanks, babe." He swallowed a sip of the tap beer. "Good stuff. Yeah. Bring me the lobstah dinner."

"Right away." She scurried to the computer to put in his order.

Her running around doing for him made him feel important. And he was, especially to Ray, who was too softhearted to do what was necessary to win all of the contracts the company needed. Kenny didn't have that problem, and he prided himself on his ability to fix things for his boss.

When Kenny got out of prison, hardly anyone would speak to him much less give him a job. Ray did both of those. If he wanted that land for his condo project, Kenny wouldn't let anything get in the way of Ray having what he wanted.

* * * *

Saturday, September 14

"I'm glad you agreed to come to the Botanical Gardens, Kate."

"I read up about it in one of the books I picked up in the library yesterday. Gardeners and tourists alike sing its praises. I even read a few comments online." She adjusted the green scarf around her neck.

"Are you chilly?" Jim wanted everything to be perfect for this visit. He reached for the temperature controls, but her hand stopped his. He glanced in her direction, and she yanked her hand from his arm. The telltale pink emerged and climbed steadily up her neck to her cheeks. She'd called it her victim's flush. He'd read about it, but had never seen one displayed the way it was on Kate.

"The temperature is fine. I'm just rearranging the scarf for now. You cautioned me that it would be warmer this afternoon and then when the sun went down, the temps would drop. I'm prepared."

"Great. And here we are." He steered the car off the highway and onto a narrow road, twisting and turning past several half-full parking lots, finally coming to a stop in one closest to the main building.

"I guess you were looking for the perfect spot." A smile tilted up one corner of Kate's mouth.

"We'll get enough walking today. We'll be glad to be this close when we head for the car later on."

"I'll take your word for that." She climbed out of the car and a gust of wind grabbed the scarf.

She and Jim reached for it at the same time. "Here, let me help." He coiled the long scarf double and then looped the material over her head. "It will stay now." He moved his gaze from the scarf up to her eyes, which opened wide. The rosy color across her cheeks evidence of something, but he wasn't quite sure what.

"Let's go." He draped his arm around her shoulders and ushered her toward the building where he bought their tickets. "Do you want to look at the gift store first?"

"No, let's go outside and take advantage of the lovely sun."

"Good plan." He held open one of the large double doors. "The children's section is this way and is quite something."

"Oh, look at this maze."

"There's another one farther into this section."

"I love the stone and the way everything looks natural."

"Yeah, that's been the plan all along." They moved on. "The kids can walk along here where all the vegetables are grown."

"Oh, my look at their art displays. These mosaic tree

displays are gorgeous."

When they finished with the children's area, they found themselves back in the central area near the main building.

"Look at this." Kate pointed toward an eagle sculpted in metal. Then her gaze fell on another sculpture. "Oh, my gosh!" She stood completely still, captivated by the movement. "The Dancing Lily." She read the small sign out loud.

"Pretty phenomenal, right?"

"My mind tells me the limbs of the sculpture aren't moving, but my eyes say otherwise."

Jim grabbed her hand and tugged. "If we don't get a move on, we'll miss out on all there is to see." They ambled down a path, stopping occasionally to read the label on a variety of green or brown growing plants.

"Oh, look at this. I've never seen a tree with droopy limbs like this." She reached a hand out and gently touched the leaves of what appeared to be a kind of evergreen.

"Some genetic thing that keeps the limbs from ever hardening," Jim smiled at the joy beaming from her face. This was such a good idea. Troubles didn't stay in your mind when you visited here.

The afternoon wore on, along with Kate's exclamations of surprise and appreciation for the offerings at the Coastal Maine Botanical Gardens.

By the time the sun dropped behind the horizon, the

temperatures did also. Jim let his arm lay across Kate's shoulders and pulled her close. She didn't resist as they made their way to the parking lot.

"What a beautiful place, Jim. This more than lived up to what I read."

"Glad you enjoyed it. We're pretty proud of what's been done here." After helping her into the car, he drove out to the main road and headed toward Griffin Harbor. When they entered the edge of town, he asked, "Lobster Pot okay with you? Or do you want to branch out? Luigi's has good Italian and not only pizza."

"Let's do the Italian if you can get by without your lobster for the day."

Jim laughed. She'd teased him. Nice. She was coming along.

"I'll survive." He parked in front of the small restaurant.

After her wine and his beer came and they ordered, Kate leaned back in the booth and appeared to study him a moment. Her eyebrows canted down and caused two little lines to form over her nose.

"Are you worried about something, Kate?"

"So what we saw today...is that what you have in mind for Aunt Liddy's property?"

"No. We've talked about leaving everything in its more natural state. We'll allow a small amount of hunting and camping, but on a limited basis with not many people at one time and not every month of the year."

She nodded and sipped on her wine. The salads and bread arrived, and they ate in silence for a while. She used a lot of pepper, but no salt.

"Explain the process to me of what has to take place if Blair and I decide to let the Conservancy Trust have the Thompson land." She dipped a hunk of bread in the seasoned olive oil and raised the piece to her mouth.

Kate's teeth bit into the bread, and Jim's gut clenched. Clearly, he needed to get a handle on his attraction to this woman who was only here for a short time, maybe never to return. Damn.

"Let me be clear about the price. You'll get more money for the land from Holland than you will from our Trust. Like the folks running the Gardens, the Conservancy Trust was started by individuals who put up their own land for collateral in order to finance the acres we've bought. We've always had our eye on the Thompson land. Liddy said she'd put it in her will for us. We were okay with waiting, but she didn't get around to doing that before she died."

"If you and Blair decide to sell the land to us for the $50,000 we're able to give you, I've got documents that you need to sign. We'll have a notary and witnesses, like you would if you were signing a will or any real estate transaction."

The waiter arrived with their meal. The wonderful aroma of the angel hair pasta with lobster Alfredo sauce he'd ordered made Jim's mouth water. Kate had ordered veal scaloppini. Her and her meat. He smiled.

* * * *

Why was he grinning? Something always seemed to be going on in the man's mind. The veal was tender enough Kate didn't need her knife. Ummm. The taste was better than she'd anticipated.

"So Blair can't get here until Friday, right?"

Kate nodded because her mouth was full of wonderful pasta with marinara sauce. Luigi couldn't have been over here from the old country long. His food was divine.

"How do you propose to spend the week?"

"Well, I don't know. I haven't given it much thought."

"Why don't you let me show you around the state? If we go out for at least two full days, we'll cover miles of territory. I'd like to get up toward the areas around Mount Desert Island and Bar Harbor, but not sure that's possible for such a short trip. We've got plenty of other port towns along the coast."

Kate stalled with another bite of the veal. What would be the effect of her spending several more days with the ruggedly handsome lawyer? His longish light brown hair with flakes of gray was different from her blonder husband. John's lean, pretty boy good looks were at odds with Jim's ruggedness. John always had to fight to get people to take him seriously. He'd modeled while he was in college and his friends ribbed him about that job. Her hair was much blonder when she was young, and people called them the golden couple. Yeah, right. She pressed her lips against the pain.

"If you're game, why don't we camp a couple of nights. I know you've camped. That's where you met Addie and Devon. I don't remember the other woman's name."

"Kim. Our other friend is Kim."

"Yeah. And didn't you say you went every summer for years?" Jim raised the beer bottle to his lips for a long swallow.

Kate imagined Jim reveled in the outdoorsyness of Maine. "We were in cabins. We slept on cots. We had inside bathrooms with their attendant scorpions."

"Well, cabin camping is an option if that's all you agree to. I know of a couple of good places. Let me check them out." He finished his pasta and leaned back in the chair.

"These cabins have inside bathrooms?" Please, please say yes. Kate hated those portable toilets. She realized she was looking forward to spending time in the outdoors. She used to love it, but there'd been neither enthusiasm nor time for that after John's death.

"Well…there are cabins and cabins. I'll make sure to get us ones that have inside facilities. What do you say?"

"Well…okay then." Kate gulped her wine. What had she agreed to?

Jim hopped up, leaned across the small table, and kissed her full on the lips. Her heart did a summersault. He sat down and rubbed his hands together like he'd won a large jury settlement.

"All right. I'll make a Mainer out of you yet."

"Don't get ahead of yourself. This is only for a couple of nights." Would they have separate bedrooms or share one? After his kiss, the idea of sharing a bedroom with the Maine lawyer sent warm tendrils spiraling down the middle of her body and between her legs. She squirmed in her side of the booth. Maybe this wasn't such a good idea. Would she look like a big jerk if she asked how many rooms?

She picked at a cuticle. She hadn't realized she'd stopped doing that until now when she went back to that awful habit which had started right after 9/11. None of the things Devon had given her helped her stop. Until coming to Maine. Then the idea of camping with Jim sent her falling back on that behavior.

"Can you take off right now?" He probably had work to keep him busy. Pushing off the activity gave her more time to get ready and to adjust to the idea.

"I need to take Monday and Tuesday to wrap up a few things and make arrangements. In addition, I want you to meet with the Conservancy Trust board on Monday. We can leave early Wednesday morning with the plan to return Friday morning before Blair arrives. I'd like to spend more time, but this will have to do. How's that work for you?"

"That will work fine."

"I'll take care of the food and beverages and linens. You need to acquire practical clothes and hiking boots." He nodded toward her soft jersey T-shirt. "That won't be warm enough. Stop by Gerard's and tell them I sent you. They'll get you outfitted."

Kate nodded. Jim's enthusiasm swept her up like a huge wave and carried her far from the shore. Scary, but exciting. She smiled across the top of her wine glass at him. Had she made a serious error in judgment agreeing to go camping with the man? Guess she'd find out.

"Hey, Jim." A portly woman with salt and pepper hair stopped at their table.

Jim hopped up and hugged her. "Mildred, how are you? I believe you've met Liddy's niece by marriage."

He gestured toward Kate, and she rose and extended her hand toward the woman. "That's right." Mildred had shared fun stories about Liddy at the memorial service. "It's good to see you again."

"Hello, Kate."

"Join us." Jim moved behind a chair.

"Are you sure I won't be disturbing?"

"Not at all," Kate added her encouragement, because it wouldn't do to let the town think she and Jim were on a date.

"Of course not." He pulled out the chair and helped settle Mildred between them. They kept up a steady stream of polite conversation, until Mildred stopped and nailed Kate with a beady-eyed stare. "You do plan to turn over the Thompson land to the Conservancy Trust, don't you?"

"I don't know yet, Mildred. My daughter's coming to visit, and then we'll decide together what we want to do with the land. It's possible she'll want to keep it in the family. Be a nice place for her to get away from the hectic-ness of New York City."

"Liddy would be pleased with either the Trust or you keeping it in the family, but she'll haunt you if you sell to Holland."

Kate leaned away. The venom in the woman's tone made Kate's heart rate trip up and her hands grow sweaty. Mildred completely believed her statement, enough to cause Kate nightmares.

"She's giving every option plenty of consideration," Jim jumped in. Was he afraid Mildred's hard sell would reverse Kate's leaning in his direction?

"I've had my say. Good night to you both."

Before Jim had a chance to rise, the older woman

stood, shoved back her chair, and left.

"Wow, is she always that outspoken?"

Jim laughed a moment, nodded, and said. "You always know where you stand with her. She's made more than a few people mad over the years. If she doesn't like a person's plans for their land, she doesn't leave them wondering about her opinion. Lots of times, they've gone back to the drawing board and come up with a better idea based on her comments."

"And if they can't win her over?" Kate sipped her wine.

"No doubt she's made a few enemies in her time on the planning board. She and Liddy were power brokers whenever questions of land use came into play. Now she's the lone vote holding off the developers."

"Enemies, huh?" She studied the man across the table from her. He and the older woman shared the same passion about the land. What would he do if she disagreed with him about what best to do with the Thompson land? What did she really know about Jim Donovan anyway? He appeared to be a man with strong convictions. What if Liddy hadn't wanted to turn the land over to his conservancy? All she had was his word and that of an equally hardheaded Mildred on the subject. A chill ran across Kate's shoulders. Surely, he was a good guy. Wasn't he?

* * * *

Saturday, September 14

Kate settled into one of the Adirondack chairs on the patio, cradling a wine glass between the fingers of both hands. When darkness crept toward the cottage, the lights on the island across from her twinkled on. The moon popped over the top of the island, rising in the sky sending a swath of white across the water, which grew shorter as the night wore on. Kate couldn't argue with how gorgeous the scenery was, but gosh, it was isolated.

And yet, peaceful.

The music from the CD playing in the cottage drifted outside. Beautiful stirring music like you found in old movies with the strings, wind instruments, and percussion sweeping you along with its intense emotion. The composer was from Maine and Jim left several of his CDs for her.

He'd checked out the house when he brought her home from the wonderful Italian meal they'd enjoyed at Luigi's. Jim bought a bottle of the wine they'd enjoyed with the meal so she'd have it to drink at home later.

He was a force for sure. He did want the Thompson land. Had she made a mistake agreeing to travel the state of Maine with him for a couple of days? Guess time would tell. She'd surprised herself by saying yes, and by how much she looked forward to seeing more of this state.

The cottage was comfortable and cozy decorated in

white with touches of lighter and darker blues. The lowering temperatures forced her inside, she flipped a switch, and the fire in the fireplace crackled on. She grabbed one of the books on the history of the area and read until her eyelids drooped. What would she do tomorrow?

CHAPTER FIVE

Sunday, September 15

After sleeping in, Kate drank coffee and ate her oatmeal on the porch. The view overcame the slight nip in the air. The beauty made her catch her breath. She understood people fighting over the property.

At the 11 o'clock service at Liddy's Congregational Church, people warmly welcomed her, and more of them confirmed Liddy's desire to turn her property over to the Conservancy. No reason to doubt Jim it seemed. She ate a yummy hamburger at a place on Maine Street called The Barn Door. They served burgers, steaks and of course seafood. The inside window overlooking the harbor gave her a wonderful view of the town and the Walking Bridge which led across the Harbor to the side where Jim lived. Should she stop by?

No. Better if she spent today shopping and chatting with friends since it was easier to use her phone in town. She set off at a brisk clip toward Gerard's, the place Jim and the librarian had suggested.

People walked their dogs on the sidewalks, taking them into cafes or at least onto the patios. A beautiful sun-shiny day, but a wind whipping off the harbor made Kate shiver and wish she'd brought a jacket with her from the cottage. Well, she'd pick up another one while she shopped.

The bell clanged when she entered Gerard's. Wood floors showed the results of years of peoples' steps. Kate glanced around. The store had a huge selection of men's and women's clothes.

"Afternoon. What can I do for ya?" A gray-haired, strongly built woman turned from behind a glass counter showcasing fishing lures. "Kate Thompson, what are you doing here?"

"I came in looking for jeans. What are you doing here, Miss Steele?"

"I told you at the service to call me Mildred. I work here part time." She laughed. "Keeps me out of trouble. Women's clothes are toward the rear of the store. I guess Jim convinced you to stay a while, huh?"

"What?"

"I figure if you're buying clothes, you must be going to stay longer than a few days. Jim Donovan promised he'd bring you back here if he had to kidnap you."

"What?" Kate sounded like a broken record, but the woman's words threw Kate for a loss. What was she implying?

"Yes," Mildred walked down an aisle. "We knew if you saw the land you'd never let the developers get their hands on it. I serve on the town's land use committee, you know?"

"Yes, I've heard." Kate followed the older woman. She'd barely gotten in a word before Mildred went on.

"Anything new needs our approval. We sure hated to lose Liddy." Mildred stopped. "With her gone, we're one vote closer to losing the battle against Ray Holland and his like. All they want to do is plow over trees and lay down concrete."

Where had Kate heard that speech before? Oh, yeah. Jim Donovan.

"We hate it, and we'll do anything to stop the activity. That's why Jim said he'd kidnap you if he had to." A large laugh boomed from the woman, and she shoved Kate on the shoulder. "Course he wouldn't. He's an officer of the court. No finer man around, I can tell you. Liddy loved him, and he looked after her."

"Yes, I understand that he did." Kate felt all kinds of bad. Guilt churned in her stomach because she hadn't made more of an attempt to keep up with John's aunt.

"Here, we can talk about the property later. Let's find the right outfits for you. How'd you happen to stop by here?" Mildred ushered Kate to the rear of the store with rows of women's clothes.

"Jim suggested the shop."

"Of course he did. We can always count on him to steer visitors our way. Okay, jeans here, shirts, sweaters, and jackets against the wall. The dressing room's behind this curtain, and we've got only the one. But I'll keep an eye out if a man comes in, make sure you're finished."

"Thanks Ms. Steele. I'm sure I'll be able to find what I need."

"Mildred to you. Your aunt and I were close."

Kate pulled a couple of pairs of jeans off a stack that looked to be about the right size.

"It was such a shock," Mildred said. "Liddy had never been sick a day in her life. We all expected her to live to be a hundred. All of a sudden she started complaining of pains in her stomach, before the doc arranged for tests, she dropped dead."

"What? Did cancer get her?"

"Your aunt was murdered."

Kate staggered against the rack of shirts. Word of any kind of sudden death still sent her reeling.

"You're kind of pale, Kate. Do you need to sit down? There's a place in the dressing room here."

Mildred guided Kate into the room, and she dropped onto the bench running against the sidewall. The back wall mirror showed her chalk-like face. She dropped her head down and drew in several long breaths.

"That's better. Can I get you a glass of water?"

Kate nodded.

Mildred hurried away without another word. Kate slowly raised her head testing whether it would spin. When it stayed on her shoulders, she rested it against the wall. Guess she should have asked Jim how Liddy died, but the woman was in her 80's, and it was normal to assume old age or her heart or cancer claimed her.

"Here you go. Take a sip or two of this." Mildred handed Kate a small clear glass.

Kate sipped. "Thanks. I'm better."

"I guess Jim didn't tell you about the murder for fear he'd never get you to come."

"He'd have been right."

"Well, I'm glad he didn't because we need you here to help fight the developers. You never told me why you were going to stay longer."

Kate blinked several times. She needed to get her head working again. "My…my daughter Blair can't get away from work until next weekend. I decided to stay longer to give her an opportunity to come and help me decide what to do with the property."

"I'm sorry I sprang the story on you that way, Kate. Not that there's ever a good way to die or to learn about a death."

Kate dug down deep for inner resources and stood.

"That is quite true, Mildred."

She walked from the changing area. "I'll come back later to shop. I'd better head back to the cottage now."

"You can take a few pieces home with you and bring back what doesn't work for you. How about that?"

"That will work fine. Thanks." She grabbed a long-sleeved teal t-shirt and a black and teal cable knit button-up long sweater to go with the black jeans. Be good on a cool evening. If nothing fit, she'd bring it all back and start over on Monday. Kate slid her credit card through the machine and Mildred handed Kate the receipt to sign.

"I'm sorry I startled you with the news, but I'm kind of surprised no one else in town mentioned it to you before now. We have a few busy-bodies." Her smile indicated she wasn't one of those. "Liddy was a good woman who worked all her life for others and for this town. She deserved better."

Was Mildred referencing how Aunt Liddy died or the lack of Kate's support for the woman?

"I slipped a CD of one of our locals in your bag. You'll enjoy the artist. He's one of my favorites."

"Thank you, Mildred." She held up the bags, "If these don't work, I'll be back."

Kate trudged up the hill toward the library where she'd parked her car, again. They had plenty of space, and she didn't have to worry about backing into the Griffin Harbor traffic. The gusting wind made it difficult for her to carry the bags. She got the car door open then wedged her body between it and the car, and maneuvered her bag inside. When she stepped away from the door, the wind flung it closed. Good grief, the wind was howling the way it did in Texas.

Why had Jim not told her about Aunt Liddy's murder? She'd have to ask him.

But not now. The emotional rush from the shock of learning how Liddy died had exhausted her. Kate wanted to lie down and rest. A picture of the wonderful cottage balcony filled her mind. Sitting there with a glass of wine would be a great place to unwind. Despite Mildred's news, Kate was glad she'd moved to the cottage. Somehow, she felt close to Liddy there.

* * * *

Jim left his desk in his home office and went to find out who was pounding on his front door in the middle of the afternoon. He wasn't expecting anyone and had been deep in reading a contract for one of his clients. Tedious but that's what his client paid him the big bucks for to make sure there wasn't anything in it to cause a problem somewhere down the line.

He swung open the heavy oak door. "Mildred, come in. All that banging made it sound like all the ghouls of hell were pursuing you."

She pushed by him before he'd quit speaking. "Jim, I told her." She huffed out the news as if she expected him to know what she was talking about, but he didn't.

"How about a hot coffee, Mildred? I have a fresh pot. Come on back here to the kitchen." He started that way without waiting for her. He'd known her a long time and coffee was always welcome. He settled her in a seat at the kitchen table and turned to get the cups and fill them with coffee. Mildred popped back up and followed him to the counter.

"I told her."

He set the filled cups on the table and eased her back into her chair, lowered himself, and stretched out his long legs. The strong black coffee gave him the boost he needed for whatever crisis Mildred had dreamed up. "Now, you told who what?"

"I told Kate that Liddy was murdered."

Jim nearly spewed a sip of coffee. He grabbed a napkin to wipe his mouth. "How'd that come about?"

She told him. He sipped the hot brew. "Well, I knew we'd have to tell her. How'd she take the news?"

"Kind of like you were afraid of. It shook her up. She got pale and nearly passed out."

"Damn. Well, it couldn't be helped. I couldn't take the chance of telling her beforehand. I had to get her up here. I counted on the land winning her over."

"We still have time to convince her to give the land to the Conservancy Trust. Her daughter is coming to visit." Mildred sipped her coffee and let out a big breath of air, apparently relieved she'd gotten the news off her chest.

"I know. I'm hoping to get Blair on our side. She was instrumental in convincing her mother to make the trip in the first place."

"Do you know what the daughter does?" Mildred twisted her coffee cup.

"She works for the 9/11 Memorial and Museum in their Communications Department."

"That's impressive, especially since her father died in one of the towers."

"Yeah, I'm pretty sure her mother doesn't quite get that, but I do. It's why I'm happy to be in Grandma and Grandpa's house. Makes them and my parents seem close." He finished his coffee, rose, and set the cup in the sink. "Guess I'd better get out there and do what damage control I can."

She rose and put her arm around his shoulders. "You've been a good son, grandson, nephew, and wonderful friend. This will be all right in the end."

"You think so?" He looked into her blue-gray eyes, lined with years and smiles.

"Sure. You know the old saying: *Everything will be all right in the end. If it's not all right, it's not the end.*"

Jim laughed. "Love your optimism, Mildred." He stood and walked her to the front door. "Thanks for the heads up. I'll keep you posted. If you hear anything from other committee people, you let me know."

"Ahyah." Mildred wobbled on unsure steps to her old 4-wheel drive vehicle, climbed in, and waved before she pulled from the curb.

"Remarkable woman." He'd known many Maine women like Mildred. He went inside, rinsed out her cup, and set it with his in the sink. Should he call Kate or show up unannounced. Surprise seemed the best bet. He'd better go deal with this now.

* * * *

Loud knocking drew Kate to her door. She'd been reading one of the history books she'd picked up at the library. Her new jeans and shirt fit, and she loved the new bulky sweater she'd found at Gerard's.

"Who is it?" Her voice came out weaker sounding than usual.

"It's me."

Even before he said his name, Kate recognized that soft Maine twang.

"Jim Donovan."

She unlocked and swung open the door. Glad she had on the new clothes. The dark teal always a good color for her gave her a touch of confidence. Now what in the world brought that idea to her mind? Damned if she wanted to think or feel anything about the infuriating man. He'd lied to her.

"Hey, Jim." She blocked the entrance with one hand on the door and one on the jamb. Not that she'd be able to keep him out if he pushed, but she was sure he wouldn't. "Got any more lies for me?"

He had the grace to drop his head a moment, but then his beautiful blues squared with her browns. "I didn't lie, Kate. You never asked me how Liddy died."

"I assumed it was old age. It never occurred to you I'd want to know she'd been murdered?"

"May I come in?"

"Sure, but only if you'll tell me what happened." She didn't budge from the door.

"I'll tell you what we know."

"Okay." She stepped back, and he entered and walked over to the windows.

"So tell me."

"Let's sit down first."

Kate nodded, curled up on the loveseat, and pulled her feet up under her. Was she nuts? Did she want to hear about a murder, especially of a family member, even if she hadn't been close to the woman? "I don't want to hear any of this, but I need the information to decide whether or not to let Blair come. So talk."

"Liddy was 88, but she was one of the healthiest people around. Everyone joked she'd make 100. People were making bets. It was only because of that and how sudden the sickness came on that the ME decided to do an autopsy. He found traces of arsenic."

"Oh, my God!" Kate sat up and planted her feet solidly on the ground, hoping that would calm her heart that seemed bent on doing double time. Her head spun a bit and she was afraid she might be sick. Her hands clasped each other in a clammy grasp. This was not stuff she handled well. "Have the police arrested anyone?"

"No. They don't have any suspects. I'm sorry, Kate." Jim rose and crossed to the loveseat. "I should've told you, but I needed you to come up to see the Thompson land for yourself, and I was afraid you wouldn't come if you knew what had happened to Liddy."

"Thanks for the apology, and you're right. I wouldn't have come. And...then... I'd have missed out on seeing amazing scenery, learning about a wonderful, strong woman, and..."

"And?" He sat next to her.

She shrugged. "Getting to spend time with Blair who's coming up next weekend. Is it safe for her to come? I was happy I'd moved out here to the cottage, but now, I wonder."

Jim's hands grasped her arms. She dared not meet his gaze. What might she read in his eyes or he in hers?

"Kate, I don't think I'd have asked you to come if I thought it was dangerous."

She backed from his hold. "You don't think?"

"I'm trying to be honest with you. This land is important." He rose and walked over to the sliding glass doors, staring at the water.

"I was married for several years, but it didn't last. I lost acres of Donovan land in the divorce and Ray Holland's company built a large condominium development on the property. He leveled our trees and laid down concrete on land that had been in the Donovan family for generations. I can't let him win this one. The Thompsons have owned this land for almost as long. I won't let him win." He faced her.

"Aren't you forgetting something, Jim? It's not your decision to make. It's mine and Blair's."

"And that's why I went to such lengths to get you up here. I'm so glad Blair can come next weekend. She'll recognize the value, I'm sure."

"Well, the value yes. But maybe she'll want to share it with lots of people rather than keep it for the family."

Jim crossed quickly to her. He pulled her into a standing position. A tingle zipped from his touch to her feet and back to her head, making the room spin again.

"But don't you see? The Conservancy Trust can make sure that happens. Selling to the Trust makes sure that not just one family gets to enjoy nature, but more importantly, it offers protection from the crowds of people who don't care about the land or the environment. Remember what you saw when we visited the Coastal Maine Botanical Gardens. Our Trust can do much to maintain and support the land and manage the animals. I want you to feel the way Liddy did. The way Mildred and many more do."

Before Kate knew what was happening, Jim pulled her to him and kissed her full on the mouth, with more passion than finesse. Her stomach dropped to her feet. Electricity shot down her arms.

He must be insane, but more insane was that she didn't push him away. When he gentled his touch, slid his tongue along the seam of her mouth, drew her flush against him, showing her what she and the project did to him, she gasped. He slid his tongue into her mouth and then along her teeth. They breathed together for a moment before he drew away and rested his forehead against hers.

"Dear God in heaven, what just happened?" Kate's words were breathy.

"I believe we kissed the daylights out of each other." He let her move back, but didn't release her.

"But I don't do that."

"But you did. Very well, I might add."

The victim's flush started on Kate's chest, rose to her throat, and then covered her whole face.

"I can't believe what happened." Her voiced trembled.

"Why? We're two free, consenting adults."

"But I'm not."

Jim let go and stepped away.

"You didn't kiss me like you were involved with anyone else, Kate. Are you?"

"My husband." She burst into tears.

CHAPTER SIX

Monday, September 16

"Hey, Jim, you're in early. What can I do for you?" Tom Jenson stepped back to let his friend enter. The Lobster Pot wasn't open for food service this time of the day, but Jim was always welcome.

"Love a cup of your coffee, and I need a favor." He settled at the bar.

"Sure." Tom filled the cup with steaming brew and set it in front of Jim. "Whatever you need, you've got it."

Hard to beat true friends like Tom. Jim was more than grateful. They lived different lives, and it would've been easy for them to drift apart. But they'd both worked at keeping the friendship alive.

"I've got to head into Gerard to meet with a client. Would you mind keeping an eye on Kate for me?"

"Not a problem at all." Tom wagged his eyebrows up and down, and twirled a fake mustache like someone in a melodrama.

Jim laughed. "Not that way, man. I've talked her into taking in the sights up toward Bar Harbor, and she's supposed to go into Hanson's today to get outfitted with sturdier clothes. She stopped at Gerard's the other day, and Mildred told Kate about Liddy's murder."

"Oh, my God. Why'd she do that?"

"I don't know." He stirred the coffee, having burnt his tongue before when he got in a hurry.

"How did Kate react?"

"She didn't take it well at all. She left without finishing her shopping and then when I showed up to explain, she ripped me a new one for not telling her."

"Can't say I blame her."

"No, but Tom, if I'd told her, I'm sure she wouldn't have come. I couldn't risk that." He gulped about half the cup.

"No, I guess, not. What do you need me to do to help today?"

"Stop by Hanson's and make sure Kate gets everything she needs. Seeing a familiar face will make her feel more comfortable."

"No problem at all. I'll ask Josie to call me when she comes into the store, and I'll show up."

"Sounds good." Jim chugged back the last coffee.

"So you're showing her more of our beautiful state? Trying to make a Mainer out of her, are you?" Tom rubbed his chin with his thumb and forefinger.

It was like a small clear bubble floated above his friend's head containing the words he was thinking. Tom thinking about the lovely Texan wasn't something Jim wanted. Did he want Kate to stay?

Hell yeah, he did, but he didn't know exactly how to make that happen. After the fiasco when he kissed her, it didn't look like he had much a chance. Still, she was worth the fight. A camping trip in cabins could help move them closer together. He felt better about being gone all day with Tom to keep an eye on Kate. He'd rearranged the Conservancy Trust's meeting for late in the day on Tuesday because a couple of the members had a conflict with the Monday meeting. That worked best with his schedule.

"Thanks, man. I owe you one." He threw down a couple of dollars for the coffee.

"This will be on the house."

Jim waved as he left the restaurant. Was he making a mistake to place Kate under Tom's eye? He'd always been something of a ladies' man, but never settled down. Nah, it'd be okay. Jim drove out of town toward Gerard.

Later in the day, after finishing his work at the courthouse, but before heading back to Griffin Harbor, he stopped the Gerard County Sheriff's office. Each little town had its own police chief, but Seth Stigler oversaw all law enforcement in the county. He'd been involved in the investigation into the suspicious death of Liddy Thompson.

"Thanks for seeing me, Seth." Jim settled into the chair in front of the sheriff's large oak desk.

"Anytime, Jim. What's on your mind?" At 55, Stigler had held the job for 10 years and his fellow law enforcement types and the general population respected him.

"Just following up about Liddy Thompson's death. You guys find out anything more?"

"Wish we had, but we've not been able to trace the arsenic and no suspicious newcomer in town caught anyone's attention. Believe me we're frustrated. You got any leads for us?"

"Afraid not. You remember meeting Kate Thompson at Liddy's funeral. She's staying out at the cottage now, and I'm working on convincing her to turn over land to the Conservancy Trust."

"Too bad Liddy never put that in her will."

"You know she talked about it often but never got around to taking the final steps. Hard to push someone on that sort of thing. We all think we'll live forever."

"How does Liddy's niece like the cottage? Well, what's not to like about that view, huh?"

"She, like everyone, is in love with the view, but she wants her daughter to come look at it before making a final decision. It's possible Blair will want to keep the land in the family."

"The daughter the niece's only living relative?"

"Yes. It sounds like after Kate's husband John was killed on 9/11 they became closer than most mothers and daughters."

"Sounds like things are moving the way Liddy, you, and the Conservancy Trust wanted them to."

"I hope so. Blair is coming in Friday. In the meantime, I'm taking Kate up toward Bar Harbor. I showed her the Gardens on Saturday. This is one more step to help her understand how we protect the land up here."

"Do you need me to do anything, Jim?"

"Just keep trying to find Liddy's killer. We'll be out of pocket for a time. If anything comes up, you can reach me on my cell."

"When are you going?"

"Just two days up and back, Wednesday morning through Friday morning. Want to be back before her daughter arrives around noon."

"You should have good weather for the trip, brisk but not yet freezing. I'll get in touch if I hear anything. You do the same."

Jim rose and extended his hand. "Thanks, Seth. Good to talk to you."

* * * *

On Monday morning, sitting in one of the Adirondack chairs on the balcony, Kate sipped her coffee. Amazing. She could just "be" here. The drive she felt at home to be active and accomplishing tasks was absent here. Made sense why the cottage was booked for most of the entire year.

She hadn't talked with her friends in a while. Maybe she needed feedback from them about what all was going on. Jim's kiss and her reaction to it…maybe she wouldn't talk about that, but she needed to hear from her friends.

Kate reluctantly left the balcony, dressed, and drove into town, stopping at the small coffee shop to place her call. It was 8 a.m. back home. Never get hold of Addie this early. She kept theatre hours. Up late at night and into work about mid-morning. Kim was on a vacation in the state of Washington. Devon was the early riser of the four of them. When they were kids at camp, she was always the first one awake.

"Morning, Kate. What's up besides the roosters and you and me?"

Her friend's wry humor always made Kate smile. "I'm still in Maine."

"This was supposed to be a short trip, wasn't it?" Her coffee cup clanged through the phone.

"That certainly was what I planned, but I've discovered

the situation is more complicated. Liddy didn't die of old age, Devon. She was murdered, but no one has a clue why or by whom."

"Murdered? Oh, hon. I'm sorry to hear that. You okay?"

"Yeah, I am. Thanks. Blair's coming this weekend to look at the land."

"Oh?"

"I don't want to make a decision about the Thompson land without her first looking at the property. It's hers as much as mine."

"Do you like it up there, Kate?"

"Well, I... It is gorgeous. The view from the cottage balcony is something."

"Send me a picture."

"Of course. Hang on. I've taken several, every morning. I can't get over how beautiful it is. Wait a minute." Kate quickly sent several photos to her friend.

"Wow. That's spectacular."

"I know. It's peaceful here. There's no better word for it. Life is less hectic. You will find this hard to believe, but I've stopped chewing my cuticles."

"Really? That is something. Nothing I've ever given you has helped you do that...so what about Donovan?"

"Jim? What about him?" Kate hated that her heart rate kicked up at the man's name. If he were standing near, her face would be pink with the emotions he easily aroused in her. Emotions she was not ready to face.

"Are you still seeing him?"

"Well, not seeing him as in *seeing him* seeing him, but we've had a few meals together. He's shown me around the town. We toured the Coastal Maine Botanical Gardens. They were amazing."

"I see."

Kate picked up her cup for a quick swig of coffee, coughed and went on. "We're taking a trip up the coast for a couple of days."

"Ah huh."

"What does that mean?"

"Just I see, and I'm happy you're having a good time."

"Devon, can you manage to come up for a few days? Maybe be here when Blair arrives?"

A long silence on the other end of the call followed her question. Finally, Devon responded.

"Don't think so, sweetie. Those last minute flight prices are killers anymore."

Huh, Devon had always had the second most money of the four of them next to Kim who'd married into wealthy oil money in Wichita Falls. Kate hated the idea that none of her friends could come up here, especially if they didn't keep the land in the family, and they wouldn't be returning. The idea brought a pang in her chest. Kate pushed it aside and went on.

"I can buy your plane ticket, if you can spare the time from work."

"Thanks, Kate. Let me check my schedule, and I'll get back with you."

They talked for a while longer and Kate left it that Devon would let her know if a trip to Maine was a possibility.

* * * *

"So boss, what's going on?" Past noon on Monday, Kenny had knocked and entered Ray Holland's office after his loud come in. His boss hadn't sounded particularly happy.

Ray circled his desk. "We gotta figure out how to get the Thompson woman to make up her mind in favor of us." He stopped and pointed at Kenny. "Go up there and scope out the situation. Maybe you can pick up something."

"Sure, boss."

"I don't want to ask for more money from the investors. She needs to be satisfied with the five hundred grand."

Ray lit his cigarette and puffed away. A sure sign the man was stressed. He'd mostly quit. No need to tell him that Kenny had already been up once.

"I can make a run over there. Let me look around to get a feeling for which way the wind blows. If it doesn't seem to be blowing in our direction, we'll figure something out."

"Thanks, Kenny. You're a pal." Ray stubbed out his

cigarette and relit another one. "Keep me posted, okay?"

"You betcha." He flicked his hand in a salute, turned, and headed from the office. He had work to do. First, he wanted to check on what Ed had on the Thompson daughter in New York. Using her to put pressure on her mom to make the decision his boss wanted and needed was a definite option. Ray, heavily leveraged on this deal, had to make a go of it. His old man would be kicked out of that high falutin' nursing home if it bombed. Kenny almost wished the old man wasn't around, but he was, so they'd deal.

Kenny packed up and headed northeast for the easy two-hour trip to Griffin Harbor again. Traffic wasn't bad. Kenny steered his car through the tight streets of the small town. The hills and a couple of one-ways made it tricky. He got himself a room at the Inn like last time. Great view. Pretty good food.

He unpacked his gear and headed out to walk the town. Small town folks talk. He'd learn how much closer the woman was to deciding what to do with the family inheritance. If he had to camp out on the property to figure it out, he would. He'd do anything to get the property for Ray.

After Kenny's five years in jail, he loved being outside in the fresh air, and walking was one of his favorite activities. A sharp wind had picked up, and he zipped up his lightweight jacket. He'd left his heavier one in the room, but the weathermen had said it would be mild. They seldom got it right. He strolled up Harbor Drive from the inn. It and Main Street farther up the hill from the water had the majority of stores and restaurants.

He smiled, and thanked the sales people who asked if he needed anything. "Nah, browsing." They talked about the weather and people were eager to talk about the Texan who was visiting. Betting was going four to three in favor of her selling the land to the Conservancy Trust and not to Holland. No one expected she'd stay on the land herself. Apparently, she was waiting until her daughter got here to make the final decision. Oh and that was Friday, don't you know?

The talk went on and on. Kenny lapped it up. How easy they made it for him. The fact the daughter wasn't coming until Friday, gave him a good chance to make an impact on Thompson's decision. He walked back to his car and placed a call to Ray's brother.

"Say, Ed, you remember the broad I asked you to keep an eye on?"

"Sure. You want me to take care of her for you?"

"In a way. Now listen carefully. Do exactly what I say."

* * * *

Kate held up a blue and green plaid long-sleeved flannel shirt against her front and looked in the mirror.

"That should do." A voice to her left said.

She spun around. "Oh. You startled me, Tom. I forget

that I know people here."

"Sorry I scared you. This looks like stuff you'd need to be outdoors. You plan on camping while you're here?"

"Not real camping, but Jim talked about going up toward Bar Harbor. I didn't bring anything but good slacks with me and jeans and flannel might be best for this trip."

"Well, this is the best place. Josie will take good care of you. The key is layers since the temps can change a lot in not much time."

"That's what she said. I was about to leave when I spied this shirt, and I'm trying to decide if I need it on top of all the other stuff I've already bought." Kate hung it back on the rack.

"You're doing tents, right? Not cabins?"

"Oh, no! I'm more of a cabin kind of woman. Jim has agreed, but he said it was almost heretical to camp in a cabin or an RV."

Tom's laugh startled her more than his earlier appearance had. "What's funny?"

"Your expression." His low laugh rumbled out again. "You look like you're not sure about going?"

"Well, I'm not. I mean, Tom, I only came up here for a short visit to look at the land. I needed to feel like I'd honored my husband's memory. Then I'd sell it and drive down to New York to visit with my daughter and on back home to Texas.

Now, I'm staying for a while, learned Liddy was killed, heading across the state with someone I don't know all that well, and Blair is coming up here to look at the land. I sort of feel like I'm out of control." She sucked in a deep breath after the long speech.

"It's understandable you'd feel that way."

"It is?"

"Sure. Things haven't gone the way you expected. It's natural for you to feel that way."

"Thanks for understanding."

"Listen, if you've finished shopping, why don't you come back to The Lobster Pot for a quick lunch. I promise you won't have to eat lobster, and I'll tell you everything I know about Jim Donovan. Maybe you'll feel better about the trip after that."

"All right it's a deal."

"Here you go, Ms. Thompson. I've got everything you bought." Josie, the store clerk, walked up with two large brown paper bags with cord handles.

"Good timing on my part, Kate. Looks like you need help with all of this."

"Thanks, Tom." She smiled at Jim's friend. "I'll give you a ride to the restaurant in exchange."

"Fair enough deal."

Kate was glad to have Tom's help with the bags. The

wind off the water was doing its thing, and she'd have struggled with the car door and the bags.

When they got to The Lobster Pot, Kate ordered the shrimp salad again. Tom sat with her for a while but excused himself when the lunch crowd increased. After she finished eating, Kate put through some calls about real estate transactions in Fort Worth. She talked with the office secretary. Both Jerry and Pam were out on showings. She'd finished her work by the time the crowd thinned out and Tom showed up with two servings of blueberry cobbler and coffee.

"Oh, my."

"House special. You have to try this because last time you were in here, you didn't. Besides, we can talk while we enjoy. I put ice cream on one and left it off the other, not sure how'd you prefer it."

"Without. I'm a purist where my cobbler is concerned. Besides the aroma drifting up convinces me I haven't eaten anything in weeks." Kate picked up a spoon and dug in. Before she got the bite in her mouth, Tom reached out to stay her hand.

"Hang on there. Those berries will scald your tongue, and you won't be able to taste a thing for days. Blow first."

"Thanks for the warning." After following his instructions, she sampled a small bite of the pastry. "Oh, my goodness." She put the rest of the spoonful in her mouth, closed her eyes, and chewed. After swallowing, she opened her eyes. "That is the best dessert I've ever tasted."

Tom smiled at her praise. "Glad you approve."

"My gosh. Does anyone not like this? You must've won awards with this recipe?"

"My grandma and mom did. I never entered any contests."

"Maybe you should." She ate a couple of more bites. "But then you'd have more people coming up here, and y'all don't really like that, do you?"

"It's probably more accurate to say we have a love/hate relationship with the visitors. The folks from away, as we call them. We're glad for their tourist dollars. It helps the economy. Fishing is a hard way to make a living. Having a B & B, a store, or running a restaurant is much easier by comparison."

Kate stirred the pastry to hasten its cooling. "Why do I feel like I'm about to hear a *but?*"

"Tourists don't always treat the environment the way we would like for them to. They tend not to be concerned about the long-range effect of their presence on the land and the animals. It's a constant battle among our citizens."

"The ones who want to allow more developers?"

"Yeah. Then we've got the ones who are more concerned about the harm to the environment."

"That's the side Jim Donovan comes down on?"

Tom nodded. "Let me tell you something about Jim. We've known each other since before we were born. Our families have always been close. We both went to college, but I came back after graduation to help with the family lobster business when my Dad was hurt. Jim went on to law school. His grandparents lived here, and he came every summer. His parents had died so when his grandparents needed help, he moved in with them."

"Doesn't he have a brother?"

"Yeah, but Phillip's an architect in Boston. His life is there with his wife and kids."

Tom sipped his coffee and eyed her over the edge of the mug. "Did Jim tell you about his wife?"

She nodded. A sharp pain made Kate suck in her breath. Was Tom going to tell a different story than Jim did?

"Jim married a gold digger to use an old fashioned term. She was a gorgeous blonde and hoped she'd latched on to someone bound for stardom in politics. Jim always wanted to be a small town lawyer helping folks out. He blames himself for losing a chunk of the family property."

"That's why he works hard for the Conservancy Trust?"

"Smart lady." Tom nodded, scooping the last of the blueberry cobbler from the bowl. He sighed. "Pretty damn good, if I do say so."

Kate laughed. "So true, and you can be excused for

being proud of your accomplishment, both with the dessert and the restaurant."

"Aw, I've just carried on the restaurant. Earlier family members get the credit."

"I bet that's not how they look at it."

"Jim has said you are kind."

Kate felt the heat rush from her neck up her cheeks at Tom's words. She hoped Jim Donovan liked her, at least a little anyway.

"I need to be getting back, but I didn't notice the bill."

"It's on the house."

"Oh. Well, thanks, Tom. This has been fun. You're good company, and the food is the best."

"You'll enjoy seeing more of our beautiful state of Maine."

"I hope it's not more of an adventure than I can handle."

"You'll be fine. You'll be with Jim. He won't let anything happen to you."

"Thanks again. See you soon." Kate walked outside and toward her car.

She'd settled in with her seat belt locked when her cell chimed. Struggling to pull it from her pocket, she caught the call from her friend.

"Hey, Devon. Please tell me you can come."

"I'm sorry, Kate. Not right now. I'd love to come and visit with you up there. The pictures are beautiful. I...I can't get away from work right now."

"Is everything okay?" The tone of worry in her friend's voice surprised Kate. Devon ran a tight ship and her make-up company made a ton of money.

"Sure fine. Maybe before you leave, I can get up there."

"Okay, I'm going to hold you to that. Take care."

"You, too." After disconnecting, the idea Devon was having trouble with work wiggled its way back into Kate's consciousness. Kate sat there a few more moments worrying about her friend.

Devon's voice had a slight tremble. This was strange for her in charge friend. She clearly didn't want to talk about whatever was bothering her, but maybe she'd open up when she came for a visit. Kate couldn't wait to share the beautiful land with her friend.

Speaking of work, Kate punched in the number for the real estate company. This time she got hold of her boss. "Hey, Jerry, I was afraid you'd be worried and I wanted to check in."

"Glad to hear from you, Kate. Peggy was asking me when you were coming home."

"Well, not quite yet. This has turned out to be more complicated than I expected. I may be here a couple of more weeks."

"That's fine, Kate. You haven't had a vacation in years. I saw where you're still handling some clients from up there. We've got the rest of your folks covered. Don't worry. Enjoy yourself. And send pictures."

Kate laughed. "I will, and thanks. I'll keep you posted."

* * * *

Tuesday, September 17

Kate woke to the sound of waves hitting the rocks below her open cottage windows. The most soothing sound in the world. She pulled her robe around her, shoved her feet in house shoes, and made her way to the kitchen. Coffee started first before anything else. Then to the bathroom where after taking care of business, she studied her face in the mirror. The lines didn't appear as pronounced as she was used to seeing them.

Her imagination must be running away with itself. Life was still stressful. She had to make up her mind about the land, but had a hard time concentrating. The peace of this part of Maine was addictive. The sounds of the waves and the birds chirping, and the view from the cottage brought her a peace she hadn't felt in years. She'd even stopped biting her cuticles, until Jim mentioned going camping. Now since he'd agreed they wouldn't be roughing it, she was doing okay again. Well, whatever it was, it agreed with her. She didn't have that drawn about-to-jump-out-of-her-skin look.

The coffee aroma pulled her from her reflection in the bathroom to the kitchen to fill a large cup. She cradled it between her hands, letting the heat warm her fingers. If anything, the news that someone had killed poor Liddy should've sent her over the edge. That's what happened with her anytime she heard of a sudden death. Her body went into fight or flight mode. Since she couldn't fight, she had to run, doing more and more. Over the years, the continued adrenalin rush had taken a toll on her body and especially her face.

She slid open the glass door, stepped out on the balcony, and leaned against the railing. The sun beat down and warmed her face. Despite the low temperature, she was comfortable. She felt safe. This was different from the way she felt when she was home in Texas. Weird. There was no other word for the feeling.

Though this was a lovely way to while away the day, she couldn't.

She had washing to do and things to get ready for tomorrow's trip, and the Maine Coast Conservancy Trust Board meeting was this afternoon.

After a morning of chores, reading a book, and soup on the patio for lunch, Kate glanced at her watch. She could grab a quick nap on the patio before she had to head out to the Conservancy Trust Board meeting. The day sparkled with a slight breeze and lots of sun. She snuggled there under a throw, and acknowledged how lucky she was in her job and her friends. Especially her new ones. Jim Donovan's face loomed in her mind's eye.

* * * *

As they prepared to leave, Kate shook hands with the six people who'd attended the meeting. They all had families who'd been in Maine for generations, and they'd donated land to the Maine Coast Conservancy Trust. They all spoke highly of Liddy Thompson, confirming again what Jim had told her that Liddy had meant to turn the land over to the Trust.

"But, Kate, if you and Blair want to keep it for your family, we'd all be okay with that." Mildred glanced around for concurrence and everyone nodded.

"Absolutely," one of the men agreed.

"I should be able to make a decision soon. Thanks for taking time to meet with me. I have a better idea of your plans and your commitment to the land."

After the last member left the room, Jim turned to her. "Thanks for listening, Kate."

"Of course, the members were informative. Not that you haven't been."

"It's okay. I know what you mean. Trust but verify. We lawyers get that." He chuckled deep in his throat. "Now can I talk you into supper?"

"Thanks, but no. I want to hang out at the cottage and

make sure my clothes are lined up for the trip." Heat began its climb up Kate's neck. Had she made the trip sound intimate?

"Let me walk you to your car then." He put his hand on her arm like there was nothing more normal in the world.

Kate's heartbeat skidded. What was it with this man that he so easily affected her? Neither had said anything about the kiss or her reaction to it.

After she'd climbed in and rolled down the window, Jim patted the door. "I'll be by first thing in the morning, and we'll head out on our excellent adventure."

Kate nodded and smiled, hoping she was up for whatever Jim had planned.

CHAPTER SEVEN

Wednesday, September 18

Kate finished her last cup of coffee, washed it by hand, and set it back in the cupboard. Jim had told her to be ready by 8:30 and it was a few minutes before that now. She'd packed her bag with the new jeans and tops of a variety of weights, and her new hiking shoes. She'd included one nice pair of slacks, and dressy shirt with flats in case they ate at one of the restaurants Jim had mentioned. She wore a good pair of athletic shoes and figured she was good to go.

The honking of a horn drew her to the door. She cracked it open first then threw it wider. A large motorhome sat half in her front yard and half on the street.

"Oh, my goodness." She tripped down the stairs and met Jim before he climbed out of the large vehicle. "What are you doing with this?"

"Do you like it? Wait until you come inside. It's got all the comforts of home."

He grabbed her hand and walked her around to the passenger side where he pulled her up and into the giant vehicle.

"Wow." Kate's gaze traveled around the amazing space. There was a place for everything. "I didn't know...I mean...have you always had one of these?" She ran her hand over the dark green leather of the banquette in the kitchen/den area.

Jim shook his head. "It's not mine. Belongs to a friend. He's loaned it to us, fully supplied. I used to have one, but got rid of it when I stayed around here more to look after my grandparents and then Liddy and didn't have to time to travel."

"When you started talking camping, I never dreamed you meant in something like this."

"This seemed more like your speed."

She opened a door to find the compact bathroom with sink, commode, and shower. "Oh, it's got an inside potty." She smiled. "I like."

Moving farther rear, she found the wall-to-wall bed. "Oh." Her hand rested on her chest where a red flush started its crawl up to her face. Did he expect them to sleep together? How stupid she was. She'd worried about a cabin without two bedrooms and this was much more intimate.

"Oh, hey" Jim put one hand on her upper arm. "See." He tilted her chin upwards. "I'll be up there."

"Oh." Kate repeated herself, but with a sigh of relief and chided herself for jumping to conclusions. "Okay."

"Let's lock up the cottage, and then we'll hit the road."

That's what they did. Driving north along Highway 1, Jim kept up a steady chatter about the sites they passed, the flora, fauna, and history of the area. With her perch in the high motorhome with its wide front window, Kate had the perfect spot to appreciate all the scenery. Her stomach growled as they pulled into the small town of Rockport.

"Sounds like you're hungry. Let's find a place for lunch."

"Where do you park this thing?"

"There's space down by the marina and there's a small café we can walk to."

"Will they have anything besides lobster?" Kate looked away afraid she couldn't keep her lips from turning up in a smile. She enjoyed teasing him.

"Yes, they will. You'll be able to get a burger if you insist, but maybe I can talk you into getting your own lobster roll."

Jim held her hand to help her from the high vehicle. Thank goodness for the steps, otherwise her only option would've been to leap into his arms. Kate glanced at him and quickly away for fear he'd read the crazy ideas floating around in her mind. What was the matter with her? She liked the feel of his hand on her back when he ushered her toward the café that overlooked the harbor. She liked a lot about him. There'd only been one other person since John. Guilt dug into her stomach making her hunger disappear. Was she interested in Jim that way? Could she be?

"She'll have iced tea with extra lemons. I'd like whatever your draft beer is."

While she'd been off in what-if-land, they'd settled into a table on the outside patio and the server had brought menus and taken their drink orders.

"Are you warm enough here?"

Jim studied her over his menu. Her behavior must've seemed strange. She'd better pull it together. No way to explain what was going on in her mind.

"Yes, thanks. This is delightful. Glad for the light jacket, but what a relief from the heat we've still got back in Texas." She rested her elbows on the table and her chin on her fists. "This is like being in another world."

"I hope that's a good thing."

Kate let out a long breath and nodded before she picked up the menu. She'd better change the subject. "What do they have here that's good?"

Jim laughed. "Everything fish. But I promise they have pretty good burgers and fries. What would you like?"

"Is their lobster roll any good?" She shot a quick glance at him and was glad she did to catch the look on his face. His eyebrows almost met his hairline, and his mouth hung open.

"Really?"

"Well, honesty forces me to confess the bite I had of yours the other day with all the butter, was pretty yummy. Can I order fries with it?"

"Of course."

The smile on his face reached in and wrapped around her heart. He seemed so pleased at her willingness to try his favorite dish that she resolved to find more things to make him happy. Oh my, but she was flailing around in deep waters where this man was concerned. She didn't know how to get back to safe, dry land. More importantly, whether she wanted to.

* * * *

What did Kate's expression at lunch mean? She looked scared and excited all at the same time. She'd loved the lobster roll and ate the whole thing, saying she'd have to learn how to make them. When he pointed out she'd need fresh lobster, she balked and said someone else would have to handle that part. She'd buy the special rolls and melt the butter. They laughed a lot, more than Jim remembered laughing in a long time.

Of course, everyone had been saddened at Liddy's sudden death and concerned about who would murder such a sweet woman. He worried a great deal about what would happen to the land. He would do anything to keep it safe for the Conservancy Trust, or for Kate's family, if that's what she wanted.

They walked along the small harbor. Jim told Kate about the various boats tied up there. "Can you do this?" He skipped a stone out across the water.

"I've never tried. We have a few lakes in Texas, but I've never been much of a water person."

"Look here." He skipped another. "See, easy."

"I'll try." She threw, and the small stone plopped and dropped into the water, not far out. Her laughter swelled his heart.

"Let's try again." He put a stone in her hand. "Now relax." He stepped behind her and grasped her hand in his. "Relax your arm. Let me guide you." The scent of her hair, a kind of vanilla, tweaked his nose. Her backside curved against his groin. He may have made an error in judgment. How could he concentrate on throwing the pebble with her near?

What did he want? He moved her arm back and then forward. "Don't let go until we hit the highest part of the arc." She glanced back, concentration, crinkling her eyebrows. He moved her arm backwards again and then forward faster. "Now." Kate let go of the pebble. It skipped twice before sinking. He dropped his arms and stepped back.

Kate jumped up and down. "Oh, I did it. I did it!" She

turned toward him. "That was fun. Thank you." She leaned on tiptoe and kissed him on the cheek. Then she backed off fast. One hand flew to her mouth. "Oh, I'm sorry."

"No need to apologize for a kiss between friends. I hope we're friends now, Kate."

She nodded a half smile on her face. "Yes, I believe we are."

"There are better places on up the road. You can practice rock throwing more, okay?"

"Sure."

Jim looked forward to helping her, but kept those ideas to himself.

"I'll race you to the motorhome." And before he said a word, Kate was several yards ahead of him. Jim set out after her certain he'd catch her, despite her head start.

He did, but they were both huffing by the time they made it up the hill to where they'd parked the vehicle. They propped their hands on their knees and leaned over to catch their breath.

"I didn't know you were a runner." Jim unlocked the door, climbed in, and grabbed them each a cup of cold water.

"Oh, I'm not. I walk a lot and do Pilates, but only a small amount of running. Our summers are too hot for me to make that my primary exercise." She gulped the water. "Thanks," and she handed him back the cup. "One of the counselors I saw suggested I take up running in an effort to make me feel safe. I didn't like it much, I can manage a short sprint like this one, but I don't enjoy it the way I do walking several miles every day. I like the feeling of strength it gives me."

He nodded. "Are you ready to head out?"

"Sure. What's next?"

"Not far. Up Highway 1 to Camden. You're going to fall in love with this small town. In my opinion, it's one of the best harbors anywhere and has great views of Penobscot Bay."

* * * *

Jim was correct. The next part of the trip lasted a smidge over 40 minutes. He found the RV Park, pulled in, and hooked up everything. They had quite a walk into the town.

"Oh, Jim." Kate stopped and stared. "How charming. It looks like a movie set."

"I'm glad you like it. I hoped you would. Wait until you get a view of the harbor from up on Mount Battie in the Camden Hills State Park. Tomorrow, we can go out in one of the ships."

"A boat?"

"Ahyah." He headed down the hill at a good clip.

Kate scurried to keep up. He was like a small boy, excited to show her a new toy. She didn't want to disappoint him. She'd better be honest about this.

"Jim, I'm not a great sailor. I almost always get seasick."

"You'll be fine."

Maybe it would be enough to show excitement looking at the boats in the harbor. She didn't know why she didn't want to disappoint him, but she didn't.

The afternoon and evening flew by. Down on the harbor, Jim pointed out the boat he said she'd enjoy sailing on. It had several masts he exclaimed and told her it was called a schooner. She'd get a great view of the town from the water. Kate didn't make any promises.

Supper was at a lovely restaurant that overlooked the water. They ate inside because the temp had dropped, but it was still wonderful. He ate a whole lobster and she had her steak, keeping her eyes turned firmly away from the red bug on his plate.

Close to ten, they started the long walk back to the motor home. Kate wished she'd eaten less. Between the exertion and nerves about how they'd manage in the tight quarters, her tummy sent out queasy messages to her brain. Not pleasant.

"How do you like Camden, Kate?" Jim's hand rested on the small of her back, and he kept to the outside of the sidewalk.

"It's delightful, of course. I loved the falls and the

harbor. My original idea about how much it was like a movie set hasn't changed. Rockland and Rockport were gorgeous, but Camden has them beat, I'm afraid."

"Camden is one of my favorites. Of course I'm partial to Griffin Harbor, but it's because of family and friends."

When they got to the motorhome, Jim unlocked the door and held it open for her. She grasped the grip and pulled herself up the steps. Following her inside, he walked to a cupboard and pulled out a bottle of wine.

"I got this special for you. Would you like a glass? It will help you sleep."

Kate nodded. Images flooded her mind. She wasn't sure how she'd shut them off to rest. She carried the glass of deep red liquid and settled on the settee of the kitchen table. "I love how compact everything is."

"It's comfortable. I've taken it out a couple of times and am always surprised. Glad you like it." He popped the top on a can of beer and settled down next to her.

Her heart fluttered in her chest. They were close, and they'd kissed, and then she'd kissed him. What were his expectations of this road trip? What were hers?

"Do you shower in the morning or at night, Kate?"

"Morning." A hasty sip of her wine made her cough. Of course, they had to talk about this, but it seemed such an intimate topic.

"I'll shower tonight then. Make certain we both have enough hot water."

While Jim showered, Kate slipped into her flannel pajamas. No one would describe them as seduction clothes. Nor her soft fuzzy socks either. Not that she planned to seduce Jim. What a silly idea. She pulled down the covers, plumped the pillows, and then refilled her wine glass. Would she be able to sleep with Jim right above her? Guess she'd see.

When Jim came out, she slipped in the bathroom to clean off what little makeup she wore and brush her teeth. Jim was already settled in the loft when she came out.

"Will it bother you if I read before I go to sleep?" she asked him.

"Not a problem. I might, too."

Silence filled the small space. They both had e-readers, so no sounds of pages turning disturbed the quiet. Kate read until her lids drooped. The last thing she remembered was turning off the reader.

* * * *

Wednesday, September 18

Blair Thompson exited the elevated train and headed for the stairs. At ten at night, several people milled around on the platform. She didn't like to work this late, but with her plans to leave for Maine on Friday, she felt driven to get ahead to make up for her time off.

People called her a workaholic. They were right. After her father's tragic death, her mother changed, becoming a worrier. She wanted to control every bit of their lives. Blair got it in her head, but she hadn't been able to keep herself from falling into similar behaviors of trying to control everything and to plan for every contingency.

Oh, she didn't bite her nails like her mom, she rode in planes, and she loved NYC. But she was for sure addicted to her work. Maybe that was because she worked at the 9/11 Museum. She experienced such joy every day she walked into the work area. She was honored to be a part of this tribute to the heart of NYC and the country and her father.

"Wish Mom would come for a visit." Blair mumbled to herself as she skipped down the stairs from the elevated to the sidewalk. Her apartment was a block away down a side street. She loved her neighborhood and the red brick building where she lived in a first floor apartment. Would she like to have more lighting on the street? Sure, but no place was perfect.

Womp! Her head exploded and down she went on all fours. She clung to her purse, which someone tried to yank away.

"Tell your mom to sell to Holland."

The guttural sounding words didn't make sense to Blair. "Oh." Someone wrenched her arm behind her back. The pain loosened her fingers on the strap, and the purse slipped from her grasp. She lay on the sidewalk whimpering, tears sliding from her eyes.

She couldn't stay there. Several minutes passed before she struggled up and grabbed her cell from her pocket. She never kept it in her purse for fear of losing her purse this way. She punched in 911.

For the first time, she wished she lived in a building with a doorman. Not that he could've protected her from the attack, but she'd have had help right away.

She let herself into the apartment with the spare key she kept under the mat in front of her apartment. It wasn't long before she heard the sirens. The police car and an EMT drove up about the same time. They alternated bombarding her with questions. She found her work ID to use for identification. Good grief. Her driver's license, medical, and credit cards were gone. She always kept spare cash hidden in the back of the closet. Guess that was a good thing. Thank God she kept her cell in her pocket.

The officer finished his initial questions, and then the ambulance drove her to the emergency room. After x-rays, the doctors put her arm in a sling and told her not to use it until it stopped hurting. Great. How did she do life like that? She popped one of the pain pills he gave her to use for not more than 4 days. After that, if she still hurt and needed them, she'd have to make an appointment with her own doctor. She'd call her boss in the morning, and gosh, dread of calling her mother made her head spin more and her stomach cramp. Mom would flip out.

It was early morning when Blair crawled into her bed. Despite the pain meds, her body ached. Her mind swirled with all the things she had to take care of when she got up later on, not the least of which was canceling all her cards. Thankfully, she'd already made her plane reservations. O, God, how long would it take her to get a duplicate driver's license? In time to get on the plane on Friday? Would she feel like getting on the plane on Friday? How was her mother...?

* * * *

Thursday, September 19

"Oh. What the...?" *My shoulder.* Last night's adventure rolled through her mind like the stupid battery bunny on speed. Blair sat up against the headboard. Her head hurt and her shoulder felt like someone was yanking it from the socket! Coffee and pain pills. Both necessities.

She crawled from the bed like an old woman, stumbled into the kitchen, and set the coffee going before hitting the bathroom. Good thing she'd left off the lid to the pill bottle. She didn't know how she'd get it open now and didn't remember how she opened it last night. Water from the sink washed down the pill. Thankfully, the woman in the mirror didn't look like she was at death's door, which was how Blair felt. Despite her major case of bedhead, a ponytail made everything look better. How would she do that one-armed? She'd figure that out later. After coffee. She needed her coffee.

Thank goodness, she'd had the presence of mind to set it to perk last night. She must've been on automatic pilot, because she didn't remember doing anything. Work. She had to call her boss.

She put her cell on speaker and called Julian Spencer, her immediate boss.

"Hello?"

"Julian, it's me. Blair."

"I was beginning to worry. Not like you to be late and not call. Everything okay?"

"I ran into a difficult situation on my way home last night."

"I've told you not to stay late."

His huff came through the speaker loud and clear. Julian looked on her like a niece and scolded her for her practice of working late when they were on deadline. Blair hated to hear the lecture she'd get from him when she told him what had happened.

When she stopped talking, the silence on the other end of the line was deafening. "Julian. I'm all right."

A long sigh followed by, "Of course, you are. The doctor told you not to use your arm until it stopped hurting? Seems an odd prescription."

"It's badly sprained, but it will heal itself if I don't use it." A quick sip of her coffee and, ugh. It had gotten cold. She emptied out her cup and poured another.

Another huff of air from Julian then he spoke again. "You were taking off Friday, weren't you?"

"Yes, I'd planned to fly up to Maine to visit my mother."

"Don't try to come in then, and maybe you should stay up there longer. There will be less opportunity to mess up your arm if you're on vacation. I know if you're in town, you'll want to come in."

He knew her pretty well. "Okay." She sounded like a petulant teen to her own ears. "I'm not sure I'll be able to go. The thief got my driver's license."

"Take the report from the police with you to the DMV and you can get a duplicate pretty quick. You probably need to stick with cabs for a while and not the subway. You'll have less chance of getting jostled."

"You're probably right. I don't see how I can get away any earlier than Friday, what with canceling credit cards, the license, and dealing with the bank for money."

"Do you have cash on hand? I can loan you dollars to tide you over."

"Thanks, Julian. I always keep a cache squirreled away in the back of my closet. One of Mom's rules. A good thing I've followed this one."

"Keep me posted on how you're doing and when you're leaving."

"Will do, and thanks for understanding, Julian."

After a full cup of hot coffee and a cookie, the easiest thing to eat, she pulled on sweats. That entailed removing her arm from the sling and sliding her bad arm with great care into the sleeve. She heaved a sigh when she got the arm back in the support. Without the pain meds, she bet that would've hurt like the dickens.

She dreaded it, but it was time to get on those credit cards. She set her laptop on the small dining room table where she normally worked. Her kitchen was too cozy to be an eat-in. She opened up the file folder with all her account info in it. Again, rules taught by her mother. Everything in its place.

The buzz at her front door made her jump. Before, she'd never been nervous in her first floor apartment. She didn't have a bellman, but the neighbors all looked out for each other. She peaked through the safety hole and drew in a short breath. A police officer. Not the one from last night, who she hoped was sleeping.

"Who is it?" Even with the uniform, it made sense to be careful.

"I'm Officer J.D. McClendon, ma'am." He held his badge in front of the peephole. "Officer Jenkins, who covered your mugging, asked me to stop by."

That was the name of the policeman from last night. This guy must be legit. Blair, slid off the chain, flipped the deadbolt, and swung open her door.

"We believe we've found your wallet." The officer held a billfold in his hand that looked remarkably like hers.

"I'm sorry. Come in." Where were her manners? She led him into the living room.

The officer held out the billfold. "This appears to be yours. Is it?"

She flipped it open. "Oh this is wonderful. My driver's license and look my credit cards. This is fantastic." She'd still report it to the credit card companies and probably need to get replacements, but now the time crunch wasn't dire.

"No money in it when it was turned over. Do you know how much cash you were carrying?"

"About $100 in cash, but that's all right by me to have everything else here. Where'd you find it?"

"A kid found it lying not far from your apartment by a trash can. He turned it into the beat cop."

"Wow, what a good citizen. If you have his name and address, I'd like to give him a reward."

"Ma'am? He may have taken the money." The tall officer tipped his head at her and quirked an eyebrow as though he considered her notion nuts.

"Maybe, but it makes more sense the guy who hit me stole the money. Why else would he have stolen my purse? Have you found my purse?"

"No, ma'am."

"So I have to get a new lock and keys made for here."

"This could've been a whole lot worse, ma'am."

"For sure, Officer. Thanks for returning this. I still want to send something to the boy."

He smiled and handed her his card. "When you have it ready, give me a call and I'll stop by to pick it up and deliver it to him. Anything else we can do for you?"

She glanced at his card. "Officer McClendon, right?"

"Yes, ma'am."

"Thanks for everything. You and Officer Jenkins have taken good care of me and my belongings."

"You're going to be all right?" He nodded toward her arm in the sling.

She nodded. "Yes, a sprain and it will be a pain for a while, both literally and figuratively, but..." she shrugged. "But as you said, this could've been a whole lot worse."

"Glad you'll be all right."

"You don't sound like you're from New York, Officer."

"No ma'am. Grew up in Kansas, but came up to school because I have family here, and I stayed. Later my parents moved up. You don't sound like you're from up here either."

She laughed. "Texas. Hard to get the twang out no matter how hard I try."

His smile spread across his face. "Not sure you need to, ma'am."

All at once, it dawned on Blair how handsome the redheaded cop was and how dreadful she must look. Heat started up her neck. She walked toward the door. "Well, I appreciate your service, Officer." She held the door for him, and he went through. "Thanks for all your help."

"You've got my card. If you need anything, call." He tipped his hat at her before heading on toward the outside door.

Blair shook her head drawing a moan. An action she should avoid. Where in the world did those reactions come from in the last few moments of her visit with the handsome cop?

She had lots to do if she was going to make her trip to Maine. She needed to help her mom out with the decision about the land. Maybe, waiting to tell her about the accident until she showed up on Friday made more sense. No reason to make her worry before she had to. She sat at the dining room table preparing to let the credit card companies know what happened and to change all of her passwords. All one-handed. Bummer.

* * * *

Thursday, September 19

Kenny answered the cell when he saw who it was. Ed was prompt. He'd better have good news.

"Yeah?"

"Kenny, I did what you told me. I hit the girl and stole her purse, grabbed the money and purse, but threw the billfold away close."

His voice was gravelly from years of smoking. On top of that, he had one of the strongest Maine accents, Kenny had ever heard. "You give her the message?"

"Yeah, said to tell her mother she better sell to Holland."

"You did good, Ed. I know your brother will appreciate your efforts. Money will be in the mail tomorrow."

"Thanks, Kenny. Let me know if you need anything else."

"Sure." Kenny disconnected and slid the phone into his pocket. He'd check in with his boss for any results yet, but he probably needed to wait longer. Kenny was up for whatever Ray needed to get this deal done.

He headed toward the Holland Building.

* * * *

Jim was surprised how well he'd slept last night. He'd worried having Kate below him in the big bed would keep him awake. It didn't, but his dreams were certainly X-rated. He smiled at the picture in his mind of her in the shower now with the water sluicing over her naked body. Maybe he'd better take his coffee outside and walk around for a while.

Last night, they'd eaten supper at a wonderful restaurant and wandered around Camden and the harbor area. Kate seemed to enjoy the town. Today they were going on the schooner Lady Belle and then up on Mount Battie. Both those experiences no visitor to Camden should miss. He wanted to share them with Kate.

Where was he with the lovely Kate Thompson? Where did he want to be? Well, for starters in her bed making love to her. But what happens when she leaves? She's sure to leave. Unless, her daughter, Blair, decides they should keep the land in the family. Then Kate would leave, but she'd come back to visit Blair and maybe him.

Was that enough? What the hell was he thinking? He threw the rest of the coffee on the grass. They needed to get a move on if they were doing the boat and the mountain today. He climbed into the motorhome at the same time Kate stepped out of the bathroom. She was dressed in black jeans, walking shoes, and a black tank top.

"Do you have a jacket?" He nodded at her arms that he noted were nicely firm.

"Yeah, I've got a long sleeve shirt to go over this, and a jacket. Layers seem to be the way to go up here." She moved to the closet area and slipped into the shirt she'd mentioned.

Without hesitating, Jim stepped close and buttoned the shirt for her. He only moved his gaze from hers when he had trouble with one of the buttons.

"Grab your jacket and sun glasses, and we'll head out."

He set out at a good pace to walk into the center of town and the harbor. The Schooner was set to leave at 10:00. They had plenty of time to enjoy the walk.

"Jim…Jim."

A hand on his arm drew his attention. Her face was red and she huffed and puffed. Ah hell. "I'm sorry, Kate. You should've said something." He'd tried to outrun his thoughts and nearly killed the woman.

"I did. When you didn't respond or slow down, I grabbed your arm. I'm up for a good walk, or run, but going downhill at this rate is setting us up for shin splints."

He stopped on the sidewalk both hands settled on her shoulders. "I'm sorry. You okay?"

She nodded. "Yeah, but at the rate we were going, my legs weren't going to be good for anything the rest of the day." She laughed and looped her arm through his. "How about we stroll the rest of the way?"

Jim patted her hand in the crook of his arm. It felt right there. "How do you feel about window shopping on our way? You up for that?"

"Always."

"First we're stopping at the drugstore." He steered her inside a Rite Aid and headed toward the section for stomach upsets. "We're getting you wrist bands that counter sea sickness. We'll make a sailor out of you, yet." After paying for the small package, he slipped the stretchy material on her wrist with the small metal ball centered on her pulse.

"I don't understand how these work, but I swear they do. Everyone I've ever known to be bothered with sea sickness puts these on and gets his sea legs fast."

* * * *

Kate's heart hammered against the base of her throat as she stared at Jim's head bent over her hand. It was hard to breathe. He cared for her in such a gentle considerate way. Yes, he sometimes bulldozed, but always in a good cause. Right now, his cause seemed to be to assure she had a great time out on the water.

"There, you're good to go." He stepped back and smiled, seeming pleased he'd taken care of the problem.

"Thank you, Jim." Kate stretched on tiptoe and kissed him on the cheek. "Let's check out this boat." She turned toward the harbor.

What had she been thinking to kiss him and for the second time. Surely, a thank you would've been enough. No, it wouldn't have been. Jim Donovan was sweet and caring. She was in for a world of hurt with him, and she'd already experienced that once and it nearly killed her. Could she survive again?

They walked along the wharf until they came to the boat Jim had pointed out last night. He helped her up on the walkway to the boat.

"I'm Cap'n Charley. Welcome to the Lady Belle. My wife Grace and I have been sailing her for 40 years."

The man was the picture of the man a fish company used in their TV advertisements all the time. The name was something like Grahams. Cap'n Charley had a gray beard, and wore his long hair in a braid. A plaid shirt, jeans, boots, and a hat completed the picture. All he needed was a pipe sticking out from between his lips. Grace escorted them to the other side of the schooner.

"I've got extra layers for you. It gets breezy out on the ocean." Dressed in jeans, plaid shirt like her husband, several layers of jackets, and a hat, the woman spoke with that lovely Maine twang.

The schooner held about sixteen people lined along each side with a few in the middle. After all were on board, the boat made its slow way out into the harbor where the wind picked up.

"Now the fun begins."

"My God, Jim, are we going to go under?" The boat

turned and angled way onto its side. Kate's fingers on the cord along the rail tightened until the knuckles shown white.

"Isn't this great, Kate?" Jim seemed to be in his element.

He pulled her close to him. She was grateful for the extra anchoring.

After a time, she relaxed, when the boat handled the sharp angles without tipping over. The view of large houses built along the coast was magnificent. The schooner slowed when it approached a small island. Kayaks lined its beach, and the people along the shore waved like mad at the folks on the boat. They all waved back. Kate laughed.

"This is fun, Jim."

"I told you you'd love it. How's your stomach?"

She smiled at him. "No problem at all. Thanks." She couldn't kiss him again, but that's sure what she wanted to do. What a mess she'd gotten herself into. She was here now, and she'd enjoy herself though she might pay a price later.

The schooner trip lasted just over two hours up and back. The views offered by the cruise were stunning. Her glimpses of large gorgeous homes perched on massive outcroppings of rock, birds swooping, kayakers in the water and along island beaches took away her breath. The sting of the wind made her glad for her jacket and the layers Grace provided.

"Very impressive, your Maine, Mr. Donovan."

Jim's smile spread across his face at her praise of his state. He nodded and clasped her hand in his. "Let's grab a quick lunch before we head for the mountain."

The mountain was something Kate didn't want to do. She hated heights, but she couldn't remember when she'd been so rejuvenated, full of energy, and ready for anything. Quite remarkable. How could she tell him no? Maybe he had something for her height fears the way he did for her queasy stomach. No way to explain to Jim Donovan the effect he had on her. Not sure she wanted to either.

She nodded to indicate her agreement to lunch and off they went.

That afternoon, they drove the travel trailer out of town a few miles to Camden State Park.

"This moderate trail to the top is listed for kids so if you wanted to hike up we could."

Judging from all the folks wearing backpacks, clearly quite a few of the visitors planned to do that.

"I'd like to drive it first." She'd prove her prowess on the trails another time.

"The nice thing about driving is you get great views the whole way up." Jim stopped at the gate, paid the fee, and steered into the line of cars, buses, and SUV's winding their way up the mountain.

They hadn't driven far up the mountain, when Kate realized she may have made a mistake, and it would've been better to hike. A couple of times the mountain dropped off on her side of the motorhome, leaving her to stare at dizzying heights. She wore her wristbands and nausea didn't bother her, but Jim didn't have anything to combat her fear of falling off the precipice. The road, wide enough for two cars to pass, didn't always have an easement on the edge or a small metal barrier to give the illusion of protection.

Jim's voice droned on, she was certain giving commentary on what they looked at. She couldn't focus on his words while her hand had a death grip on the armrest, all the while praying the brakes worked on the way down.

After what seemed hours, though later Jim assured her it was less than fifteen minutes, he pulled into a parking lot.

"Let's get out. The views are spectacular from up here."

She'd made it this far, Kate figured she had to climb out. What she found when she did made her glad she'd taken a chance--a giant outcropping of rock, bigger than the motorhome. Kids had climbed up on the top, and parents used cell phones and cameras to capture their images. Others less adventurous posed in front of the rock. A person's significance dwindled standing by a boulder of that size.

They passed by it and climbed a few steps higher. Kate gasped. Not because the wind whipped right through all her layers making it decidedly chilly, but because of the amazing view spread out in front of her. She was far enough from the edge she appreciated the site without fearing she'd fall. Camden Harbor lay below, sailboats bobbed in the white caps, lobster boats, and other motorized boats putted to and fro. The church steeple with sun glinting against the gold dome made her remember an old saying from one of the books her mother used to read. "God's in his heaven. All's right with the world." Of course, 9/11 had given the lie to that belief. But still….

"Oh, Jim. I'm grateful you dragged me up here. It's perfect."

"Come look at this monument. It marks where the poet Edna St. Vincent Millay penned her poem *Renascence.* She describes turning around and *'all she saw from where she stood, was three tall mountains and a wood.'*"

Kate ran her fingers over the inscription and the words from that stanza. "This is weird, but I know this poem."

"Lots of people do."

"No, I mean I have a personal connection to it. Addie practiced saying this all one summer at camp. She planned to use it in a poetry reading competition. I can't wait to tell her what I found." Kate threw her arms around Jim and hugged with all her might.

What might've been awkward seemed normal especially

when Jim hugged her right back.

"Are you up to climbing up into the turret?"

Kate swung her gaze in the direction Jim pointed.

"You go. I'm fine right here with Edna." She slipped her cell from her pocket. "I'm going to take a picture to send to Addie."

"Okay." He headed off. Nice that he let her do her own thing and she him. They had a comfortable relationship.

Later Kate survived the drive down the mountain, but only because she kept her right foot shoved against her imaginary brake, and because Jim was a real gentleman. He slowed down so others who drove faster could more easily go by, while he moseyed on down the curving road, never saying a word to Kate about her lack of trust.

Back in Camden, they left the van in the RV lot and walked down into the town, stopping at a small pizza joint. They selected a large with everything except anchovies. Jim ordered a bottle of beer for himself and Merlot for Kate. He remembered her tastes.

He tipped the bottle for a couple of good swallows. "How are you holding up, Kate?" His arm slid along the back of the banquette. He squeezed her shoulder once and let go. "You've had a lot of new stuff coming your way right now."

Her shoulder tingled where he'd touched her, and Kate fought the yearning to lean into his strong body. She sipped her wine to buy time. "I'm doing much better than I expected. I've stopped biting my cuticles, a nasty habit I never had before 9/11 and one I've never been able to stop since." She fiddled with the napkin, folding it and unfolding it. "The view from the cottage is calming, like you said. I love sitting out there on the balcony, and have all day long and done nothing."

Jim clapped his hands and laughed. Kate jumped at the loud noise.

"You've fallen under the spell of the cottage! That's great. I knew you wouldn't be able to resist it. No one can." His smile seemed to spread past the edges of his face. It appeared his enjoyment of her reaction to the cottage filled his whole body and the restaurant.

Maybe the spell she'd fallen under was Jim Donovan himself.

CHAPTER EIGHT

Friday, September 20

"Oh." Blair couldn't keep the moan in when the man pushed past her to get up the jet way at the Portland Airport. He didn't stop to say he was sorry. Good grief. For a carry on, she'd slung one of her medium-sized purses over her good shoulder. Normally she'd have made this trip with one larger bag and carried it on, but she didn't figure she'd be able to shove it into the overhead compartment with one arm in a sling. Sometimes people were helpful. Sometimes not. Best to be able to do it yourself. Mom lesson number 15.

She'd texted her mother the plane landed, and told her which baggage claim area she'd meet them in. Apparently, Jim Donovan had driven her here. Be interesting to meet him.

Quick stop in the restroom which ran longer than usual with the line and her arm, but then she passed through the glass doors into the baggage claim area.

"Blair."

She turned toward the voice. Her mother made her way

toward her followed by a tall man with brownish hair streaked with silver. *Wow, Mom looks great. Better than I can ever remember seeing her in a long time.* Her mother had color in her face, and her eyes twinkled. Hmm. Blair kept her body angled away from her mother. No reason to freak her out, but hiding her arm only worked for a short time.

"Oh, Blair, what's wrong?"

Jig's up.

"Are you hurt? Were you in an accident? Why didn't you tell me?"

The man with her laughed. "Maybe if you slow down a minute, Kate, she'll tell you." He stretched out a hand. "Hi. Jim Donovan. I was your great aunt's lawyer."

Blair extended her hand. "Nice to meet you, Mr. Donovan. I confess I've been curious about the man who shook my mother out of Fort Worth."

"I believe it was a joint effort. Please call me Jim."

Nice name. Good old fashioned, strong.

"If you point out your bag, Blair, I'll grab it."

"Sure. It's bright red. I got tired of fighting over whose black bag belonged to whom."

Blair showed him when it slid along the carousel, and Jim grabbed the bag and led them out to the car. They left Portland International Airport and headed for Griffin Harbor. Two hours later, they arrived at the town, and Jim drove them around, pointing out the sites.

"It's a beautiful little town." Blair agreed.

"Look, Blair." Her mother gestured out the window to a white building with columns sitting at the top of a grassy rise. "It smells like a library, you know? Newer facilities don't have that great aroma."

"I'll have to make time to go inside." Blair noticed how Jim continued to keep his eye on her mother, making sure she was comfortable.

"Jim, do you always play tour guide?" Blair leaned forward to get a better look from the backseat.

He laughed and said. "The town council doesn't pay me, but they appreciate my services."

They chatted about the scenery on the way out of town to the cottage, less than 15 minutes from civilization. Not bad at all. A charming cottage overlooked the water.

"Oh, Mom, this is lovely. Way nicer than you led me to believe before you came up here."

"I didn't know Aunt Liddy had substantially remodeled the cottage before she set it up for a rental property."

Once everyone was inside, Jim said. "I'll carry your bag upstairs."

"Thanks." What a considerate man. Hmm.

"There's a bathroom upstairs in the loft plus the one down here. Come with me. I want to show you the best." Her mother grasped her good arm and led her toward the windows through which she caught an awesome view. She slid open the door and they stepped out into the sunshine on a balcony overlooking the rocky coast of Maine.

For a moment, she couldn't say anything. Her eyes drank in the scene before her. "Wow. What an amazing view, Mom." Blair sank into one of the Adirondack chairs. A loud sigh escaped her lips. "Okay, all I need is a glass of iced tea, and I'm set." A smile spread across her face. No wonder her mother considered keeping the land in the family. It was glorious.

"She's discovered the lure of the cottage."

She glanced over her shoulder. Jim had stepped out on the balcony.

"So who wants to do what with this land?" Blair asked.

"Hey, you don't get to change the subject. No more excuses, tell me exactly how you hurt your arm?" Her mother sat in the other chair. Jim leaned against the railing.

She'd stalled as long as possible. Best to get this over. Blair pulled in a deep breath and pushed out the scary words. "I came home late one night and a man grabbed my purse—"

"Oh, my God. You were mugged?" Her mother interrupted her.

"Well, people might call it that."

"What else would you call it? You were mugged. I hate

you living in that city." Her mother turned away and toward the water, but not in time to hide a tear sliding down her cheek.

"It's okay." Blair reached for her mom's hand. "They didn't take my credit cards or driver's license. A kind police officer returned my billfold to me the next morning. Money was gone, but that's nothing compared to if they'd taken the cards and ID."

"If you girls have everything you need, I'm heading back to town," Jim said. "Work demands I get a move on. How about I take you to The Lobster Pot for supper this evening?"

Blair kept quiet to let her mother answer, but she didn't say anything.

"If you want to be alone, I understand," Jim spoke into the silence that followed his question.

"No. That's kind of you to offer, Jim. We accept." Blair wasn't leaving the invitation on the table. Why didn't her mom accept his friendly offer right away? She'd need to check out her mother's relationship with the Maine lawyer.

"Yes. Thank you. I'll walk you out, Jim." Kate led him into the cottage.

"I'll stay here if that's okay with y'all." Blair settled more comfortably into the chair and enjoyed the view. She dreaded it, but the time had come to tell her mother what the guy said to her, or at least what she thought he'd said.

Blair blinked her eyes open when her mother set two glasses of iced tea on the small table between the two Adirondacks.

"Ah, Mom. Thanks."

"Don't get a chance to spoil you much anymore."

Blair picked up the glass and sipped. "Yumm. This is your special tea blend. Did you bring it with you?"

"No, I didn't originally plan to stay here longer than a few days. Addie sent me a pouch of the tea when I asked her. I'm not blaming you for me having to stay longer. It wouldn't have been realistic to expect you to drop everything at a moment's notice. I'm happy you were able to come see the property that's been in your father's family for generations."

"So how far does our land go?"

"It's this whole end of the peninsula."

"Well, this is gorgeous, Mom. I'd kind of like to have a place to get away from the city for a change. Aunt Liddy rented it out?"

"Yes, an agency handled all the details. She has a caretaker who looks after it between leases and if something comes up while the renter is here."

"Tell me again who wants the property?"

"Jim would like it for the Maine Coast Conservancy Trust. He can tell you more about it this evening at supper."

"Why didn't you say yes to his invitation right off? You

left an awkward silence."

"Well…I…"

"You should have said how good looking the man is. Hey, am I cramping your style by staying here?"

"Oh, Blair." Red rose up her mother's throat covering her face.

"Mom, I had to tease you, but he is handsome, don't you agree?"

Her mother glanced down and then looked at her from under her eyebrows. "I can't in all honesty disagree with your assessment."

Her mother hadn't dated much at all since her father was killed. Blair sure didn't want to scare her off if there was the smallest possibility of something happening between her and the man from Maine, better cut her slack on this one.

"So Jim wants the land for a Trust. Someone else wants it?"

"Yes, a developer named Ray Holland wants the land for construction of condos."

"What's he offering for it?"

"$500,000."

"Wow!" Blair sat forward. "Is the Trust group offering anything?"

"Jim and several others tell me, that Aunt Liddy intended the Trust to have the land. She never got around to changing her will. They can only pay us $50,000."

"Whew. Big difference."

"Yes. But if Aunt Liddy promised them the land...and then...anyway I wanted to ask you if you would like to keep it in the family."

"Well, it's yours, Mom."

"Sweetie, if something happened to me it would be yours."

Blair squeezed the tea glass until her knuckles turned white. Her mother's words reminded her of what the mugger said. Better tell her. She hated to upset her, but better for her to have all the information.

"I want to tell you something, Mom."

"Sure, dear, anything." She leaned forward to pick up her tea.

"The man who mugged me said to tell you to sell to Ray Holland."

Her mother's tea glass crashed on the balcony. "Oh, my God. Are you sure?"

"I'll get the broom, Mom. You stay there." Blair slipped through the open doorway.

* * * *

That meant someone had singled out Blair. It wasn't a random act. Kate couldn't decide if that was good or bad.

Blair stepped out of the cottage with a broom. "I can't

carry everything."

Kate rose. "Of course, I'll get the dust pan. It's always easier with two people anyway." Kate swept and Blair knelt holding the dustpan.

"I couldn't have done this alone. Guess I forgot about my arm. "

In quick order, they finished the job, Kate returned the broom and pan to the closet in the front hall and returned with another glass of tea. She sat again on the patio. Drew in a deep breath before asking, "Are you sure, Blair, that's what you heard?"

"Pretty sure."

"Did you tell the police?"

"Huh-uh. I was shaken up at first. I couldn't make sense of the words. I worried I wouldn't be able to come up here because I'd lost my driver's license."

"I'm glad you made the trip, sweetie."

"Me, too. This view takes my breath away." She rose and walked to the edge and leaned over. "Pretty straight down."

"I don't worry about anyone climbing up."

Blair laughed. "I guess that's true."

The comfortable silence continued for a few moments then Blair turned and faced her mother. "Have you met the Holland guy?"

"Yes, two times, both briefly. He seemed like a decent man. He wanted the land to build his condos, but…Oh, my God. The last thing I said to him was I wasn't going to decide anything until my daughter got a look at the property." She set her glass on the side table, rose from the chair, and joined her daughter at the rail. Placed her arm around Blair's waist and squeezed. "I'm sorry. I think this," she gently touched the sling, "is my fault."

"You couldn't have known, Mom. I'm fine and can take the sling off any time now. I sort of like to remind myself to not try swinging through the trees." Her lips curved up in a smile that said she might still try that.

They both stared at the soothing vista for a few moments.

"What's your call on any of this, Mom?"

Kate shrugged her answer. "Let's get ready to meet Jim for supper. We'll drive in to town early to give us time to introduce you to Griffin Harbor. Maybe it will help us make up our mind what to do with the land."

"Well, $500,000 is a lot of money."

* * * *

"Griffin Harbor is as charming as you said, Mom."

Kate parked in the lot near The Lobster Pot, and she and Blair climbed from the car. "Glad you like it. You'll love this, too. It's Jim's favorite place to eat. The owner Tom is his best friend from birth." She pushed through the door and they entered the restaurant with wooden beams coving the walls.

Blair scanned the room. Wooden tables filled the center with booths with wooden benches along two of the walls. A long bar filled in the top of the U. The smell of burning wood from the fireplace mixed with the tantalizing aromas coming from the kitchen. The restaurant was about half-full and a soft hum of conversation from contented patrons rounded out the scene.

"Kate, good to see you." A man, Blair presumed to be the owner hugged her mother. "Jim is running a bit late, and asked me to look out for you."

"Tom, I want you to meet my daughter. Blair this is Tom Jenson, the owner of this charming restaurant."

Blair shook hands with the man. "Nice to meet you."

"I've saved the best table for you."

Blair couldn't tell what made this particular table better than any other, but she took him at his word. Tom held the chairs for each of them and left to get their drink orders.

He returned quickly with her mother's Merlot and her Chablis. "How are you liking our small town, Blair?"

"It's as delightful as Mom told me."

Jim blew through the front door and made a direct line for their table. He settled in between Kate and Blair.

"Sorry to run late. A last minute call came through I had

to take."

"No problem, Jim. Tom has taken good care of us."

"Of course he has. I'm having lobster. Your mother doesn't want that, Blair, but how about you?"

"I'd love to have lobster, or the bug, as Mom calls it." She and Jim smiled at each other.

"Hey, no ganging up here." Her mother poked each of them on the arm. "Tom makes a really good steak, and I'm having one of those."

The evening went on with a lot of banter and chuckles. Blair couldn't remember hearing her mother laugh this much in a long time. Jim was solicitous of her every need, and listened intently whenever she talked, leaning toward her as if he didn't want to miss anything.

"What can you tell me about the Trust thing, Jim?" Blair stirred her coffee toward the end of the meal.

"Its official name is Maine Coast Conservancy Trust. Trusts like ours exist all over the country and throughout the world to protect the flora and fauna of a region. Sometimes they are private, as is ours. Sometimes they're run by a government. They raise funds to protect the land and ensure that future generations get to enjoy nature. There are even trusts set up to protect a ship or a bridge."

"What do you plan to do with our land, Jim?" Blair sipped her coffee and set her cup back in the saucer.

"I took your mother to see the Coastal Maine Botanical Gardens the other day. It's also a trust, but they've set up an educational experience for visitors with sections where they've planted specific items."

"The children's section was as impressive as the rest of the Gardens." Kate sipped the last of her wine.

"Would you like another glass?" Jim asked.

"No thanks. I've got to get us home." Kate smiled and glanced up at him from under her eyelashes.

My gosh, is Mom flirting with him? Huh. He's so conscious of her every need. Interesting development from her trip to Maine.

"We're planning on keeping everything more natural. We'll allow camping on a limited basis. What do you think of the cottage, Blair?" Jim focused his attention on her.

"What's not to love? The kitchen and bathrooms are spot on for what you'd expect in a Maine cottage, but with all the latest and greatest technology. Soft comfortable furniture and a fireplace you can turn on with a switch."

"Most important is that gorgeous view out the windows and sliding doors. My gosh, that just blew me away when I first walked in. Don't think I'd ever get tired of enjoying that view."

Jim laughed. "Another conquest for the view. Have you decided what you want to do with the land?" His gaze fixed on each woman in turn.

Blair glanced at her mother. She'd let her respond.

Kate shrugged her shoulders. "Not quite, but we're getting close."

"You know where I stand on this. Let the Conservancy Trust have the land or keep it yourself."

"I know. I know. The difference in money is significant though, Jim."

"Yes, but turning the property over to the Trust is what your aunt wanted. Okay, enough on this for now. How about desert? Next to the lobster, Tom does that best."

"I encourage you to sample his blueberry cobbler, Blair. It's truly to die for."

＊ ＊ ＊ ＊

"When I first arrived, the cottage seemed far away from anything. But now, I can make the drive at night." Kate capably steered her small SUV down the dark and twisting road after supper with Jim. "I'm not bothered by the distance or the emptiness."

"Proud of you, Mom."

Blair's smile, visible because of the moonlight coming through the windshield, said more than her words did.

"I like Jim Donovan, and the town is charming."

"Isn't it? Jim's a good man if on the stubborn side. I'm still amazed he convinced me to come up here."

"The change of scene has been good for you. I haven't noticed you bite your cuticles once this evening."

Kate lifted a hand from the steering wheel. "No, I don't do that much anymore."

"The people here are friendly, not at all the stuffy stand-offish Yankees you're always hearing about."

"They're a proud, hardy bunch of folks. They have to be to weather their hard winters. But it also makes them conscious of their neighbors, and looking out for each other seems to be a natural tendency."

"And Tom served the best lobster I've ever eaten."

"Where have you eaten lobster before, Blair?"

"You remember the six weeks during college, several of us spent in Canada to work on our French?"

"Yes."

"Well, we drove down into Maine one long weekend, and ate it several times."

"Gosh, I should've tried to get you to visit Aunt Liddy then. It never crossed my mind. I'm sorry, Blair."

"Don't do that, Mom."

"What?"

"Guilt yourself. You hang too many *shoulds* on yourself."

Kate laughed. "It comes with being a mother."

"You do it to excess." Blair squeezed Kate's shoulder

once. "I can't tell in the dark. Are we getting near the house?"

Kate blinked on the bright lights. "Yes, around this next turn." She maneuvered into the small front yard missing the large boulder with space to spare. Indeed, she was becoming an old pro.

The front porch light spread a warm welcome. Kate unlocked the door and they went in, leaving their coats in the front hall closet.

"Would you like a glass of wine, Mom?" Blair headed for the cabinet that stored the wine and glasses.

"That would be lovely. Thanks. We can sit by the fire and talk more about the land and what we should do with it." Kate flicked the switch on the gas fireplace. The glow warmed more than her body. It warmed her spirit. This whole trip had touched her in unexpected, but pleasant ways.

"Here you go." Blair handed her a glass of Merlot and sat in the chair next to the fire. She exhaled a long breath and then drew air in. "This is wonderfully pleasant." She sipped her glass. "I bet Aunt Liddy didn't have any trouble keeping this place rented."

"She didn't. Jim showed me a calendar with the majority of weeks booked for this year. The people who had reserved last week and this week canceled due to illness. Because of Liddy's death, Jim didn't get the management company to rebook with anyone."

"How sad to have this place booked and then not be able to come."

"Well, it worked to our advantage. The Griffin Harbor Inn is charming and comfortable, but we'd not have the space to move around there we have here. While the view of the harbor is lovely, it doesn't compare to this one."

Kate glanced through the window into the dark, pierced by the small lights on the porch, the stars, and the sprinkling of lights from the houses on the island across the way. Eventually, they'd be gone and it would be the moon, stars, and porch lights. The soft darkness of night cocooned Kate in safety.

Blair leaned forward, cradling the wine glass between both hands. "So, Mom, what do you want to do?"

"When I started up here, I planned to sell to the highest bidder. I'd stop by to visit you—"

"I still hope you'll do that."

"I plan to, sweetie. I'm close and it would be stupid not to. I can't promise I'll return after this one trip."

"I'll take that. Go on. I interrupted you."

"After I visit you for a day or two, I'll get on a train heading back toward Fort Worth." She tipped her glass. The red liquid made a path down her throat, warming her. "But," she gestured with her glass at the cottage and toward the view, "this place is captivating. I know of no other word for the magic it's spun around me. I feel safe here. I love the ties to John's family. Everyone has spoken highly of Aunt Liddy and shared in our tragic loss of your father."

"Several people have mentioned Liddy's desire to leave the land to the Conservancy Trust. Even though she didn't put anything in her will, one part of me would like to honor her desire to do that."

"So why didn't you follow through already?"

"I decided you needed a chance to come up here and see the place yourself. I didn't want to make the decision without your input."

"Well, there's no question I love this cottage." Blair set down her glass, walked up to the sliding doors, and gazed out into the darkness. "It's truly an inspiring place. I wish I wrote songs or fiction. I could do seriously good work here. And then rest and recharge and write more."

Kate smiled at her daughter's flight of fancy. Blair barely sang and always hated English in school.

"But $500,000 is a lot of money. Think of what we could do with that?"

"What would you do with it, Blair?"

"Ha, I'd buy a larger apartment and pay off some bills. I'd make a large donation in Dad's name to the 9/11 Memorial Gardens and Museum. After that, I'd invest a good-sized chunk. But it's not my money, Mom. It's yours. What would you do with it?"

"Oh, gosh. I don't have a clue. I've got what I need. I guess I'd make lots of train trips up to New York. I've missed you."

"Ah, Mom." Blair got up and gave her mother an awkward one-armed hug.

"Here's something else I've been thinking." She sipped her wine and then set the glass on the coffee table. "What if we keep the land the cottage is on in the family? With access to it, of course. The Conservancy Trust can have the majority of the land. That will please Jim. His main desire is to keep Holland from getting his hands on it and spreading his condos all over the land."

"What about the threat from the man who knocked me down? Maybe we just need to take the money and run."

"That's certainly been the way I've thought in the past, but the cottage has changed me. We both need to be cautious, but maybe it's time to get on with our lives."

"Are you sure, Mom?"

Kate nodded, rose from the chair, and joined Blair at the windows. She hugged her daughter close.

"Would you come up again? It would be selfish to keep it just for me. I'm pretty busy right now."

"Someday, you'll marry and have kids of your own to bring here. And yes, I'll probably visit then. I can get a train to

Chicago and then over to Boston and then to Portland where I'll rent a car."

"You wouldn't come back before then?" Blair returned to the chair and sat. She picked up her wine and gazed over her glass at her mother. "Maybe to visit Jim Donovan?" Her eyebrows canted upwards in question, and she raised her glass looking over the top at her mother waiting for a response.

Kate's breath caught in her throat for a second. "I don't know. There might be a spark of something there, but maybe he only appears interested because he wants me to sign over the land to the Conservancy Trust."

"Don't sell yourself short, Mom. You're a good-looking, intelligent, woman. Yes, Jim wants the land, but he doesn't seem like the sort to act in such an ugly manner." She finished her wine and rose ambling toward the kitchen. "I'm bushed. I'll take one to sip on upstairs."

"Tomorrow you can tell everyone we're keeping this part of the land. We can continue to rent the cottage. We'll pick out when we want to come during the next booking year and mark off those times. It will be fun to read the reviews on the rental site and realize that's our cottage they're talking about."

Kate rose, raised her hands over her head in a long stretch. "I'm relieved to have reached a decision." She followed Blair into the kitchen. "Another glass to celebrate seems appropriate. I'll read for a few minutes before going to bed." Blair refilled Kate's glass.

"Thanks."

"How about we meet up here for Christmas if it's not already booked?"

"Oh, my goodness, Blair. That's in the dead of winter."

"Yes, but we'd have fun." She laughed then kissed her mother. "Goodnight."

"Sleep well, Blair. Thanks for coming and helping me figure out what to do with Aunt Liddy's land. You won't miss the big bucks too much?"

"Nah and it's our land, Mother. Our land." Blair headed for the stairs.

Kate stepped out on the balcony for one final look. The temperatures were low enough she wished for her coat, but she didn't want to take time to get one. What a beautiful, serene place. Eventually, shivers forced her back inside. She'd heard they'd have their first freeze tonight. So different from Texas where they prayed for the September temperatures to drop into the 60's at night.

She closed the sliders, and sank into the stuffed chair closest to the fire where Blair sat earlier. Kate propped her feet on the hassock and dreamed.

What about Jim Donovan? He certainly seemed interested and goodness knows he got her hormones jumping around like no one in many long years. There'd been one other man since John died. Her friends didn't know about him. He looked a lot like her husband, and that was probably what led to the attraction in the first place. It was early after John's death when carrying on alone seemed beyond her capacity. The man wanted her to send Blair to boarding school up east somewhere. Even now, Kate's stomach clenched at the idea. She refused, and that ended the relationship.

After reading a chapter in one of the history books, she rose to turn in. She went to her room, and pulled on her long-sleeved mid-thigh sleep shirt along with leggings. After a last sip of wine, she set the glass on the table, and closed her eyes.

* * * *

Fire. She must be dreaming about fire. The fright jerked her right up in bed; her heartbeat doubled; she gasped for breath and coughed. Terrible nightmare. So real. Unexpected after settling everything last night with Blair. She glanced at the clock on the bedside table. The face was dark. My gosh, what's going on? Must be the remnants of the dream making her groggy.

"Mother." Blair's screech reached through Kate's muddied brain. What was wrong? Blair always called her mom. She threw her legs over the side of the bed, coughed again as something in the air made it difficult for her to breathe.

Reaching the hallway, her feet abruptly stopped. Oh, my God. Fire blazed at the front of the house.

"Blair get down here, fast. The house is on fire." Kate headed for the stairs.

"Stay there, Mom, I'm coming." Black smoke billowed from the roof overhead. "We've got to get out."

"We can't use the front door; the fire is there and overhead." A timber crashed in the loft right after Blair reached the ground floor. "Dear God!"

"We gotta go over the balcony, Mom." Blair headed in that direction.

"Will you be able to do that with your arm?"

"Don't think we have much choice." Blair joined her mother in the living room. No sling on her arm.

"Don't open the slider yet, Blair. Let me get the sheets off the bed." Kate crawled back into her room. Flames engulfed the far side, the heat intensifying with each minute. *Dear God, let me get my child out of this inferno.*

She dragged the two sheets behind her. "I'm going to tie the ends together. When we go out, we need to stay low and do it fast. I'm afraid the extra oxygen will draw the fire toward us. I'll close the slider the moment we're through. We've got to get over the railing, before the glass shatters."

Snap. Crackle, Pop. Not the friendly sound of cereal from her youth.

Blair coughed and wiped her eyes then scooped up the sheets when Kate finished connecting them together.

"When you get outside, tie the end of a sheet to one of the poles on the porch."

Her daughter nodded.

"Let's go." They crawled to the door. Kate pulled open the door and shoved Blair through. Kate followed her daughter and closed the door fast. Blair struggled with the sheets.

"Here you hang on with one hand and then we'll both pull. That should make it tight enough to hold." Kate's muscles strained against the material. "You go first, Blair."

"But, Mom."

"Don't argue. Despite your arm, you're in better shape and can help me get down." And if the glass blew out before they were off the balcony, Blair would be farther away.

Her daughter slid down the sheet hand over hand. On her way down, her grunts and moans announced the strain on her arm and the times she bounced against the rocks.

"Okay, Mom. Come on." She was breathing hard.

More crashes from behind Kate. It must be more of the ceiling falling in. Kate glanced over her shoulder once. Through the glass door, the fire warmed her face. Her heart raced. She could hardly catch a breath, and she hadn't gone over yet. How could she manage this?

One step at a time, like everything else in life. She

hoisted one leg over the balustrade, then got the other one over, squatted down. How had Blair done this with one bum arm? Kate reached between her legs and grabbed hold of the sheet in both hands, praying not only that it would hold, but she wouldn't crash to her death in front of her daughter. If—when—she got out of this, she determined she'd do more upper body strength training. Better off than lots of women her age, but right now three times a week at Pilates instead of only two seemed a no-brainer.

Would the sheet hold? Would she be able to hang on? Her heart battered against her chest like a machine gun. She loosened her grip and slid down. Pain shot through her legs when she bunged her knees against the rocks.

"Keep your feet in front of your body, Mom." Blair instructed in a breathy voice.

That makes sense. Kate pictured sports reports of people repelling down walls and mountains. They always seemed to push off with their feet before going down. Then they slowed their descent with their feet. "Oh!" Watching and doing were two different things. Her feet smashed into the rock.

She wasn't strong enough to go hand over hand the way Blair did. Kate loosened her grip, slid, tightened and slowed, slid again. How much farther?

"I've got you, Mom." Blair's arms wrapped around Kate's

thighs. What a relief. Kate let go, and they tumbled a foot or more to the rocks and slid to the beach below where the waves lapped.

"*Boom.*"

They lay on the sand, breathing heavily. Shards of glass cascaded around them.

"Mom, are you okay?" Blair's voice was a hushed whisper.

"Yes. Bruised I'm sure, but so far as I can tell, nothing is broken. You?"

Blair's head nodded against Kate's back. "Say something, sweetie. A nod doesn't cut it."

"Shh. Keep your voice down. Like you. Bruises, a few cuts when the glass hailed out on us, but nothing broken, not even my arm, which hurts like a son-of-a-gun."

"You cushioned my fall, Blair. You're probably hurt worse."

"We can't lie here. I don't know if you've noticed, but it's cold and we're wet."

"And I'm still lying on top of you. Sorry. Let me roll off without hurting you more. Why are we whispering?"

"Don't stand. Stay low. Doesn't it strike you odd the house caught fire? I know we only this evening decided to keep the land, but we did get that warning before I came. If the fire was set, someone could be hanging around."

"The fire fighters will catch them."

"Do you hear any sirens, Mom? And don't you read? Arsonists like to stay around and admire their handiwork."

"Dear God, Blair, what have I dragged you into?"

"I don't know, but we can't deal with your guilt right now. We need to get out of here. Then we'll figure something out. Damn, I wish I'd put on my sneakers. Which direction?"

"Let's go that way. It's toward town. There's a house about a mile away. It sits right above the water, like ours does...did." A full body shiver shook Kate's body. The wind had picked up. She couldn't fall apart now. She dragged in a deep breath. "I've walked along the beach but only half-way. I stopped when the rocks got to be steeper than I wanted to crawl over, but the other direction is several miles to anything."

"Okay, let's go then." Blair grabbed Kate's hand, and they set off.

After a while, their eyes adjusted to the darkness. She'd have welcomed a full moon rather than the sliver of white in the sky.

Boom. Her heart constricted. Adrenalin shot through her system. *Boom.* Kate dropped to her knees dragging Blair with her.

"Is someone shooting at us?" Kate whispered the words.

"Maybe explosions from the fire. We had a gas fireplace and stove."

The roar of the fire brought to mind a rushing train. After a few moments, Kate gathered herself together, ignoring the way her nostrils stung from the fire. The way her muscles ached. The way her feet stung.

They had to keep moving. She pulled into a crouching position and motioned for Blair to follow. They set off after one last glance at the glow in the sky.

They didn't talk, but used hand signals to help each other avoid holes in the ground or the jagged boulders. Water lapped at their feet. The cold stinging as much as the rock cuts. The earlier trembles were nothing to what set in from the shock and the cold wind gusting around them. Blair's teeth chattered in the silence.

"This is…as far as…I've gone, Blair. We've probably got…another half…mile. You…make it?"

"Sure, Mom. I can do anything you can do."

A smile slipped past Kate's mouth at hearing her competitive daughter's slogan from when she was a young girl. How had she raised such a brave girl, and her be such a coward?

The terrain got rockier, but many of them were flat boulders, which didn't gouge out their feet, but the mist made them slippery. Kate slipped and Blair helped her up. Blair slipped and Kate lent a hand. Kate gritted her teeth to keep from biting her lip. They had to keep on.

* * * *

Jim sprang from his bed at the special ring on his cell lying next to his bed. Adrenalin spiked. A fire some place. He was one of the many town volunteers who helped the fire department. It was his month on. He threw on clothes and grabbed his makeshift equipment. The volunteers paid for their own gear. He climbed in his truck and stopped to read his cell message for which direction to go.

His heart jumped to his throat and pushed his blood pressure off the charts. The address on his cell was for the cottage. Kate and Blair were there. Oh, no. He floored it, caught up with the fire engine lumbering its way along the narrow road. He wanted to zoom ahead, but there wasn't a lot of room to pass. He couldn't take a chance of making the truck crash.

His first sight of the cottage sent his heart into a downward spiral. Blackened bricks surrounded an empty shell. A few flames attacked the neighboring trees, but the cottage itself?

The stone fireplace angled into a dark sky. The roof was entirely gone.

He stumbled to the side of the road, knelt, and threw up until only bile remained, and then he threw up that. Kate was gone. Kate and her daughter both died inside the cottage. He prayed it was smoke inhalation. They wouldn't have known as much of the horror that way.

Someone patted him on the shoulder.

"Hey, Man."

He glanced up to find his best friend leaning over him. "Tom, she's gone."

"Well, you don't know that for sure. The firefighters haven't made it in yet to confirm anything like that."

"Not much consolation, Tom. Where else would they be in the middle of the night?"

"The neighbor up the road heard an explosion and called it in."

"Dear God, Tom. This is my fault. I insisted she come up here to look at the god-damned land. And her daughter's, gone." He dropped his head in his hands, tears slid down his cheeks.

"Hey, Chief. We've not located any bodies yet." The fireman's shouts barely penetrated the bleak hell Jim found himself in.

"What?" He grabbed hold of Tom. "Help me up." He strode toward the Chief. "Andy, what did Pete say?"

"No bodies on what's left of the ground floor of the cottage. We haven't made it into the basement, yet. But from what we can see, we can't make out any bodies there."

"Why would they be in the basement in the middle of the night?" Tom asked the question troubling Jim.

"They wouldn't be unless someone dragged them down there. Are you seeing signs of arson, Chief?"

"It appears to have started in several places at once. Unusual for an accident, but I'm not ruling that out yet. Two women staying here, right?"

Jim nodded.

"Either smoke?"

"Not that I ever saw."

* * * *

Driving away from the inferno, Kenny laughed to himself. He'd handled Ray's problem again. That other old woman, Mildred Steele, who served on the town committee the way Liddy Thompson had, still remained. He'd checked minutes of the meetings, and she was the lone holdout insisting on turning the property over to the Maine Coast Conservancy Trust. Stupid bitch. Little by little, Kenny was mowing down the obstacles to his boss getting hold of the land for his development.

He rolled down the truck windows. He reeked of smoke and not like from his cigarettes. After a while, he wouldn't notice it, but now he'd tough out the chill temperatures to have the fresh air. He neared the loop at the far end of the peninsula and followed the road. He'd come out up north of what remained of the cottage. Could he get the Steele woman tonight? Maybe. The authorities seemed to be kind of busy right now. He chuckled and then lit a cigarette. Yes, things were moving in the right direction for Ray Holland Development Corporation.

Cruising into Griffin Harbor, he found houses and businesses dark. Why the hell would anyone want to live in this small town with no action? Well, not his problem. When he finished up with Steele, he'd head back to Portland. Poison. Fire. Maybe strangling this time? He had a three-foot piece of rope in the back of the truck that'd work fine for the job.

Steele's house was up ahead. He drove past and turned a corner, parked, and grabbed the rope from the back of the truck. An alley presented a way to reach her house without worrying about anyone who might still be up in the dead of night seeing him from the street. No lights on in Steele's house or the neighbors'. Looking good. He'd be glad to end this tonight and pick up his life in Portland.

He pulled gloves on before he stepped into the darker shadows provided by the bushes and moved toward the house. A neighbor's swing creaked in the wind. The back porch ran all around the house, allowing him to look in the windows. There's old lady Steele's room. The back door provided an easier and quieter access than smashing in one of the windows. One less chance someone would hear him. He reversed directions to the screen door, which surprisingly was unlocked. Maybe he'd get lucky and the door would be that way. He'd heard talk of folks in small towns like this not locking their doors. Stupid assholes.

Damn. The door slid open without a peep of sound. She must take good care of her house. He stood for a moment to figure out the layout. After one wrong turn, he found her room. The door stood open. Kenny checked the closets to make sure no one else was there. There shouldn't be, but he wasn't a fool. He tiptoed to her bed.

Mildred Steel snored. Not that annoying kind that could wake the dead. Kenny nearly laughed. Focus. He looped each end of the rope around his hands, leaned forward, crossed his arms, and slid the rope behind her head. She jerked, and bright brown eyes glared at him. One hand reached under her pillow and came out holding a gun.

Kenny knocked it away with his elbow and tightened the noose at the same time. Her fingers came up to pull the rope away, but he was stronger than the old woman. Her legs kicked out as she tried to scoot away. He held on. She gurgled several times then lay still. Kenny checked her pulse. Nothing. He pulled the rope from around her neck and then grabbed the gun. He watched the TV shows and knew how good the cops could be at finding evidence. He wasn't leaving anything for them.

His rapid steps made no sound on the hardwood floors. He retraced his steps, glanced through the window before he pushed open the back door and stepped out. A quick dash through the yard and he hit the alley, and then all he had to do was get to where he'd left the car. Not even a dog disturbed the silence. Portland, here he came.

Eagerness to tell Ray his project should go through now without any hitches, kept Kenny's foot heavy on the pedal. He only slowed when passing through small towns, which were speed traps. Even though it was late at night, he wouldn't take any chances on screwing this up for his boss. Ray would get his project, and his daddy could stay in that nice nursing home where he was happy.

CHAPTER NINE

Saturday, September 19

"The Barton house…can't be far now." Kate barely got the words out through chattering teeth. Her daughter didn't respond. "Blair, do you…need to stop?" If she did, Kate feared they'd lie down and go to sleep never to wake.

"Okay. Saving my breath…for climbing."

"I'm not sure I can make this next leap." Kate paused. Blair joined her.

"Let me go first. I'm gonna put my butt on that rock and then swing my feet around." Blair demonstrated. "Ouch. Be careful of the jagged place."

"Oh, honey, you're bleeding."

"Don't worry. You try. I'll help."

Kate nodded. Except for the dangerous rock, Blair's idea worked. "Ugh."

"Give me your hand."

Kate reached out and Blair used her good arm to pull Kate into a standing position, about three feet higher from the lower outcropping they'd stood on. Sure enough, the rock bit Kate, too. She pressed her palm against the wound, warm blood oozed on her fingers. Damn. That hurt. In fact, she hurt all over. Cuts on her hands and feet stung like the dickens, but they had to keep going. She'd come to love this rugged coast of Maine, but they weren't dying out here.

"Which way, Mom?"

"Up."

"Okay."

Kate patted Blair's hand where it rested on her shoulder. "Let's go. Glad you don't have a camera with you. My rear is going to be right in your face….Ha. I made a joke. Come on, Blair. We're going to make it."

Moans and grunts accompanied their efforts, hand over hand, helping each other when either needed a boost. With Kate leading sometimes and other times Blair, they climbed over the top and collapsed on Barton's grass. The silence broken only by their heavy breathing blending with the whoosh of waves below them.

"Whew. Mom, you should've told me we'd be doing all this rock climbing. I'd have brought my hiking boots."

Kate reached for her daughter's hand. "Sorry, forgot to mention that. I'd like to lie here for a while, but we'll freeze to death if we do. Come on. Let's find out if Mr. Barton is home." Kate pushed up on all fours and then staggered straight. She leaned a hand down to her daughter. "Don't be lazy. Let's go."

"I'm coming. Don't be bossy." A surprising laugh came from them both. "What do we do if he's not home?"

"I'm breaking a window, but I see a light on inside." Kate couldn't remember whether she'd heard anything about Mr. Barton heading back to Florida where he spent the colder months. Surely, the light meant he was home. She prayed he'd be here, because then the house would be warm. Right now, her whole being focused on finding the quickest way to get warm. Shivers wracked her body all the time. Blair wasn't doing any better.

Barton's house sat on the land in a different position from the way the cottage did. An expansive grass garden ran from the back of the house to the cliff they'd climbed. A deck surrounded his back door. Kate knocked, but not loudly. If he was home, he'd not hear. Using her cold hands to beat the door shot white-hot pain through them. She glanced around the garden. Good. He'd used small boulders to line the different beds. The scent of dead roses tickled her nose when she leaned over to claim a rock. Kate slammed it against the back door a couple of times before dropping it. It hurt to hold on. More cuts to her hand. God, it would be worth it if Mr. Barton opened the door.

A light flipped on bright enough to illuminate the entire back yard, almost blinding them. Kate made out a form through the glass in the top half of the back door.

"Mom, that sounded like a shotgun being cocked."

"Everyone has guns up here, Blair."

"Who is it?" The gruff older voice reminded Kate of what a bear might sound like.

"Mr. Barton. It's Kate Thompson. I'm staying down the road from you. Liddy's cottage caught fire. We escaped over the balcony. Please let us in."

Before she'd stopped talking, the sound of a key turned in the lock and the chain slid out of its holder. Mr. Barton swung open the door with one hand, a shotgun held in the other. "Come in. Come in." He leaned it against the wall, stepped back for them to enter. "What in the hell are you doing here this time of night? You're wet. How'd you say you got here?"

"Along the shore and then up the rocks." As the words passed Kate's lips, the details of the trip blurred in her head.

"Mr. Barton, I'm Kate's daughter, Blair. Could we bother you for towels and maybe blankets?"

"Where are my manners? I'm sorry. My daughter, Mr. Barton." Kate slid to the floor. She'd used her last once of energy to get here and now she'd given out. Thankfully, it looked like Blair was taking over.

"Where's my brain? I must be half-asleep. Let me turn up the heat." Barton scurried toward the wall thermostat. "Nice to meet you, Blair. There are towels and blankets in that front hall closet. Get them while I get the fire going then we'll move your mother closer over here."

Everyone had a task except Kate. A tear slid down her cheek. She'd surprised herself holding it together for the length of time they'd been out there. A crisis, most of the time, sent her into flight mode. Guess that's what this one did. Flight to escape.

She must've drifted for a moment, because the next thing she knew Blair was patting her dry with a towel.

"Move over here, Mom. You'll be more comfortable."

With Blair on one side and Mr. Barton on the other, Kate struggled to get her feet underneath her. She made it, but each step was agony. She settled into the high backed chair set close to the fire. Someone had draped a towel over the chair. Mr. Barton pulled up a footstool and Blair wrapped a quilt around her. "Th-thanks." Lovely, the aroma of a real fire, her last thought before her eyes drifted closed.

* * * *

"Mr. Barton, could you call someone for us?" Blair drew the quilt around her shoulders and suppressed a shiver.

"Of course, but first, I'm putting on the pot. Hot tea will hit the spot. Whenever your mother wakes we can give her a cup."

"I love the idea of hot tea. If I can get it inside my

body, I might start warming up sometime in this century."

"Tell me who you'd like me to call." He set the full pot on the gas stove and turned the flame to high.

"Jim Donovan. Do you know him?"

"Well, of course. Everyone in town knows Jim. I've got his phone number right here." He paused in his search through cards on his desk when the teapot whistled and made quick work of fixing her a cup.

"Lots of sugar whether you drink it that way or not, missy."

Blair smiled. "Yes, sir."

"I've got the number. Let me get hold of him if I can. Phones tend to be iffy out here."

Blair moved over to the fire and settled on the raised hearth. Her mother appeared to be sleeping. Should she try to wake her?

"Well, I've never heard a more relieved man when I told him you were both here. He's on his way."

"Thanks." Blair pulled her feet up under her and leaned against the side of the fireplace. How wonderful the warmth felt. The tingles indicated her body had begun to warm up. Hurt? Yes. But those pains meant she was alive. For a while on the trek to Barton's, she'd had her doubts. Not just about whether her mother could make it, but whether she would as well.

The tea Mr. Barton gave her was sweet and hot, both of which helped pull Blair out of the slump she felt herself falling into. Mr. Barton puttered around, not seeming to know what to do with his guests.

Her mother moaned and jerked awake. "Blair?"

"I'm right here, Mom." She dragged her quilt with her and knelt by her mother's chair. "We made it." She rubbed her mother's hands, which were still chilled. "Mr. Barton, can you get Mom one of these great mugs of tea? She'll be better after we get her to drink it. It sure helped me."

"I got it right here, kept the pot hot for her."

He handed the mug to Blair, and she held it out to her mother. "If you can hold this yourself, it will help warm your hands. Getting this yummy tea inside of you will do the rest."

"I can...do this."

"I'm sure you can." Blair breathed a sigh of relief when her mother swallowed the sweet liquid. "Mom, I asked Mr. Barton to get hold of Jim Donovan if he could. He's on his way here."

"Good idea, dear. Jim will know...what we need to do. I wonder if there's anything...left of our belongings. And the cottage. What a shame. It was such a cozy place with those incredible views."

Blair was glad to hear her mother's speech was better with fewer pauses. Mr. Barton had refilled both their cups when a pounding came from the front door.

"Excuse me." Mr. Barton hurried to let in his visitor. Jim Donovan rushed past the man, leaving a trail of smoke smell behind him. He went directly to her mother.

"Thank God, you're alive, Kate." He knelt by her chair and gathered both her hands in his.

She winced, but Blair was certain he hadn't noticed. He was in shock himself if he'd believed them to be dead. "We all believed the worst. The firefighters haven't made it into the basement yet. They were looking for bodies. My God." Jim shuddered and drew a hand down his face, fingering tears from his eyes.

My goodness. He does care for mom. Is she going to be up for a relationship with this man?

"What happened? Are you all right?" He spared a moment from her mother to glance at Blair.

Between them, they told the story of their discovery of the fire, their escape over the balcony, and the trek along the water's edge, over and around the granite boulders, and finally up the wall of stone below Mr. Barton's land.

Jim had been so thrilled to find her mother was alive, that the extent of their injuries hadn't registered.

"Josiah, I'm glad you hadn't gone back to Florida yet and that you called in the fire."

"I was getting ready for bed when I heard a boom!

Startled me for sure. I was already calling 9-1-1 when the second explosion came."

"Thanks for getting hold of me."

"The young lady asked me to."

Jim smiled and nodded at her. "Thanks, Blair. Okay, we need to get you medical attention and then clean dry clothes."

"How bad is the cottage?" Kate asked. "What about the rental car?"

Blair drew comfort from her mother stirring herself to ask. She'd been quiet, causing Blair's worry headache to pound. Her mother had no reserves for handling a crisis. It was as though she'd used up her lifetime supply when Blair's father died.

"I'm afraid the cottage may be gone, Kate." He leaned in to wipe the tear sliding down her cheek with his thumb, leaving a sooty smudge. "It's possible the car can be salvaged, but we'll know better tomorrow. We'll go out in the daylight and check out what's what."

Jim stood. "You feel like walking to the car? Or I can carry you."

Her mother's victim's flush spread quickly from her chest up her cheeks.

"No, thank you. I'll walk. I may moan, but I'll walk."

"Good for you, Mom. Mr. Barton, thanks for the hot tea. That did the trick."

"You're welcome, Blair. Glad I was here to help out you and your mother."

"Thank you, Mr. Barton." Kate pushed herself from the chair on wobbly legs. The moans she'd mentioned fully in evidence.

Blair groaned right along with her mom. "We'll return the quilts after we get them cleaned."

"Don't worry about that. You get to feeling better."

Blair and Jim, one on each side, helped her mother walk outside to his truck. It was still dark out, but a sliver of light on the horizon indicated dawn wasn't long off. Blair's gaze kept drifting toward her wrist and the watch she'd left on the bedside table. It wasn't an expensive one, but not having it or her cell left her off kilter. My God, they had nothing here. All the belongings they had were what they had in her condo in NYC and her mother's house in Fort Worth. Better off than the poor souls who lost everything when their home went up in flames. But right now, they had nothing.

Blair's mind wandered through all the problems facing them with no identification and no money or credit cards. What the hell were they going to do?

Jim must've called the medics because an ambulance with its engine on sat in front of his house when they pulled up. Blair was hoping they had pain medicine with them or she was afraid neither she nor her mother would be able to sleep tonight.

The medics tended to them, cleaning their wounds and bandaging the worst ones. And yes, thank you, God, they had pain meds. Blair's body ached in places she didn't know she had. Frankly, she was amazed how well her mother, who only walked and did Pilates twice a week, managed. Blair actually worked out at a gym four times a week, and obviously was younger, but still this experience nearly did her in.

Apparently, Jim had worked miracles while the medics had tended to them because he magically produced sweat pants and t-shirts they could sleep in.

"I'm going to put you in my grandparents' room. They had a king-size bed before it was a standard. I'll be down the hall. Holler if you need anything."

Was Jim going to kiss her mother goodnight? Sure looked like he wanted to. Hmm. Interesting development. She'd have to think about that tomorrow. She barely managed getting herself and her mother into the soft clothes. Between the pain meds and their exhaustion, she and her mother drifted into dreamland when their heads hit the pillows.

* * * *

"It appears to me like we've got serious shopping in our future." Blair's voice wasn't strong the way Kate was used to hearing. God, she had to be all right. Kate pulled herself together to respond.

"Well, we certainly need to, Blair, but I don't know what we'll use for money. I'll call Jerry, and ask him to wire us money to the bank. That will take several hours, but we're out of luck for our immediate needs." She shook her head and picked up the coffee mug in front of her. Maybe after a gallon of the strong liquid, she'd feel more herself.

"Don't worry, Kate. Besides the land, Liddy had money in her bank account. We've not talked about it, because everyone understood it was going to you."

What a relief.

"If the bank manager makes any kind of a fuss, I can take care of it. In fact, let me do that in the first place. Whenever you feel like getting out, you can shop for whatever you need." He pulled out his billfold and handed over a couple of $100 bills. "This will get you started."

"Thanks, Jim. I hope we don't scare anyone showing up looking like this." Kate's image in the mirror startled her. Maybe it shouldn't have based on the way her body screamed when she rolled out of the bed. Exhausted last night, a shower had been the last thing on their minds. Now, they'd slept in the warm-ups Jim had rounded up for them and they were a sorry sight.

"I found a couple of jackets around here. If you tell me your shoe sizes, I'll run out and pick up tennis shoes for you." Jim head slapped the side of his head. "Well, duh, let me call

Mildred Steele. I bet she'd be willing to pick out underwear and jeans and shirts and bring it over in under thirty minutes."

Jim pulled his cell from his pocket, clicked her name in his contacts. "This won't take but a second. When I get her, you can give her sizes."

"Sounds like a plan, and we don't have to move much." A smile tipped up the corner of Blair's mouth. Maybe the effort to summon up a whole grin was beyond her strength. She rose and limped to the counter for the coffee pot and filled her cup. Then she raised the pot toward her mother in a silent question.

Kate nodded to her daughter, and Blair topped off her cup.

"That's odd. She must be out." He slid his cell back into his pocket. "Well, looks like you're stuck with me." He grinned. "Write down sizes. I'll pick up the basics, underwear, and new sweatpants in a size much closer to your own than what you're wearing."

Kate had been out of it last night, but now she realized she and Blair must be wearing Jim's warm-ups. That would certainly account for how long the arms and legs were. While she'd dithered, Jim had stepped out and returned with pens and papers he laid on the table in front of them.

"Make out your list of basics. I'll stop by Mildred's. I'm sure she'll want to help."

Kate felt the victim's flush begin its steady crawl up from her chest to her cheeks. How could she write down a bra and pantie size and give them to Jim?

Blair apparently didn't have any qualms. She picked up the pen and wrote a list.

Kate held the pen in her hand, but the page in front of her remained bare. Revealing such intimate details to the man who filled up more and more space in her mind made her toes curl.

Jim stepped over to her, lay his hand on her shoulder. "Fill this out, Kate. I won't look. I'll hand it over to Mildred or if she's not available, to a clerk in the store."

His sensitivity to her concerns amazed Kate. She smiled at him and turned to fill out the paper with what she needed for now until she could go out herself and gather the essentials for a couple of more days.

Kate didn't know what she and Blair would do next, but top on the list was a shower and to dress in the new clothes when Jim returned with them. While she waited, she'd pop another of the extra strength OTC meds, the medics had encouraged her to take to keep the pain at bay.

Jim strode from the house with their lists in his fist, a man on a mission. Blair heated up her cup and asked her mother if she wanted more.

"No more, thanks, honey. It's a good thing I can't walk

fast. I'd slosh."

"So what do we do next?"

"I don't know about you, but I'm taking a nap. Don't want to shower until Jim returns with the new clothes, and a nap's about all I can do without hurting myself."

"I vote for that. Mom, Glad you're able to get around so well this morning." Blair helped her up from the chair. "Last night's adventure was quite something."

Kate put her arm around her daughter's waist and gave it a squeeze. "But we made it. I'm sure anyone would excuse us for a morning nap. Let's go."

* * * *

Jim's relief at finding Kate and her daughter alive with only minor injuries…well, he'd never stop thanking God they'd survived. He steered his truck to a stop along the curb in front of Mildred's house, an old historic one, she was justifiably proud of.

The sun scattered its beams across the porch, but the front porch light burned. Hmm. She never left the light on after the sun rose believing it to be a huge waste of resources. No paper lay there, but this wasn't the day for the weekly Griffin Bay Bugle. It only came out Sunday and Wednesday. He knocked on the door.

Mildred had grown hard of hearing. He'd tried to get her to put a bell at the front, but she'd refused. The house didn't have a bell originally, and she wouldn't agree to the change. Neighbors were used to hearing pounding on her door anytime someone came to visit. So Jim pounded. And pounded. And pounded.

Mildred cleaned her house on Saturday. Said she wanted it nice for Sunday and didn't want to work on the Sabbath. One of the few modern conveniences she'd agreed to use was the vacuum cleaner, but no whirring sound met his ears. Where the hell was she?

Jim walked across the porch and looked through the windows into the front of the house. No lights on. He continued checking the windows, working his way through to the back. Again, he saw no lights in the kitchen and no coffee pot perking on the stove. None of the fancy drip pots for Mildred. She'd have been perfectly happy to have the old ice boxes with ice delivered weekly. Mildred Steele was the definition of an original.

He made it to Mildred's bedroom and glanced through the window. She lay unmoving in her bed. My God, had she had a heart attack? He pulled his phone from his pocket and got the home of Bill Stanley, the town's Police Chief. Because they were a small town, they didn't have a regular 911 system. One call to the local police chief put you in touch with emergency services.

"Bill, I'm outside of Mildred Steele's house. It looks like

she may have had a heart attack. Send the ambulance. Tell them to come in the back. It's closer to her bedroom."

"Okay. We'll have someone there in a few minutes, and I'm on my way."

That's what folks in small towns did. They helped each other. Jim returned to the door. He'd try the handle before knocking out one of the windows. Of course it was unlocked, Mildred's usual custom. Regardless of how many times he and others told her she needed to lock the door. Jim entered and hurried to her bedroom.

Mildred Steele lay in her bed, the covers awry. Her eyes were open. Jim leaned over and checked her pulse anyway. Nothing. Removing his fingers from her neck, he noticed what looked like a reddish ring around her neck. Dear God. This couldn't be happening. Had his friend been murdered?

The whoop-whoop of the ambulance drew his attention from his old friend. Mildred hated that sound. Said it reminded her of the sirens in old movies about the bombing in England. Creepy was her word.

He backed out of the room to greet the paramedics. "She's dead, and it looks suspicious. Don't disturb anything."

"We'll wait for the Chief to get here then. I'll put in a call to the county coroner."

In a few moments, Bill Stanley himself arrived. It didn't take him long to come to the same conclusion Jim had, and Bill contacted the county sheriff, Seth Stigler. He promised to send a detective.

Jim hated to leave Mildred, but he wanted to get the clothes for Kate and Blair. He knew those present would give her the respect she deserved. He told Bill everything he knew and asked to leave. Bill dismissed him with the words the county detective would want to speak with him.

"You've got my cell. Please tell Seth I'd like to make a donation toward an award for info leading to the arrest of the person or persons who did this."

He glanced once more at Mildred Steele. Damn this was a nightmare. He trudged out the back door and around to the front. He hated to tell Kate. She'd never want to return, believing Griffin Harbor was a hotbed of crime and violence.

* * * *

Not perfect clothes, but a much better fit than the too-large warm-ups Jim had loaned them. Mildred had done a good job selecting the clothes and the sneakers for them. With one decent outfit each, they could go out for more shopping. They'd see for themselves the extent of the damage to the cottage.

Jim hadn't said much when he returned and handed them their sacks. They'd said thanks and hurried to the shower.

Blair had finished first. "Mom, I'm going to try to rustle

us up a small lunch. It will be interesting one armed."

"Thanks, sweetie. I'll be there to help after my shower." The hot water made her cuts sting, but soothed her muscles, something of a fair trade off. Kate finished blowing dry her hair. Nice she didn't stink of smoke any more. Limping only a little, she left the bedroom and headed for the kitchen.

"Blair, what can I do to help?" Kate came around the corner to find her daughter sitting at the kitchen table and Jim leaning against a counter. No signs of food preparation taking place.

"Sit down, Mom." Blair's voice had a strained sound, as if her vocal cords didn't have enough space to do their job.

"I can help with lunch, Blair."

"Please sit, Kate." Jim held a chair for her.

"What's up?" She didn't move to the chair.

"Please, mom." Blair drew her mother down to the chair next to her. "Jim has bad news."

"What can be worse than the fire at the cottage?"

"Mildred Steele is dead." Jim delivered the news in flat tones.

"What? When. I'm sorry, Jim. She seemed like such a robust woman. Did she have a heart problem she didn't know of?"

"Kate, I found her in bed when I went by this morning. Her death is suspicious."

"What?" Kate couldn't make his words compute. "Didn't Mildred help you buy these clothes?" She glanced down at her shirt and jeans.

"I found her before I did the shopping."

"Well, but…" Kate squeezed the space above her nose with her thumb and forefinger. She glanced up at her daughter and then at Jim. "Are you suggesting…someone…" she struggled to pronounce the word…"murdered Mildred?"

Jim nodded his head. "I'm not an expert, but it looks that way to me. We'll know more after the county sheriff investigates."

"I can't believe this. What was suspicious about how you found her?"

Jim glanced at her daughter and then back to her before saying, "It appeared she had rope burns around her neck."

Kate stood quickly knocking over the kitchen chair and dashed to the bathroom where she threw up.

"Mom, let me in." Blair's voice reached her through the closed door.

"Mom."

"I'm all right." What a lie that was. "I'll be out in a few minutes."

"If you don't come out soon, I'll get Jim." Her daughter's threat had the hoped for result. Kate couldn't stand for Jim to see her like this.

"Hang on, Blair."

Kate blew her nose and used a face cloth to wipe off her face. She opened the door. Blair was standing outside with her arms crossed over her chest.

"Are you going to be okay?"

Kate nodded.

"Then let's go back to the kitchen. There's more Jim wants to talk with us about."

Good lord, what else could he have to say? Kate's mind whirled with the events of less than twenty-four hours.

When she and Blair entered the kitchen, Jim turned from the refrigerator a can in his hand. "This soda will help settle your stomach." He put it on the table in front of where Kate had sat before. His grip on her shoulders comforted. She settled into the chair he held for her.

"Kate, Blair and I have talked, and we've decided it's best if you and she return to her home in New York."

"I understand Blair; she lives there. Why do I have to go?" Was he kicking her out? Apparently, the bit of interest was all on her side. Get a grip, woman. Serious stuff was happening, more important than this crush she seemed to have on Jim Donovan. Kate focused her attention on the Yankee.

"Consider what's happened. Your cottage was set on

fire. Blair told me what the guy who mugged her said. And now someone has killed Mildred Steele."

"All bad things, I agree, but why should I leave?"

"Use your head, Kate. What do they have in common?"

Kate looked at Blair and at Jim. "Oh, my God. You're implying it has to do with the land, aren't you?"

He nodded. "I hate to say this, but it would be safer if you let it be known you're considering the offer from Holland Development."

"But I'm not."

"Mom, Jim wants everyone to have more space. Sheriff Stigler needs time to investigate Ms. Steele's murder with us not around to distract."

"But you were attacked in New York. How will going there keep us safer?" Kate had told her daughter she'd visit, but whether she could make the trip was still up for discussion.

"That's the point of you letting it be known you're leaning toward the Development. That should keep you safe." Jim's lips thinned into a straight line.

"Is Holland behind all of this?" Kate raised her hand to worry the cuticle around her thumbnail. So much for stopping a bad habit.

"I don't know. He never struck me to be a violent man, but I guess any of us can do violence if something we want badly is threatened." Jim rose and went to the counter and poured himself a cup of coffee. He turned and leaned against the counter, one foot cocked over the other.

"All right. Before we leave, I'd like to take a look at the cottage first."

"Are you sure?" Blair glanced between her mother and Jim.

"Yes. If we're going to do this, we'll make it look real. After I look at the…burned out cottage…I can say this was a sort of sign against giving the land to the Conservancy Trust. I'm going away to recover from the trauma of the fire."

"That sounds good, Mom."

"Can you take us to the cottage, Jim?" Kate met his gaze. His face creased with worry for her.

"If you're sure you want to, we can go now."

"Yes. Let's do this."

It didn't take them long to get to the cottage. Yellow tape marked off the car and the remains of the building to the cliff on either side.

Jim stopped his truck, but they all sat there a moment, absorbing the magnitude of the site in front of them.

Blair was the first one to get out. She stood for a full minute. "God, we were lucky to get out of that alive."

Jim reached for Kate's hand and squeezed it. "You ready."

She squeezed his hand back. "Yes." Not knowing how

you'd ever be ready to look at something like this. Generally, she avoided news stories that showed burned and bombed out homes and businesses. The images quickly brought to mind the dreadful scenes of 9/11.

Blair joined her and Kate slid her arm around her daughter's shoulder. "It's something, isn't it?"

Nothing remained of the walls or the roof. The cement basement seemed to be intact, the stone fireplace angled toward the blue sky, testimony of what had been.

"You can walk closer if you want, Kate, but don't try to enter what's left of the building." She nodded. Jim lifted the tape and she eased a few steps inside the perimeter.

The smoke smell still hung in the air. The stone steps to the front door remained, but led into emptiness. Kate couldn't stop the tears that formed. "Oh, my goodness all the people who'd made reservations to stay here…"

"Yes, we'll let them know and refund their money," Jim said.

"I hope the caretaker has something else he does. We certainly don't' need him here anymore."

"You're a good person to be concerned about him, Kate. And yes, he has several families he works for."

"I'm sorry, Liddy." Kate glanced up. "I planned to do what you wanted with this beautiful piece of land, but it wasn't to be."

"I'm glad she's not around to see this. The cottage meant a lot to her. She'd modernized it, and didn't live here anymore. Still it was where she'd spent most of her life."

Kate turned her back on the contrasting views—the ugly remains of the cottage and the gorgeous sea and island. She grasped Blair's hand in one and Jim's in another. "Let's get this show on the road."

"We've got lots of details to take care of before you can leave." Jim's take-charge attitude comforted.

"Well, it won't take us long to pack." Kate's attempt at humor fell flat.

"Let's start with a late lunch at the Lobster Pot and get the word out you're leaving and not planning on turning over the property to the Trust."

"With the difference in sale price between $50 thousand and $500 thousand, no one will hold it against us, Mom." Blair clasped her mother's hand in both of hers.

Maybe not. But the pain in Kate's heart said she would hold herself responsible.

CHAPTER TEN

Monday, September 23

Kenny breezed by his boss's secretary, not bothering to tease her because he was eager to see if Ray had heard the news from Griffin Harbor. He tapped on the door and entered, closing it behind him.

"Good morning, good morning, Kenny. How was your weekend?"

For a moment, Kenny was taken aback. Could Ray know what he'd done? "It was okay. You seem to be in an especially good mood, boss."

"I am. I am. Do you know why?"

"Not a clue." Best to play dumb.

Ray got up from his chair and walked around to the front of his desk where he sat on the corner. Kenny recognized his boss's position of power. When things were going great with a deal, this was where he perched to announce the news.

"I've heard the Thompson woman has seen the wisdom of our dollar signs and is going to work with us!"

"Congratulations, Ray. That's great news."

"I went out this morning to tell my father he didn't have to worry now about staying where he was, I'd have plenty of money for his care." He rose and returned to his desk chair. He rocked back and propped his feet on the desk. "I don't know how much he understood, but I know what it means for him."

"So when do we get moving on the project?"

"Oh, papers aren't signed or the deal finalized. Thompson went to New York to spend time with her daughter there. Apparently, the cottage caught fire—I heard it was a short in the wiring."

"Well, we'd have to tear down the cottage to make room for the condos anyway. Seems to me that saved us a bunch of money."

"True. I don't know how, but I suspect you've helped make her change her mind. When the dough starts rolling, I'll make sure you get a nice bonus."

Best not to deny or confirm anything. "Thanks, Boss."

"Kenny, why don't you take yourself a couple of days off for a vacation. Time to celebrate."

"Great idea. You know how to get hold of me if you need me."

"Sure do. Thanks again. Enjoy yourself."

A flight to Florida and a few days with booze and babes and warm weather sounded like a great way to unwind.

* * * *

Wednesday, September 25

Blair had insisted on turning over her bedroom to her mother, saying she was fine on the sofa bed in the living room. The size of her daughter's apartment pleasantly surprised Kate. A living room large enough to accommodate a round dining table, sofa, and two chairs. The smallish kitchen with a window looking out to the wall of another building was more New York apartment stereotypical. The one bathroom included a tub shower combination. None of it updated and modern, but it seemed to suit, Blair.

"Honey, I can't get over the size of your closet. It's huge."

"It's the single factor which decided me on this apartment. Yes, I have to catch two trains to get down to where I work, but it's a short walk to the station. A wash-a-terria is nearby. Tonight we're getting the best Chinese in the town delivered. You won't believe how good it is."

Kate laughed. It surprised her she could laugh here in NYC, but listening to her daughter go on…well, it lightened her mood. "I can tell how happy you are."

"I am, Mom. And I'm happy you've come. I'm sorry Aunt Liddy died, and I can hardly believe someone murdered Ms. Steele to get our land."

Kate nodded. Not a subject she wanted to pursue, but

her daughter deserved honesty. "Actually it was two."

"Two? Two what?"

"Two murders. Jim didn't tell me before I traveled to Maine, but Aunt Liddy was also murdered." Kate astounded herself with how calm she sounded making that statement as if she were commenting about someone's trip to the grocery store. Now her heartbeat kicked up and judging from the heat on her chest, she was about to go into a full-blown victim's flush.

"That's horrible, Mom. Jim should've told you."

"But then, I wouldn't have come. We wouldn't have seen the cottage nor had the opportunity to enjoy the gorgeous view from our land."

"You wouldn't have gotten to know Jim Donovan."

Kate chose to ignore her daughter's provocative comment. It wouldn't do anything to help her get a grip to have to spar with Blair about the handsome Mainer.

"And I wouldn't be sitting in my lovely daughter's apartment in New York City."

"I guess not."

Blair's smile filled Kate with warmth and hope. Time to change the subject. "What time do you have to go into work?"

"Normally, I'm on the train by seven every morning. That gets me to the office before eight, but I'm not going in for the next couple of days. My boss said to take a couple of more days off while you're here. I'll have to pay it back over one of the holidays, but that's okay with me."

Blair slid her fingers between Kate's and drew her to the sofa in the living room. Her brows drew down, causing frown lines above her nose. This looked serious. "What is it, honey?"

"Mom, when you lived here with Daddy and me before…well, did you like New York?"

Blair had never asked her that question, and Kate had never given it a thought. But now good memories rushed in. Memories she'd apparently suppressed because of the events of 9/11.

"I loved New York, Blair. I'd forgotten." She rose and crossed to the window to look out on the sidewalk outside Blair's apartment. "The hustle and bustle. The sounds, smells, the different languages you could hear anywhere. And oh, let's not forget the food or the Broadway shows. And the lights during the holidays."

Kate moved to the end of the sofa. "The grocery store on the corner from where we lived always had Christmas trees. It was an annual journey to march down there the first of December and drag the perfect tree back home."

"I remember those times, Mom. I didn't know if I'd dreamed them. You never spoke of them."

"I'm not sure I remembered them until right now. We were happy then. Thinking about them only reminded me of what we'd lost. So I stopped. I'm sorry." She sat next to Blair. "I didn't realize how that would also cut off your memories." She squeezed Blair's hand. "Forgive me?"

Blair put her good arm around her and squeezed, gently to avoid hurting either of their injuries from the night of the fire. "It's okay, Mom. You did the best you could. That's all any of us can ever do."

"Thanks dear."

"I do have a favor to ask though." She took hold of one of Kate's hands in hers. "I want you to go with me down to the Memorial Garden."

Kate went to pull her hand from her daughter's grasp, but Blair tightened her hold. Kate did the next best thing; she straightened on the sofa away from Blair.

"Now wait. Hear me out. I've talked with lots of people who passed through the memorial. Mom, it's peaceful there. The flowing waters. The trees and flowers. The monument itself with all the names. Many people have told me touching the name of their loved one, brought them such peace."

"Blair, I..."

"It did for me, Mom. Please, at least go down there with me. I'll show you my office. If you want, we can go in the museum store. Please do this for me. I want my whole mother back. I lost my dad on 9/11, but in a way I also lost you."

Tears fell. Kate pulled her daughter to her. They both

sobbed. A thing they'd never done together before. Kate had maintained a stoic calm around Blair when she was little, hoping not to scare her with the intensity of her emotions. Oh, when Blair wasn't around, visiting her grandparents or at school, Kate regularly broke down. But for her daughter she held it together.

"I'm sorry, Blair. I didn't want to distance myself from you, but when I cried back then it was violent, out of control. It would've frightened you."

"Grandma and Grandpa, tried to explain it to me."

"We were both lucky to have them."

Blair nodded.

Kate gulped out a short laugh. "Good thing we didn't plan to go out to supper tonight. I bet we'd never get rid of our raccoon eyes. Here's a tissue."

"Thanks." Blair dabbed at her eyes. She rose from the sofa. Walked to where she kept her wine. "Want a glass?"

"Yes." Silence hung in the room until Blair handed Kate her glass. "Thank you."

She raised hers filled with a beautiful ruby red liquid. "To my beautiful, brilliant, and understanding daughter." They clinked the crystal.

"Aw, Mom. Don't make me start crying again."

Kate gulped her wine. "I'll go with you tomorrow, Blair."

* * * *

Jim had spent Wednesday in his office in Gerard catching up on work he'd let slide while he'd been caught up with Liddy's property and Kate's problems. He'd squeezed in time to talk with Sheriff Stigler before heading to Griffin Harbor and lobster with Tom at his restaurant. It was a few minutes before nine, and the number of patrons had thinned out giving Tom the opportunity to eat his meal with Jim.

"I don't guess I'll ever eat too much lobster." Jim pulled off his bib and signaled the waitress for another beer.

"Especially, when it's my lobster and you know it's cooked to perfection." Tom removed the bib and wiped his hands on one of the small towels he provided his guests.

The waitress brought them both two beers and then cleared away their plates.

"I understand you spent the day in Gerard."

Jim barked a short laugh. "The grapevine is alive and well."

"It's one of the criteria of being a great small town to have a great grapevine."

"I had tons of paperwork to file both for other clients and with Mildred's estate."

"Did she have much?"

"Nah, because she'd turned over her property to the Conservancy Trust already. The rest is going to a grandson in New Hampshire. I stopped by and picked Seth's brain on what's going on here. He shared that his office was making progress toward figuring out who killed Mildred. They theorized it might be the same person who killed Liddy. It's odd for two wonderful old women to be murdered in a small town like Griffin Harbor. One has to suspect they're related."

"The tie that binds must be the Thompson land." Tom tipped his head back for a couple of large swallows. "Ah."

"I forced Kate Thompson to come up here, putting her and her daughter in danger. When she returns from New York, I'm going to tell her to go home to Texas."

"Is she going to return after visiting in New York?"

"Before she left she told me she wanted to come back for Mildred's funeral. That's scheduled for Saturday." Jim turned his bottle around and around on the table.

"How'd she get temporary papers to replace those lost in the fire?"

"One of her friends, Addie I think, went into her house and faxed copies of her birth certificate, drivers' license, and insurance papers up here. Kate's organized. Addie had no trouble locating them. It will take a while before the new official documents to arrive. She had them sent to my address. She'll have to return for those."

"Jim, even though the cottage is gone, isn't there some one she might return for?" Tom looked at Jim over the top of his beer bottle.

"Well, I admit, I'd like there to be someone, but she's not over the loss of her husband."

"It's been over fourteen years."

"Different people take different amounts of time to heal."

"Sad. Hope it works out for you somehow, man."

"I've been alone a long time and made my peace with this life." He ran his hands over his eyes picturing the cottage devastated by fire and believing the worst. "Hard to trust someone responsible for nearly getting you and your daughter incinerated in the cottage fire. It's my fault for asking Kate up here in the first place."

＊ ＊ ＊ ＊

Thursday, September 26

Kate had forgotten the diversity of people in New York City. The subway ride to downtown was in its own way exhilarating. Still no one made eye contact, and now the gazes of lots of passenger were glued to cells, e- readers, or pads. Apparently, her legs hadn't forgotten how to balance with the rocking motion.

Blair seemed thrilled beyond anything Kate could've imagined to have her mother in New York City. How sad she'd denied her daughter this joy. *Please, God, don't let me fall apart.* She'd prudently stuffed tissues in her purse, which she'd safely looped across her chest. It was one of her new purchases along with a new cell phone.

They came up out of the subway and walked for several blocks until Kate noticed long lines snaking around a corner. "What's all that?"

"The visitors."

"My goodness. Is there significance to this date?" Past September 11, Kate was surprised to find such large crowds.

"It's always like this, Mom. Of course, on the anniversary, we give preference to the survivors."

They walked on the other side of the street, moving toward the entrance. "Isn't the end of the line back that way, Blair? We appear to be going the wrong way."

Blair waved the badge around her neck. "You've got people, Mom. We'll skip to the front of the line and get you a special badge. Then we'll still have to go through the metal detectors."

Kate swallowed. She hadn't realized, since she'd avoided all coverage of the anniversary each year, preferring to stay holed up on her own.

"Pardon me," Blair smiled at the two people at the front of the line. "Jennifer."

The guard looked up. "Hey, Blair. You can come through here."

Blair shoved Kate in front of her. "This is my mother, Kate Thompson."

"Ms. Thompson, it's nice to have you here. Get her a badge, Blair."

"Sure thing. Thanks. This way, Mom."

Blair tugged her along. They got her a special pass and then headed through the metal detectors and wound around a few more twists and turns. The farther they walked into the gardens, the more Kate struggled to breathe. Again, the numbers of people stunned her. That this many people still cared this many years later nearly brought on the tears. She gritted her teeth.

Standing under the shade of a tree, Blair pointed out the layout with the museum itself at the farthest point. Then she indicated the giant pools.

"Daddy's name is engraved on one of the walls of the North Pool. I can't tell you the sense of pride it gives me to see that and know that he will always be remembered. Long after we're gone, Mom." Kate's hand slid up and brushed at her eye.

Kate drew in a deep breath and let it out. Then another. "Okay, Blair, I've come this far." They headed toward the North Pool. People snapped pictures. Others stood silently. If they talked, it was in hushed tones. Some leaned against the granite wall to peer into the deep pools with the ever-flowing water. Blair stopped and then Kate did. It was as if she'd given over her will to her daughter.

"Here's his name, Mom." Blair laid her hand gently to

the left of carved letters on the stone.

Kate hadn't focused her eyes on the name. The closest she'd gotten was to look at Blair's hand. She didn't make eye contact with her daughter either. The rate of Kate's heartbeat had increased with each step, and now she feared she'd pass out. She had to drag in a breath.

"Come on Mom, you can do this." She slid her right arm around Kate's waist and drew her forward. Then Blair lifted Kate's left hand and placed it on top of the granite where her own had lain.

Almost without her willing it, her gaze traveled to the carved words.

"John…Wendell…Thompson." Kate whispered the names, and the tears fell. Blair's soft sobs joined hers. They turned and embraced.

They cried for a time, but finally the tears slowed. Kate dragged out the tissues, handed several to her beautiful, brave daughter, and sopped up the moisture and wiped her own nose. She dragged in a deep cleansing breath and let it out. She straightened and looked around.

"This is incredibly beautiful, Blair. Tasteful, strong, and sensitive. A great honor paid to all those we lost." They linked arms and went around the pool. Kate glanced at other names. She recognized ones from John's office and more tears spilled, but she kept breathing and kept moving.

"This was years in the making, Mom. I've only been here a short time, but I feel such pride to have a small part to do with showing respect to all we lost."

"I'm proud of you, Blair. I'm sorry I haven't been there for you."

"Oh, Mom. You've always been there for me, just not here." She glanced around at their surroundings. "I'm more than pleased you came today. I'm proud of you for being able to do this."

"Damn, here come the tears again."

"Tears are okay, Mom. They're cleansing and healing. They show how much Daddy meant to us. If we didn't care so much, we wouldn't need the tears."

"My wise daughter."

CHAPTER ELEVEN

Saturday, September 28

"Kate, I want you to sell the land to Ray Holland."

Jim's first words to her when he picked her up at the train station in Portland last Friday evening had taken her by surprise. Now, here he was saying them again. What was going on with him? His advice went against everything that was important to the man.

Kate put him off last night, saying she was tired and they could talk about it after Mildred's funeral. Another service packed with many people from Griffin Harbor and the surrounding towns. Mildred had been a powerhouse and the town would miss her drive.

They'd returned to Jim's house after the service. Kate hadn't eaten anything from the spread laid out in the church fellowship hall. Now she wished she had. She could have a fight on her hands with Jim.

His stance, arms across his chest and his legs spread, indicated a man bent on getting his own way.

"Before we begin this, how about we have a glass of wine?" Kate rose, heading in the direction of the kitchen, hoping to lighten the tone of the discussion. Jim apparently was having nothing to do with a delaying tactic. He stepped in front of her.

"No, we're talking now. Right now."

Kate huffed and flopped into a large wingback that flanked the fireplace. "Okay, talk." She crossed one leg over the other, but when she couldn't keep the leg still, she set both feet firmly on the floor, needing a façade of control.

"I've been thinking, and it seems to me the only way to keep you safe is for you to sell the land to Holland. Not pretend like we've been doing, but to sell it to him." He sat in the matching wing chair, but stiffly, not relaxed.

Kate didn't say anything, stared at him, gritting her teeth to keep from yelling at him for his stupidity.

"Before you left for New York, I told you you'd be okay as long as you didn't turn over the land to the Maine Coast Conservancy Trust. If you kept it, you'd be okay. Now, I've changed my mind. You need to sell to Holland for real."

Kate leaned forward. "Jim this is my land. Blair's land. I won't sell to Holland and let him build his damn condominiums! I'm not saying the Conservancy Trust is getting all of the land. Before the fire, Blair and I had decided to keep the land where the cottage sat in the family. We've talked about rebuilding.

We'll want to keep an access to the property, of course."

"No." He rose and crossed the room, putting his back to her. "You have to sell and get back to Texas where you'll be safe." His hands clenched at his side.

His words pierced her heart, which had only recently taken to beating with something like that of a normal human. Pre-9/11. She didn't much care for the hurt. Wasn't sure she could push through the discomfort. Did he feel nothing for her? They'd never been intimate. Maybe he was a good man, concerned for her safety and not for her.

Was she brave enough to take a shot at this? At connecting with Jim Donovan?

Her hands grasped the armrests and she pushed herself up. Slow steps carried her to stand behind Jim. She placed a hand on his back. "Jim." The muscles in his back contracted.

"Look at me…please."

"I can't or I'll change my mind and try to convince you to stay. But I couldn't live with myself if something happened to you."

Kate nodded her head. "I understand. Let me assure you that you would live. Oh, maybe not as fully as before, but we do go on living after the worst of disasters."

Jim turned then. His hands grasped her forearms. "I'm sorry, Kate. I haven't forgotten what you went through, but what happened to your husband wasn't your fault. If something happened to you, it would be on me."

"And how is that?" Her hands rested on his chest trembling with the effort to not grab his shirt and pull him closer.

"I dragged you up here. I bullied you into that road trip. Did everything I could to make you fall in love...with Maine."

"Jim you didn't hold me at gun point and kidnap me. I have free will, and I had a say in my coming and going. I wanted a chance to visit Blair. You provided an opportunity to do that. Do I have regrets? Sure. I'm, sorry someone murdered Liddy and Mildred." Kate silently congratulated herself she said that sentence without a tremor in her voice. "I hate that someone attacked Blair."

Kate stepped closer into Jim's space. "But I don't regret coming here. Seeing this beautiful state. Meeting such wonderful people. Visiting with Blair and seeing for myself how happy she is in New York. And the Memorial. If it weren't for you, I'd have never gone there or had the chance to see how lovingly the dead have been honored. I can move on now."

She stretched on her tiptoes and slid a hand around his neck. "What about you, Jim? Can you move on?" She pulled his head toward hers and his right hand moved up to caress the side of her face. She kissed his palm. His thumb slid along her jaw line and then slipped across her lips. His gaze left hers and fixated on her lips. He lowered his head and placed the softest, most tender kiss she could imagine. His tongue touched the corners of her mouth and slid along the seam. Kate opened to delicious feelings, his tongue dueling in slow motion with hers.

After a time, Jim lifted his head, his breathing heavy. He stared at her for a moment. "Wow. That was more than I anticipated. The earlier kisses pale beside that one."

She smiled at him. Her knees decidedly wobbly she held on.

"I'm glad you agreed to come to Griffin Harbor, Kate Thompson. Liddy would be pleased."

Kate nodded. "I believe she would be."

Jim tightened his hold on her and drew her flush against him, his erection pushed against her lower belly. This time his lips ravaged hers before he moved to her neck and the spot behind her ear, sending chill bumps down her entire left side. He returned to her lips, and her breathing went completely out of her control when they breathed together, becoming one.

Her head spun, warmth spread from their lips through her middle and lower. She held him close. If she let go she'd probably drift off the planet. And she didn't want to do that. She wanted to stay right here wrapped in this man's arms. Emotions swirled around and through her. She'd forgotten what this felt like. This wonderful losing of yourself in someone else.

Again, Jim pulled back. His gaze seared into hers. He scooped her up and carried her to the sofa where he lowered her. She lay back with him partly on top of her. His erection pressed into her thigh. His hand slid from her neck down and caressed her breast. Her nipples perked and ached for more of his touch. God, she was flying apart. His hand moved lower and his fingers slid beneath her skirt.

Oh, my God. She ached for him to touch her down there. And he did. His hand slid between her legs. She arched against him, straining for release. She kissed him deeply. Her tongue touching his, sucking on his. She slid her hand down his chest and played across his muscles, her fingers sought the buttons of his shirt.

His palm pressed against her mound. She ground against his hand. "Open for me." His words against her neck, followed by hot kisses sent chill bumps all down that arm and her side. She shifted to spread her legs. Then his fingers slid inside her panties and found her moist with yearning. Slowly a finger slipped in and came out. He put the finger in his mouth before he slid it in again, this time farther. She gasped for breath and strained against his hand and fingers craving more of those wonderful sensations flowing over and around and through her.

Then his thumb brushed once, twice, three times across her sensitive nub. She moaned and thrust against him. "Oh,

Oh. Don't stop." And he didn't, and she burst into a thousand shiny pieces of sparkling glass, screaming out her release.

He held her gently while she settled back to earth.

She blinked, waking from a dream, but it wasn't a dream. It was real, and Kate wanted to pleasure Jim in many ways. She wanted to feel him inside of her. She pushed against his chest. Frown lines formed between his eyebrows.

"What?"

"Come with me." She continued to push and moved them from the sofa, drawing him with her toward his bedroom. "We're not finished yet." Jim's only response was a deep laugh.

* * * *

Sunday, September 29

They stayed in last evening, choosing to keep their newfound closeness to themselves. Jim gave up trying to convince her to sell the land to Holland. She flat refused to listen every time he raised the issue. Then she'd kiss him and that was the end of the discussion.

The view from his front window always drew a smile, but now the smile came from inside and exploded outwards stretching his arms above his head. God he couldn't remember when he felt this good. Normally he couldn't function without his morning coffee, let alone feel so—well, like he could conquer the world. The aroma from the perking brew tickled his nose. His stomach growled. Last night Kate and he had eaten squash soup Mildred had made for him, and that he'd frozen. They hadn't wanted to go out even for more food.

He'd have to do a better job of keeping the pantry and fridge stocked. Jim returned to the kitchen and pushed aside worries about how long Kate would stay and how everything would resolve about the land. He wanted to revel in the good-to-be-alive feeling flowing through his whole body, mind, and spirit. Live in the moment was his new motto.

After filling two cups with coffee, he reached for the half-n-half Kate loved. He'd stocked it before she returned from New York. He drank his black.

When he pushed open the door to his bedroom, Kate's blonde hair spread across her pillow drew his attention. She'd thrown one hand over her head. One foot stuck out from the covers. Before he walked out of the room in search of coffee, he'd turned the fire up in the fireplace, giving thanks for the gas he'd put in during the remodel he'd done on his grandparents' home. Kate was naked under the covers and he didn't want her to get cold.

In fact, he never wanted anything to hurt her again. He set the cups down on his side of the bed and climbed in next to her. He trailed his fingers across the top of the sheet dipping under to touch her breasts. The nipples perked instantly. Kate's eyes fluttered open.

"Oh, Jim. You crazy man. You want to do this before

coffee?"

He laughed. "No, that would be crazy. I've brought the coffee." He leaned against the headboard on his side of the bed and held out her cup.

She sniffed and sighed. "Hold that for a moment." She got up, flung a robe around her naked body, and headed for the bathroom.

Jim sipped his coffee and thanked his lucky stars that he'd gone to Texas. He couldn't imagine what lay ahead for them. Kate lived in Fort Worth, in a large metropolitan area in Texas. Portland was the largest city in Maine, but was small by comparison. Could she be happy here in rural, small town Maine? What about the winters? Brutal by anyone's standards. Could she survive those? Neither had spoken the L word, but he was pretty sure that's what he felt for Kate.

How she could ever forgive him for dragging her and Blair into this mess, he didn't know. What about Blair? How would she feel if Kate and he developed a long-distance relationship? Of course, Blair wanted to keep the land. Who wouldn't? Kate said they'd talked about building a new cottage out there. Would Kate stay there when she visited or would she stay with him?

More coffee. He'd swigged half the mug in one gulp. The questions were making him nuts. The door opened and Kate returned. She had a touch of lipstick on and she'd brushed her lovely hair, leaving it less tangled, but no less bushy. He loved the effect.

"Just what I need." She climbed into bed and relieved him of the extra mug. She swallowed about half the contents in a single gulp. "Thank you. I could get used to this."

Jim grinned. "Yeah." He pushed aside questions about them and made every effort to keep things on balance. If you don't ask, you don't get no. Of course, you don't get yes, either.

"What do you want to do today?" Apparently, Kate wasn't afraid of the questions.

"I'm all yours." She didn't know how true that was.

Her low chuckle rolled out. "I can figure out something. But after a second cup of coffee." She leaned over and dropped a sweet kiss on his lips but pulled away before he could respond. "First a quick shower and then we can strategize over breakfast."

His gaze followed her walk toward the bathroom. She stopped in the doorway and looked over her shoulder. "You coming?"

Jim couldn't remember ever moving faster, or a more enjoyable shower in his life.

* * * *

It was noon before they got out. Bundled against the cold front that had come in overnight, they crossed the walking bridge to the main part of the town. They stopped and chatted with the people they met. It seemed to Kate, most folks were happy she'd decided to keep part of the land and give the rest to the Conservancy Trust.

She'd convinced Jim they couldn't live their lives in fear of all the bad that can befall a person. She'd done that most of her adult life, and since her visit to the Memorial Gardens, she'd changed. It was like she'd broken out of a chrysalis. She wanted to spread her wings and fly. Well, maybe not literally in planes. Would that taboo also fall away? Guess time would tell. If they were going to find out who was doing all this, they needed to live out loud as the saying went.

That didn't imply she and Jim would take crazy chances. They'd be cautious. Before they set out on their walk, Kate called Blair to alert her about their plan. Blair also needed to be especially cautious. Her daughter agreed not to travel alone, especially late at night. She'd investigate a security system for her apartment, but she wasn't moving into one of those high rises with a doorman. Entirely cost prohibitive. She refused to let Kate help make up the difference. Damn her independent daughter. Kate couldn't stop her lips spreading into a smile. Pride for Blair warmed her insides like a hot air balloon. She could almost lift off the ground.

Oddly, Blair asked no questions about Jim or when Kate planned to return to Texas or to arrange another trip to New

York. Not that Kate had answers for her. She was taking a wait and see attitude. She knew she couldn't return to Texas until the murders were resolved. Otherwise, she'd be looking over her shoulder the rest of her life, wherever she lived.

A couple hours later, Jim and she returned to his house over the walking bridge.

"How about a nap?" he asked.

"That sounds good to me." She'd stifled a couple yawns on their walk back. Apparently, he'd noticed.

Jim peeled down the comforter, and they climbed in snuggling close. She'd take this as long as she could get it. At some point, she'd come back to reality, which might mean a return to Texas. Well, from a practical standpoint, even if something worked out to allow her to stay, she'd have to go back to Texas to closeout her business and the house. Probably the best she could hope for was to split time between Griffin Harbor and Fort Worth. She knew people who did that. Could she? Her eyelids drifted down, batted, a couple of times then she relaxed.

* * * *

Monday, September 30

Jim insisted Kate ride with him to Gerard. He had business to attend to, and he wanted them to stop at the Sheriff's Office. He'd talked about wanting her to practice shooting a gun later in the day.

The man was nuts. No way was she touching a gun. Guns killed people. Of course other things did. Liddy was poisoned, and Mildred strangled with a rope. She got that they had to be careful, but didn't agree to going in the direction of using a weapon. She suspected she hadn't heard the end of the discussion.

Kate had spent the morning on the porch at Jim's office, bundled up, and sipping hot coffee. She loved the view down the street. Sidewalks lined with all the old houses and the trees with their leaves beginning to turn. Gerard was a lovely town, much larger than Griffin Harbor, of course, but still a town and not a city.

Now they waited to meet with Seth Stigler, the Gerard County Sheriff.

A tall, barrel chested man walked toward them. "Hello, Jim. Nice to see you, Ms. Thompson. Sorry for the circumstances."

"You can call me Kate, Sheriff."

"Let's go back to my office." He led them down a short hall, ushered them into a small office, and gestured to the two straight chairs in front of his desk. "So are the rumors I've heard correct, Ms.—Kate? You're planning on keeping a small portion of the land and selling the rest to the Conservancy Trust?"

"The grapevine is alive and well in this part of Maine."

Kate smiled and nodded. "You've heard correctly. My daughter and I plan to rebuild the cottage."

"Normally, I'd say congratulations and welcome to Maine. But, Kate, is that wise given all the circumstances?"

"I've tried to change her mind, Seth. She's a stubborn lady."

"Sheriff, I've lived my adult life looking over my shoulder waiting for the other disaster to happen. That's not a healthy or full way to live."

"To be blunt, you're alive and not dead like Liddy and Mildred. I wish I could guarantee you that we'll catch this fellow, but I can't do that. Maine's a big state and if someone wants to, they can hide out for a long time."

"What about staff to keep an eye on her?" Jim crossed one leg over the other.

The sheriff shook his head. "Afraid not. You can check with the police in Griffin Harbor."

"We'll do that." Jim's tone was subdued. The chances must be slim for that.

"The Griffin Harbor Inn is lovely, but I'm not certain of how good their security is," the Sheriff tapped a pencil on his desk.

"She's staying with me." Jim's words brooked no argument or censure.

The Sheriff nodded. "Good. We'll keep you posted if we

come across anything. You do the same."

Kate felt the dismissal. She rose and extended her had. "Thanks, Sheriff." Jim followed.

They were quiet on the walk back to Jim's office in the old house. They went in briefly to collect their belongings, and then he closed the windows and locked the door. "Let's head home," was the last thing he said to her all the way back. Kate studied the scenery and dithered about whether she was making the right decision. She didn't want anyone else making decisions about her life. If she turned tail and ran, she'd be giving in to whoever was behind all the mayhem in her life right now. That's what she did after 9/11. Let the Taliban steal her life and steal Blair's. She wasn't about to let that happen again. Reaching the resolution, she rested her head against the seat back and dozed.

"Hey, sleepy head, we're home."

She stretched and smiled over at Jim. "Nice words."

"Glad you got a rest, cause after we change clothes we're heading out to a shooting range."

Kate slammed her door to emphasize her "No."

Jim slammed with equal vigor. "Oh, yes we are. If you want my cooperation on this misguided strategy to flush out the culprit, you have to do it on my terms. That means you have a gun and you know how to use it."

They stared at each other over the hood of Jim's SUV.

She wanted to live her life on her own terms now and that meant catching the bastard who'd killed Liddy and Mildred and threatened Blair. If that meant she had to learn to use a gun, that's how it would be. She gave one short nod and headed for the house.

CHAPTER TWELVE

Tuesday, October 1

"Ms. Thompson, I wanted to follow up with you about your land. I'd heard you'd had a change of heart and decided to sell your land to my company. I'd have gotten back with you quicker, but had family health issues." The man's voice seemed older than she remembered it.

"Sorry to hear that, Mr. Holland." Kate's fingers tightened on her cell. She hated telling people no. Everyone in her office knew her to be a sucker for Girl Scout Cookies or anything else kids or grandkids sold for their schools. She was genuinely sorry about Mr. Holland's family matter, but it was time to gut up.

"Some time ago I considered selling to you, but since then, I've decided to keep the part of the land where the cottage sat in the family. The rest will go to the Maine Coast Conservancy Trust the way my aunt intended."

"I'd heard there was a fire, Ms. Thompson."

"Yes. The cottage burned down." Her words were met

by silence on the other end. Drawing in a deep breath, she continued, "Right after that was when I decided to sell the land to you, but things have changed, and we're keeping it in the family." More silence.

"Mr. Holland, are you all right."

The sounds of Holland clearing his voice came through the phone. "Yes, I'm all right. I'm disappointed to hear your decision. I guess the timing was off for this deal. Enjoy your land." He disconnected.

Well, that wasn't the hard sell she'd expected. Kate settled on Jim's porch with a cup of hot coffee in her hand. Maybe all that had been missing in the past was for her to be definite instead of wishy-washy.

* * * *

Wednesday, October 2

"What kept you? You've been gone forever." His boss' tone sounded like he held Kenny responsible for the worst disaster.

"I headed out for a couple of days of vacation, like you suggested. I had difficulty making flight connections because the storm across the middle of the country threw off flight schedules."

"Didn't you tell me you'd heard that Thompson was ready to sell to us?"

"Well, I did. I told you weekend before this last one."

Kenny rubbed his hand across his face. What could've gone wrong? Both the Thompson broad and the old lady were gone. No more roadblocks should block his boss getting the land.

"I talked with Thompson yesterday and—"

"You did what?" Kenny's blood turned to ice through his veins. He didn't believe in ghosts, but he was certain, Thompson and her daughter died in the fire. How could they have gotten out?

"I said I talked with Thompson, and she's keeping the land, at least a piece of it. The rest she's selling to the Conservancy Trust."

"The hell you say."

"Yeah, I do say, Kenny. What made you sure we were going to get it?"

He hopped from his chair to pace. What could he say to that? Because I killed her? Not hardly. He turned and faced Ray. "It was the rumor on the streets of Griffin Harbor. When I picked it up, I passed it on to you."

"Because of Dad's stroke, I couldn't contact Thompson right after I heard from you. Yesterday, when I talked with her, she said no."

"Is she still staying out at that cottage?" Kenny needed more info to figure out what to do next.

"I wouldn't know how she could. I told you the cottage burned down." His boss cocked his head and studied Kenny.

"You wouldn't know anything about that, now would you?"

"What makes you ask?" Kenny paced to the window and stared out. Things didn't appear to be going the way he'd hoped. By now, he and Ray should've been celebrating the conclusion of a great deal.

"I remember back when we were kids you got into trouble starting fires."

Damn him for bringing up those times.

"No, I didn't try to burn down the cottage." He couldn't quite face Ray and deny his involvement. He threw words over his shoulder. "It was old. I bet it was the wiring."

"I'm glad to hear that, Kenny. You're a good buddy. I appreciate how you stop by to visit with my father, but well…just glad you didn't have anything to do with the fire. I'll figure out another way to take care of Dad. Another deal will come along. At least I hope so."

"Me too, boss." Kenny rattled the change in his pocket and considered what else he could do to help.

"I've got to make calls. Close the door on your way out." Ray picked up the handle on the phone on his desk.

The dismissal curdled Kenny's insides. Ray didn't know how much he owed him. There'd been lots of jobs over the years that needed a nudge to make'm come together. Kenny had supplied the nudge.

Of course, Ray loved his old man. Hell, Kenny loved

him. He was more like a father to him than his own. The old man had needs that made it important for Ray to get the Griffin Harbor land. Maybe it was time for old man Holland to go. That would relieve the strain on Ray's financial situation. After this last set back, the old man couldn't be in good shape. Most of the time Holland didn't recognize Kenny when he stopped by. Now it was his time to move on. To help his son.

What was with the Thompson woman? Was she a cat with nine lives? She should've burned up in that fire. Her and her daughter. After he handled Ray's old man, he'd deal with Thompson.

He steered his truck toward the nursing home. He should've done this before, but the old man gave him shelter when no one else would. Treated him like one of his sons. Kenny turned out a damn site better than Ray's brother. Though he did have his uses.

Kenny parked his truck, and headed through the double doors of the retirement center. Spaced at regular intervals made the security cameras easy to spot and avoid. He made his way through the facility with long halls and doors opening into the many rooms. Ray's dad had moved back into his old room after being in the hospital wing. Stepping into the room, Kenny shut the door, which had been partially open. The old man was awake, but his eyes didn't register that he recognized who'd entered. Probably just as well. He looked a lot worse than he did two weeks ago when Kenny had last seen him.

Kenny picked up one of the extra pillows. "Good night, Daddy." He pushed the pillow down on the old man's face and held tight. Kenny's muscles strained to hold it down as Holland kicked, but only for a short time. Then he was still. No mistakes like with Thompson. She'd get hers next.

Before Kenny rose, he placed two fingers on the old man's neck. Nothing. Kenny breathed a long sigh then placed the pillow underneath the old man's head. He looked like he slept peacefully if anyone looked in on him.

Now for Thompson. Should he try for the daughter again or go straight for the mother? He hopped the commuter train toward New York City. Daughter first then the mom. If Ray ended up with the land after all, maybe Kenny would get one of those condos with the great view.

* * * *

Friday, October 4

JD McClendon had picked up Blair, and they'd gone to Sardi's for supper. She found it surprising how quickly their relationship had developed from that first morning visit after the purse snatching. He'd called a couple of times. When she returned from Maine, he stopped by. They'd gone for coffee. Then ate dinners at mom & pop restaurants he knew about.

Sardi's was a step up for sure. Blair loved this restaurant for the food and the ambiance.

"Doesn't seem crowded in here tonight" Blair picked up her coffee cup. The lovely scent of Bourbon tickled her nose and warmed her insides when she sipped. What a great way to end a meal.

JD glanced around. "Not particularly. There are a number of empty tables. Surprising for a Friday night, but we've managed to get here between the before and after theatre crowd."

"Sometimes I sense all the folks who've passed through here." Her gaze sought the caricatures on the walls. "They go back over a long time."

JD studied her across the table. He lifted his cup and sipped. "How many times have we gone out, Blair?"

"Four or five times. Why?"

"I've never detected this kind of "ooey" quality before. Are you into the mystical?"

"Well, I do read my horoscope every morning while I drink my coffee." She chuckled. "But mostly I find it amusing. Don't you sometimes sense the presence of those who've gone on? I'd think in your business you would."

"If you're asking me do I feel anything when I visit the 9/11 Memorial Gardens and Museum, yeah, I do. Not so much at other places."

She nodded. "Mom felt it there. I was relieved. We had a great visit. We made up for the one when I was seventeen."

She'd told him about that trip. He'd shared stories about people he'd lost. While he'd grown up in Kansas, his father's brother was a police officer and another one was a firefighter in New York. One uncle was injured, but recovered, physically anyway. JD had told her how much he worried about him.

"Are you up for walking around?" Blair glanced at JD. "You had a hard day." He'd told her about a robbery that ended in the death of a teenager by a gang member.

"I love Times Square and the people. I get a kick out of all the tourists gawking at the sites."

"Don't make fun. I was a tourist once." She loved how he helped her on with her coat and how when they got outside he drew her arm through his and kept her on the inside of the walkway. An old world type of gentleman. Was it wise to date a police officer? Maybe not. JD had told her his goal was to be a homicide detective. Sounded scary, but he assured her it was safer than the job of a beat cop. Which wasn't terribly comforting, but she was rushing things for sure. He was a nice young man and they enjoyed spending time together.

"This has been fun, but I know you have to get up early in the morning."

"Yeah, when I get a break, I'll call you." They climbed in a taxi and headed to Queens.

"This is expensive. You know I could've done the subway, and you'd have gotten home sooner."

"You crazy woman. I wasn't putting you on a subway by yourself. We agreed you'd take extra precautions until the perp bothering your family is captured."

"Well, we did, but I'm not going to stop riding the subway. It's how I go to and from work. I'm being mindful and put extra locks on the front door."

"Good." He smiled. "I don't want anything to happen to you." He kissed her on the lips then, a sweet kiss that stirred something deep within.

"Twenty bucks, mister." The cabby said, pointing to the automated price machine.

"Can you wait while I walk the young lady in? Extra tip if you will."

"Sure thing."

They walked through the lobby entrance to Blair's door. She unlocked the three locks. "See. I'm safe. Thanks for this evening, JD. It was lovely."

"Glad you enjoyed yourself. I sure did. Let's do a repeat when we can get it scheduled. You pick where we eat next time."

"I look forward to that. In the meantime, I'll come up with a special place for us to go and one not especially expensive like tonight."

JD pulled her close and kissed her again. This time with much more passion, enough to make Blair's legs go all rubbery.

He released her. "Lock up. I'll wait right here until I hear all three locks click."

"Yes sir. You be safe, now here."

Click. Click. Click.

Blair leaned against the door. She hadn't felt this way about a guy in a long time. She loved spending time with him. Didn't hurt he was such a great kisser. She turned to her left and hung up her coat in the front hall closet, a nice perk of her apartment.

She turned around at a sound and excruciating pain hit her stomach and spread through her body. Oh my God. She floated to the ground. Warm wetness met her fingers where they clutched her middle. What was wrong? She hurt all over. Darkness filled her peripheral vision telescoping in. And then nothing.

* * * *

Friday, October 4

Kenny laughed. He was getting good at this. Maybe he needed to start charging. He could pull in some big ones. Up to now, he'd killed with poison, rope, pillow, and now with a knife. He glanced down at the still body. Didn't take long to bleed out from a knife wound in the belly. Yeah, she'd be dead soon enough. He didn't need to hang around. He glanced through the window he'd broken to get into the apartment. A taxi pulled away from the curb, but nothing else. He crawled out through the window and headed for the subway.

Now for the Thompson woman. She's one of the main problems in all of this. He headed for the train and a ride to Portland where he'd grab his car. Sometimes it was easier to do things yourself.

* * * *

"Blair, I wasn't expecting to hear from you. How are you dear?"

"It's not Blair, Ms. Thompson."

A deep voice came from her phone with her daughter's name and picture attached, sending trembles deep in the center of her soul. Her heart rate jumped. Something must be wrong.

"I'm JD McClendon, a friend of Blair's."

"What's wrong with my daughter?" Kate's voice rose two octaves and her breath caught.

"She's in the hospital. She's been stabbed."

Kate's knees gave out, and she sank to the floor of Jim's kitchen. "Oh, my God."

"She's going to make it. You hear that, Ms. Thompson? She's going to make it."

"Which hospital is Blair in? And tell me who you are again."

"New York-Presbyterian Queens Hospital. I'm a police

officer, Ms. Thompson. I met Blair when her purse was stolen. She's been taking extra precautions. We thought she'd be safe in her apartment. I feel—"

"Officer McClendon, you keep Blair's phone on you. I want to be able to reach you. I'll be on my way within thirty minutes. If anything changes, let me know."

Kate still sat on the floor, not able to find the strength to rise. She punched in Jim's number. She needed to let him know she was going.

"Hey, Kate. Sorry I'm running late. This project in Gerard ran longer than—"

"Blair's been stabbed. She's at New York-Presbyterian Queens. I've got to get to her."

"I'm leaving now. Wait for me."

"I can't. You're forty-five minutes away. I can be halfway to Portland before you get here. I can catch the train there to New York."

"I'll meet you in Portland then. I don't want you going to New York by yourself."

"Thanks, Jim." Kate disconnected and using both hands pushed herself off the floor. Not graceful, but it worked. She pulled a small bag, one of her replacement purchases, from the closet and put in overnight essentials. While she and Blair replaced skin care products and toiletries when Kate had visited her daughter in New York, still she didn't have much, and it didn't take her long to throw together a small bag. She grabbed her coat, purse, and keys to her new rental and set out toward Portland, praying the young man was correct and Blair would be all right.

* * * *

Saturday, October 5

Blair blinked her eyes. Oh jeez, she ached. What was wrong? She wanted to move her body, but it didn't respond to her brain. Ohhhh. She hurt.

"Blair. Blair, honey. You're in the hospital. You were stabbed. You're going to be okay, but you've lost a lot of blood. The blade missed vital organs, but…"

That sounded like JD. She turned her gaze toward the sound of the voice she loved to hear. He lifted her hand and kissed the palm.

"You had me pretty scared."

Sweet man. Like she'd thought. She wanted to ask him something….

* * * *

She batted her eyes open. Where was she? Had JD been here? Had he kissed her hand?

"Well, Missy, it's about time you came around." The brisk voice scolded her.

"Water?"

"Ice chips are all you get for a while, then water," the

voice declared.

Had she spoken? Or was the nurse clairvoyant?

The lovely ice chips soothed her parched throat. Her gaze followed the gray-haired woman busying around her bed, looking at the wires and tubes, writing on the chart.

"Mom?"

"Your mom's not here, sweetie. She's on her way, and your young man has only left you when we insisted. He's outside in the hall waiting for me to let him back in. Feel like sitting up?"

Did she? Only way to know was to try. After raising the bed, the nurse slid her hands under her arms and Blair swore the woman must work out. She was certain the nurse did all the work of repositioning her. Blair went along for the ride. The nurse went out the door and then JD entered.

She smiled, but maybe not. JD looked worried. She concentrated. There she must've done it.

He smiled back at her. "Have I ever told you what a beautiful smile you have?" JD brushed his fingers across her hand.

* * * *

Kate was grateful Jim had insisted on meeting her. She hadn't been looking forward to navigating the subways by herself. Oh, she'd had no problem when she and John lived in the city. She'd found it a challenge to figure out what the fastest way possible was to make a trip requiring multiple changes. You could cut the commute time if you knew exactly where to stand on the platform. She'd been quite good at the game. But now...well, a lot had changed.

Thank God for cell phones. She and Jim found each other at the train station in Portland with no problem.

"Thanks for coming with me, Jim."

"Of course. I wouldn't let you go through this by yourself."

His grip on her hand was comforting. She'd make it through anything with him by her side. Oh, my. She could be in a great deal of trouble here. It wasn't good to depend on anyone that much. She knew better than others how quickly a loved one could be ripped from your life. The devastation. The emptiness. The yawning chasm in front of you. To realize you'd never ever see that person again. Touch him. Hold him. Be held by him. The aching void could devour you.

She'd let that happen to her after John's death. It should've helped that she wasn't alone in her loss. But that didn't help. It was like her loss got swallowed up in the country's loss and then paled into insignificance. Except to her.

"We're here, Kate. Let's get to the hospital and check on Blair."

Within another thirty minutes, they walked into the hospital, and a volunteer showed them to Blair's room.

"I'll wait here if you want."

He was always considerate of her feelings. "No, you come to."

The white sheets had nothing on the whiteness of Blair's face where she lay in the hospital bed. A red headed young man in a police officer's uniform sat in a chair next to the bed, holding her daughter's hand. He rose, but retained his hold.

"Ms. Thompson, I'm JD McClendon. Blair's doing well." He spoke in soft tones not to disturb her daughter.

Kate mentally noted the young man's interest in Blair while she made the introductions, then she moved to the left side of the bed and lifted her daughter's other hand. She brushed hair from Blair's forehead. One tear after another slid from Kate's eyes. She'd almost lost her beautiful girl. That indeed would've killed her.

Jim's arm around her shoulder brought comfort. Clicks and wheezes from machines broke the silence in the room. Her daughter had an awful lot of tubes connected to her for someone JD said was going to be fine.

"Hmm." A small noise from her daughter. Blair's eyes blinked open. They sought JD first.

"Hey, you've got company." JD didn't speak with a New York accent. Kate would have to ask where he was from. Apparently, Blair found his voice charming, judging from the grin she sent him.

"Blair." Young love was wonderful, but Kate wanted to see Blair's eyes herself. Her daughter rewarded her.

"Ah, Mom. Thanks for coming."

"Sweetie, you thought I wouldn't?" She leaned in and kissed Blair's cheek.

"And Jim. Thanks for getting Mom here."

"Do we know what happened?" Jim the practical one asked.

"We drove to Blair's in a taxi after supper, and I asked the driver to wait while I walked her inside. All three locks were secure. I heard them all click when she re-locked them. I'd climbed back into the cab and we pulled away when I noticed Blair's phone lying on the seat. Thank God, she dropped it and I found it. I made the cabby turn around. When I went back to return it, she didn't answer my knocks. I kicked in the door and found Blair lying on the floor by her closet with a stab wound in her stomach. Called 911 and did what I could to stop the bleeding."

"Do you remember anything about the attack, Blair?" Jim asked.

She shook her head. "Hu-uh. Last I remember is hanging my coat then waking here."

"Now, Missy, time for you to catch up on your rest." A nurse bustled in. "I knew your mom needed to see you, but she can come back tomorrow. We'll keep a close eye on her.

She's not out of the woods, but definitely improved over where she was when she arrived. Her young man saved her life for sure. If he hadn't returned, I'm afraid our young lady would've bled out."

Her stark words sent pain spiraling through Kate's insides, and her knees grew wobbly. Her fingers clutched Jim's strong arm. It was one thing to worry your daughter might die and another to hear a medical professional proclaim how close she'd come to losing her daughter.

Like a drill sergeant, the nurse rushed them out with assurances they could return the next day. Kate found herself outside her daughter's room with Jim and JD.

"Thank you hardly seems sufficient under the circumstances, JD." Kate shook his hand. "Would you like to join us for breakfast?"

"Yes, thanks. We can compare notes on what's been going on. Blair's told me some. There's a small Mom & Pop cafe not far."

"Comfort food sounds great to me. Do you know of a place that would be close to the hospital where we could stay? I'm sure Blair's is off limits for a time."

"Right. It's a crime scene. There's a Hallston Inn not far."

"That'll work." Jim said. He kept Kate close. Between the two men, Kate felt safe.

Over the crispy sizzling bacon, fluffy pancakes, and hot coffee, she dug for clues about Blair's relationship with JD. The men mostly talked about what had been going on back in Griffin Harbor. The officer impressed her with his clear-headed thinking.

"If the deaths in Griffin Harbor are connected to the land development deal—"

"Which we all believe." Jim interrupted.

"I knew I was taking a chance by telling everyone I was keeping part of the land and turning over a portion of it to the Conservancy Trust. Despite the earlier attack on Blair, it never crossed my mind this could spill over on her again."

"The first was sending you a message, Ms. Thompson. This was different."

"Is there any chance it's not connected, and this was a thief who broke in?" Jim sipped his coffee.

"Nothing was taken. Not a thing. All her appliances are intact, television, laptop, all the way she left them. The apartment isn't torn up, no drawers pulled out or belongings scattered in the rooms. We found a pane in a side window that had been cut out where the perp made his entrance and exit." His hands clenched recounting what he'd found.

"Damn." Jim set his cup down. "This is my entirely fault. I shouldn't have practically kidnapped you and forced you to go to Maine."

"You didn't kidnap me." She patted Jim's arm and shot a grin at JD. "Jim's exaggerating. It's true I didn't want to go to Maine, but I did want to visit with Blair. You assisted me in doing that, and I'm grateful. I don't fly," she threw in the young man's direction.

"Blair told me. I'm sorry for your loss, Ms. Thompson."

"Thank you. Call me Kate, please."

JD nodded. "So let me summarize to check if I've got this right. Your aunt was killed. She left the property to you. She was opposed to letting a development company get hold of it, but never put that in her will."

The waitress stopped at their table. "More coffee?" Everyone nodded. After refilling their cups, she moved to another table.

"She told people in Griffin Harbor that was her plan." Jim jumped into the story. "She and Mildred, the other woman who was murdered, both served on the town committee that made land use decisions."

"Who benefited from their deaths?"

"Well, I guess I did from Liddy's. I inherited the land."

"No one suspects you had anything to do with this, Kate." Jim squeezed her hand. "The developer Ray Holland should've been the one to benefit after Liddy was killed. The numbers were evenly split between supporters of development and conservationists. After her death, the odds increased in his favor of getting the approval he needed for his project."

"I assume your police or sheriff's deputies looked into his alibi?" JD asked.

"He's solid for the time of both deaths."

"So maybe he has someone working for him. Can you check the background of everyone working for him?" JD sipped his coffee.

"I'll ask the police if they've done that. I assume so, but maybe not."

"Trust but verify is my motto. Well, it's my mother's, but I've seen it work out so many times, I adopted it."

"Are your parents both alive, JD?"

"Yes. Dad's a professor at NYU and Mom writes children's books. They moved up here from Kansas after I got my job, and we've got other relatives here."

"What made you decide to be a police officer? If you don't mind my asking."

"I lost one uncle on 9/11 and another was badly injured. One was a firefighter and one a police officer. Family members fought all the time over which service was best. Lots of people did a ton of good work that day and in the days and months that followed. I connected with the police officers."

"How did your folks react to that idea?"

"They were proud and scared. I'm not always going to be a beat cop. I'm planning to become a homicide detective."

"Good for you, son. I'm going to call Seth and make sure he checked on Holland's employees." He stepped outside the café.

"So you and Blair have only known each other for a few weeks?"

"That's right. I returned her purse to her the morning after the mugging."

Kate repressed a shiver at his terminology. Certainly better than the stabbing Blair was now victim of.

"Why do you ask?"

He was certainly a direct young man. She decided to respond that way. "You seem close to Blair. The nurse said you'd been there since the ambulance brought her to the hospital."

"Sometimes it's not the amount of time that counts."

Hard to argue with him on that. Look at her and Jim. She nodded. "I appreciate all you've done for her. You did save her life."

"I've been kicking myself for not going in and checking out her apartment before I left her there. She's in a fairly safe neighborhood, and all three of her locks were good."

"Don't second guess yourself, JD. We all do the best we can in any situation."

He nodded. "Thanks."

"Well, we've got movement on the case." Jim rejoined

them at the table. "Sheriff Stigler had news. When they were checking on Holland's employees, they learned that Holland's father had died. Ray Holland was in pretty bad shape. He kept mumbling about a man who worked for him, saying, 'He better not have. He better not have.'"

"Who was the man?" JD asked.

"His name was Kenny Gouge. The cops found out he'd been in prison. He'd known both Hollands for his entire life. The senior Holland had been like a second father for him."

"The police believe Gouge killed Mr. Holland's father?" Kate shoved away her cold cup of coffee. She'd had enough she'd be wired for days now. "That doesn't make sense. From the story you told, he would more likely have been fond of the man."

"How did Mr. Holland die?" JD asked.

"It looks like natural causes. He had Alzheimer's, and recently had a stroke. The thing was he was particular about his pillows. The nurses said he wanted his head on one and not the other. When they found him his head was on the pillow he didn't like on top."

"Any surveillance cameras in the nursing home?"

JD's questions were right on. He'd make a good detective. Did Kate want her daughter tied up with a policeman or detective? Probably not what she would've chosen, but she didn't get to choose.

"Not many, but they're running them now."

"Poor Mr. Holland. Lost the land he wanted and now lost his father."

"You're a kind hearted person, Kate. Holland is a rough and tumble businessman." Jim patted her hand.

"You say your aunt was poisoned and the other woman on your town committee was strangled. Do you suppose there's more than one suspect?"

"Good question, JD. You're thinking if it was one killer he'd use the same method?"

"Yeah, that would be standard for a serial killer. This is either more than one person or someone who is not a regular murderer."

His words sent ice through Kate's veins. How could she be sitting here with someone calmly talking about this. She put both hands on the table and pushed herself up. "I've had enough. All this talk about regular murderers makes me gag."

Both men rose. Jim's arm came around her waist.

"I'm sorry, Ms. Thompson. I should've checked my language."

She swallowed a couple of times before finding words. "Nothing to apologize for, JD, except I'm Kate. Remember?"

He nodded. "I've got a shift to fill. How long do you plan to stay? I'd like to touch base with you before you return to Maine."

"I'll stay until Blair can move home. Can you stay that long, Jim?"

"I can't stay but another day. Let's get you set up where I feel comfortable leaving you, and I'm sure you can get around safely."

"Jim, I'm not an invalid. I'll manage. I'll do whatever Blair needs."

"I can help." The young officer seemed committed to her daughter.

"Okay. Thanks, J.D. Well, let's find a place to sleep tonight."

"The Hallston Inn is around the corner from the hospital. It's got suites. You'd be comfortable there." JD led them out of the café.

"Let's head over there then and get settled." Would she ever get tired of Jim's hand on the small of her back? No and she'd miss it when it wasn't there.

CHAPTER THIRTEEN

Friday, October 11

Kate sat on Jim's porch and enjoyed the view. The last week had been a marathon of worry about Blair, who thanks to being strong and in great shape made a quick recovery. They'd searched for and found Blair a new apartment. JD had been invaluable. He'd brought along his police buddies, and they got her moved with what looked like little effort at all.

The new apartment was located on the second floor and the building had a doorman. Everyone agreed it was much safer. More expensive and smaller than her other one, but the safety factor was of primary importance.

Blair was pleased with their choice. The apartment needed her touches of course, and the stronger she grew the more she'd be able to focus on that. She had visitors from work. Kate got to meet Blair's immediate boss. It made her proud to hear all the good things everyone said about her daughter.

So now, Kate was back home. Oh, well, not exactly

home. She was here at Jim's house. If the cottage hadn't been burned down, she'd be there, but it had. Before Kate left New York, she and Blair talked again about the land. Both wanted to keep that small piece where the cottage looked out over the water. The rest could go to the Conservancy Trust if they promised to maintain an access for them to get to the property.

Columbus Day holiday weekend brought an increased number of visitors to Griffin Harbor with its apple and lobster festivals a big draw. The festivities ran through Monday. Tuesday she planned to sign the papers, and then it would be time to go home. Home to Texas. Where her heart might break.

But this time, she knew she'd recover. Given time, the heart always healed.

"Hi, Kate!"

Her heart rate kicked up at the sound of Jim's voice. "Hey. You were gone longer than I expected."

He set a bag on the table in front of her—the sweet cinnamon aroma made her stomach growl—and he settled onto the loveseat on the front porch next to her.

"The walking bridge is single lane both ways and moving slowly for folks stopping to take pictures. Just nuts. Nobody bothered you, did they?"

"No. We've had more tourists than usual walking by, but

who can blame them on such a gorgeous day? Want a cup of coffee to go with the sweet rolls? I want to reheat mine."

"Thanks. That'd be great. I promise not to eat them all while you're gone." He stretched out his long legs in front and leaned his head against the back of the loveseat.

"You better not. Be back in a jiffy."

Kate maneuvered through the darkened living room and made for the kitchen toward the back of the house. If she were to stay here, not that Jim had asked, she'd want to take on a remodeling project and make the space more open. What Jim had done was okay, but he basically stuck with the old layout. From her personal experience and from watching HGTV, moving walls was a definite option if you wanted to and had enough money.

She loved the convenience of the quick perk machines, where you popped in a small container and voila! Out came a perfectly perked cup of coffee. Hers was ready, now for Jim's.

"Don't scream. Come with me."

"Not funny." She whirled around to find not Jim but a strange man standing by the back door. In his hand, he held a gun. Her heart jerked, lightening zapped down her arms. "Who are you? Get out of here." Going with this guy wasn't an option. He could kill her here, but she was dead for sure if she let him drag her off somewhere.

"Why couldn't you sell my boss your land? Nice and

easy. What do you want with it anyway? You're not from here."

"But it's my land. I get to decide. I'm sorry your boss was disappointed, but there must be plenty of other gorgeous parcels of land available." She was proud not a whit of trembling that coursed through her body showed up in her voice. If she could keep him talking, maybe Jim would get suspicious about how long she was taking and check on her. But then he could get hurt. Her heartbeat fluttered at the base of her throat at the picture of Jim lying on the floor, bleeding.

She wanted to look around for a weapon, but was afraid to take her gaze from the man with the gun. The cast iron skillet sat in its usual spot on top of the stove, but she'd have to move toward the crazy man to get close enough to make a grab for it. She didn't want to get closer to him for fear her movements would make him suspicious.

"But he wanted this land. He could make more from this land. He'd needed it to keep his old man in that fancy nursing home."

"I've heard his father died. I'm sorry for his loss." Maybe not a safe topic, but staying in the house and talking was preferable to leaving with him.

He nodded. "Yeah. Finally exhaled his last breath. It was quiet, you know? Less trouble than with the old lady."

Kate's mouth went dry. The earlier trembling was

nothing compared to what she felt now. How long would her legs support her? She put out a hand and grasped the counter. A whimper struggled to escape. She clamped her jaws together.

"With your daughter dead, and you gone, he can have your land and build his condos. I may get one of them. Nice view from your land."

He waved his gun at her. "Come with me. We've talked enough."

"You can't get away with this. The town is full of folks here for the holiday." Her feet wouldn't move. It was like they were set in concrete.

What could she do to stall? Should she tell him about Jim? Should she scream? The man had told her not to, and he had a gun. Her palms grew sweaty. Her breathing became erratic. Not a good thing. If she screamed, would he kill her and then go after Jim? Dear God. What should she do?

"What if I sign the land over to your boss right now?" If she kept him talking, she'd be better off, right?

The man cocked his head at her. His eyebrows drew together. "Can you do that?"

"Sure. It's my land." She gulped in a shallow breath. "I can do anything I like. The contract's in the front room." She backed away one step. How would he respond? Her heartbeat fluttered in her throat. She rubbed her palms down her pants as she eased another step away from him.

"My boss would love that. But I can't let you live even if you give him the land because you know what I look like."

Kate swallowed on a dry mouth, nearly gagging at his words. "I have a very bad memory. Like you said, this isn't my home. I'll sign over the land and return to Texas." Kate continued to inch away. The man with the gun stalked her. Dear God, please let Jim have left the porch so he's not visible to the gunman through the windows.

"My boss will be really happy with me if we can make this happen."

Kate stopped at the desk in the large living room and never let her gaze slide to the windows. "I've got the contract right here in this drawer."

The man studied her closely. "Pull it out slowly. Don't try anything."

Like what could she try? All she knew to do was stall for time. "Here it is. It's made out to the Maine Coast Conservancy Trust. I'll scratch out their name." She grabbed a pen from the holder on the desk and drew a line. "See, it's done. Now I'll write in your boss' name. Ray Holland. My initials mean I approve this change."

"You gotta sign all of the damn pages. I don't want any confusion."

"All right." Kate leaned over and with her hand shaking,

she signed each page. Where was Jim?

"Hurry up."

"There are a lot of pages." Did she hear a floorboard creak? Did this crazy man hear it? Was it Jim?

"Here you go." She spoke loudly and swished the papers, hoping to distract him. "Now your boss has to file the papers at the courthouse, and then the land will be his."

"Good deal." He raised his gun. "I don't need you anymore."

Whomp! The cast iron skillet came down on his head with enough force to kill him. The gun went off, and a sharp pain stung Kate's head. She collapsed to the floor.

* * * *

"Kate, Kate. Talk to me. Open your eyes. Tom, she's not coming to."

Tom put his hand on Jim's shoulder. "It will be okay. Looks like a graze. The ambulance is on the way. It's taking longer because of all the people in town for the holiday."

The siren in the distance was a comforting sound. Jim cradled Kate in his arms. She had to be all right. How could she consider staying here with all the bad that had dogged her steps? Not that he'd asked her. What a fool he was, and now he'd gotten her shot.

"Sir, step away. Let us look at her."

The police and emergency personnel arrived.

Jim rose and backed away, not taking his gaze from Kate.

"What happened, Jim?" Tom asked.

"Kate was gone a long time getting the coffee. I had a bad feeling."

"Good thing you paid attention to your gut."

"Yeah, but I shot her, Tom."

"You didn't shoot her. Stop saying that." He looked at the police officer and shook his head.

"Go on." The officer encouraged.

"I came in through the back, but she wasn't in the kitchen. I heard voices from the front room. Her voice trembled. With all that's been happening, I decided I needed a weapon, but my gun is locked in a drawer in the bedroom, so I picked up the skillet, figuring it was better than nothing. The guy lying on the floor held a gun in his hand pointed at Kate. He was going to shoot her. I swung, and he dropped like a net broke on a ton of fish."

"Excuse me, officer. We're moving her to the hospital in Gerard."

And they whisked her away. That was comforting. If she'd been serious, she'd have gone to Portland.

"The man is dead, but when she regains consciousness, if she confirms your side of the story, we probably won't file charges," the officer said.

"Is he free to go right now?" Tom asked.

"Yeah. Not like we don't know him."

"Let me drive you to the hospital, Jim."

"Thanks."

"We'll probably meet you there. We want to hear the first thing Ms. Thompson has to say."

"What? You're concerned we're going to put words in her mouth?"

The officer touched his finger to his hat in a salute and left Jim's house.

"Jim." Tom patted his shoulder. "It's okay. They're doing their job. Let's go."

* * * *

It was the longest forty-five minute drive Jim could remember. Worse than when it snowed and the trip literally lasted more than two hours.

The police talked with Kate before they were able to see her. The good thing about that was it meant she'd come to and when the officers came out, they stopped and nodded to Jim.

"She confirmed your story. Don't expect any charges to follow."

"Thanks. That's a relief, but I was terrified he was about to shoot her."

"It certainly appears you're right based on all Ms.

Thompson told us."

"Are you Mr. Donovan?" a starchy nurse asked.

"Yes."

"Ms. Thompson can see you."

"Thank God."

"One at a time, okay. She's going to be okay, but it's been a trauma."

"You go on, Jim. I'll wait here." Tom slouched into one of the chairs in the emergency waiting room.

Jim nodded and followed the nurse who held open a door. She led him to a curtained cubicle. When he pulled the curtain aside, Kate's sparkling brown eyes rewarded him.

"Hey." She spoke softer than her usual strong tone.

"Hey, yourself. What am I going to do with you? Can't let you roam off by yourself in the house without you getting into trouble."

She smiled. "I told the police officers you saved my life." She looked down then up at him. "They said the man was dead."

"Yeah." Jim nodded. Hadn't this woman had enough trauma in her life? Damn. "I called Blair to let her know what happened. She wanted to come. I told her to wait to hear what the doc said."

"Good she needs to take care of herself."

Kate reached her hand toward him. He clasped it in

both of his. "I told the police this, but I want you to know. He confessed to killing an old lady. I assume that's either Mildred or Liddy. He also killed poor Mr. Holland's father."

"Poor Mr. Holland?"

"Apparently, this man wanted to help Holland and decided when it looked like the land deal wasn't going through to get rid of his father, eliminating a financial burden. All the other murders and attempts were to get me to sell the land to Holland. I'd signed the papers to Holland just before you crept in through the kitchen. I couldn't reach the skillet or I'd have taken a swing."

"Remember our discussion about you learning how to shoot and to carry a gun? I'm sorry I didn't push you on that."

"But Jim I was home. I probably wouldn't have been walking around with one strapped on my hip."

"Speaking of home, when do they say we can spring you?" His heart swelled at her reference to his house as home. Maybe there was hope yet for them.

"Any time now. I need someone to keep an eye on me and to occasionally wake me up."

"I volunteer for that job. And on the way back, I'll sit in the back seat and cradle your head on my lap."

"Do you have a chauffeur since I last noticed?"

"Tom drove me. He was afraid I'd run the car off the road in my haste to get here."

"Well, for heaven's sake. Go get him." She fluttered her hands at him.

"Ahyah."

She laughed but grabbed her head.

"Sorry."

"Go get him."

Jim stuck his head out of the door. "Come here. Kate wants to see you."

"Yep." He stepped through the door. "Hey, pretty lady. How're you feeling?"

Kate gripped his hand, drew him down, and kissed his cheek. "Thank you for driving Jim here."

"You're welcome. Glad to be of help. He was pretty much a nut case." His chuckle spoke of a long-time friendship.

"All right, Ms. Thompson. We're ready to kick you out. Have sicker people in need of this bed. You're going home with one of these gentlemen, I presume? Or perhaps both?" The nurse chuckled. "My, my."

"She'll be going home with me." Jim stated in his courthouse voice.

"Well, here are your instructions." She handed him a sheet of paper. "Follow them exactly, and if there are any complications, bring her right back here."

"Got it."

* * * *

Sunday, October 13

Kate sat on Jim's porch talking on her cell with Blair. Hard to believe what all had happened in such a short time. "Glad you're doing okay, sweetie."

"How are you, Mom?"

"About good as new. My headache's gone and I feel amazingly well. Jim and I are going into town later for the lobster fest and fair. I've promised Jim, I'll try to eat a real lobster."

"Really, Mom? This thing y'all have must be serious if you're talking about eating a bug." A chuckle from Blair. "You're so funny to call it that."

"That's what it reminds me of." She paused, drew in a deep breath. "How would you feel about it if something developed between Jim and me?"

"I'd love it, Mom. Your friends and I have always wanted you to find someone."

Kate thought about all the men her friends had thrown her way. None of them stuck. Now she'd been in Maine right at a month and...well anything was possible.

"I'm sorry all this has happened to you, Blair. It's my fault for coming here and dragging you into the decision making."

"Hey, Mom. It's okay. Good things come from bad stuff. You've met Jim and I've met JD. I probably never would've if the guy hadn't snatched my purse."

"He did seem pretty taken with you. You like him a lot?"

"Yeah, Mom, I do. I'm pretty sure it's mutual."

Kate chuckled. "I agree based on the way he looked at you and how he hovered. He's a keeper."

"Well, see. It's all good then?"

"Yes, it's all good."

"You let me know how you do with the lobster."

"Will do. Take care." Kate disconnected, smiling at what might be ahead for her daughter.

"What's all good? Didn't mean to eavesdrop. I came out to tell you it was time to walk into town, and you were on the phone. I didn't want to interrupt."

Kate patted the seat on the swing next to her. "Life is all good."

He sat and spread his arm across her shoulders and snuggled her close. "Glad to hear you say that. I haven't wanted to push you, but what are we going to do about us?"

"Us, like in you and me?"

"Yes, us. You and me together. We'll sign the land papers on Tuesday. Do you and Blair have plans to start to rebuild the cottage right away? Are you heading back to Texas right away? Can I convince you to stay?"

"That's a lot of questions, Jim."

"Yeah, I want to know where we stand. We've known

each other a month, but—"

"It's been pretty intense. Can we agree we've had at least three-months-worth experience wise?"

"Works for me. People get engaged after three months all the time. It's not so unseemly fast which a month would be."

Kate turned and looked at him. "Jim?" Was he doing what she hoped he was doing?

"I'm not doing this well. Let me try again. Kate Thompson, will you marry me? I promise not to require you eat a whole lobster."

Kate cocked her head at him. Guess he didn't have a lot of practice at this. A good thing. "So if I say no, do I have to eat the whole lobster? Interesting bribe. Either way, I say yes, I will marry you, Jim Donovan."

He grabbed her and pulled her to him in a crushing embrace, smothering her lips and face with kisses, sending chill bumps scampering along her arms. Then he trailed kisses down her neck while his hands wandered down between her legs.

"Wait, wait!"

"No, you can't change your mind. You've said yes."

"I'm not changing my mind, only our location." She slid off the swing and drew his hand to her mouth where she sucked each finger. "How about we take this discussion into the bedroom."

"I'm right behind you."

* * * *

Later when they were deliciously sated with each other, Kate leaned across his chest. "Does this mean I don't have to eat the bug?"

Jim laughed. "How about a lobster roll instead?"

"Works for me." She flopped back on the bed. "You know, we have lots of decisions to make. Like where will we live? How do I keep working? I love my job. If I stay here all year, how will I manage winter? What about my friends in Texas?"

Jim propped up in the bed. "We don't have to answer those all right now, Kate, but we'll have some explaining to do if we don't show up for the lobster fest."

"And my lobster roll. Yes sir." She hopped from the bed and made for the shower, but he followed her, and they did come near to missing the lobster fest, which drew a few raised eyebrows from the townspeople.

CHAPTER FOURTEEN

Friday, November 1

The whole town had celebrated on hearing the news three weeks ago that Kate and Jim were getting married. Blair was thrilled for her mother. Apparently, she'd been more worried about her than Kate ever realized. They'd decided to rebuild the cottage, with the goal of having it ready for a Memorial Day picnic. Kate wasn't sure they could pull that off. A lot depended on the weather and how much time she spent back in Texas dealing with things there, but it was good to have goals.

In the past, Kate's goals revolved around buying and selling homes and taking care of her parents and Blair. That didn't leave much time for any personal goals after she factored in being there for her three friends. The way they'd been there for her.

Blair was right. Bad stuff happened, but good could come from that. Kate settled back in her comfortable train compartment. She'd come a long way since her life imploded with the attack on the World Trade Center and the Pentagon. Would she have been as brave as the people who crashed the plane in Pennsylvania? Hopefully, she would, but she didn't know….God bless all their families.

Jim hadn't rushed her for a decision, but everyone in town kept asking those same questions she'd asked. Blair asked. Addie, Kim, and Devon asked. How would they live their life? Would they fly back and forth between Maine and Texas? (Not that Kate flew, but Jim flew.)

Kate traveled on the train about three-and-a-half days. A day to get to Chicago with an overnight and then two days to Fort Worth. Jim had wanted to drive her, but she insisted on doing the trip by herself. After all, if they decided to keep two residences, her traveling options were limited. She couldn't expect Jim to take off from work whenever she wanted to see her friends. She had two choices. Get used to the long train trip by herself or fly.

Well, that wasn't happening. Kate sipped her iced tea. Riding the train provided a variety of scenery and plenty of time for reflection, which she needed. Reflection and seeing her three good friends to get their input on how to make her life work.

The train chugged into the station in downtown Fort Worth at almost five in the afternoon. A wreck on the track had delayed them three hours. One of them would be there to meet her. Kate packed and gathered up the remnants of snacks from her trip and stuffed them into a side pocket of her suitcase. She walked into the terminal pulling one bag behind her. More people than she expected and slowly the crowds parted and not one but all three friends swarmed her.

"Oh, Kate, you look fantastic." Addie hugged her first. Her long brunette hair flew around her perfectly oval face.

Kim, in a full-length mink hugged her next. "We're glad your home, but Hon, you need a heavier coat." She eyed Kate's khaki car coat.

Devon with red wisps of hair escaping a cap pulled low against an early cold front held her the longest. "I've missed you."

"All of you didn't have to come, but this is such a lovely surprise. I've missed you. Where's everyone staying?"

Laughter loud enough to turn heads burst from her friends. "Your house."

"Well, great. That will give us all plenty of time to catch up. Do I have anything to eat there or should we stop on the way home."

"We've got it covered, Kate." Addie linked an arm through Kate's.

"Are you staying here, too, Addie?"

"You betcha. This is a regular girls' weekend. Mike understands I'm not available, but he sends his love and congratulations. He says he's looking forward to meeting your Yankee."

"Aw, he's a sweetie."

Addie laughed. "I won't tell him you said that. It doesn't fit his homicide detective persona."

"We'll keep it a secret then. Oh, I can't wait to catch up with all of you and to get your advice."

"Well, we're always glad to share that." Kim laughed. "Did you have lunch on the train?"

"Just snacks."

"Well, let's get home and eat. Then we'll be happy to give you the answers you seek." Kim led the way to her large SUV.

"No driver, Kim?" Kate asked.

"I gave him the day off so we could talk and giggle to our hearts content. If we go out at night, he'll drive, and we don't have to be careful about how much we drink."

They all laughed. None of them were huge drinkers, but it paid to be safe. Kate sighed. She'd missed them. While Addie was the only one in town, they all kept up with each other's lives through social media. They shared meals once a month or so, plus their girls' trips a couple of times a year, when they'd traveled all over by train or car in deference to Kate's fear of flying.

They chatted the whole trip and before she knew it, Kim

pulled up in the driveway of Kate's house. Nice to be home. She led the way inside. Everyone carrying something meant they got everything inside in one trip.

"You don't have much, Kate." Devon lifted a bag onto Kate's bed.

"Everything I packed for the trip burned in the fire." Her friends shuddered.

"We're grateful you're okay." Kim hugged Kate again.

"Kate, you unpack." Addie stuck her head around the door. "Gals, you help me finish up the meal. Then we can give her the third degree while we devour the wonderful stew I've made." The other two friends nodded and they left Kate alone in her room.

Several years after losing John, Kate had redecorated the bedroom. It had always seemed cozy to her, but now it felt cold and empty. She missed Jim.

Well, she couldn't have everything. Her friends here or Jim in Maine? It was Jim of course. She'd have to figure a way to come back for frequent visits, and they'd have to come to Maine for the wedding for sure. Kate unpacked quickly and hurried to join her friends.

Addie had outdone herself. Steam rose from the bowls on the dining room table. If no one had been hungry, the lovely aroma of onions and garlic wafting through the room would've made them ravenous. They settled in to do justice to her efforts. Addie had paired the stew with a mixed greens salad and French bread toasted in the oven.

Kate loved hearing about their lives on the ride from the train station but now it was her turn. She brought them up to date on the happenings in Maine, emphasizing her relationship with Jim and with seeing Blair and the breakthrough she'd had in New York City at the 9/11 Museum and Memorial Gardens.

"So all of the troubles, the murders, attacks, and the burned house were because of the misguided loyalty of a friend of the developer?" Addie went right to the point.

"And because Aunt Liddy never put in her will that she wanted the Maine Coast Conservancy Trust to have the land. Let that be a lesson to us, ladies. If we want something done with our property, we need to put it in our wills."

"But if she'd done that, Kate, Jim wouldn't have written or come to get you. You'd have never met." Kim sipped her wine.

"You might never have gone to New York and resolved your fears." Devon wiped away a tear about to slide down her cheek.

"Devon, are you all right?" Kate studied her friend. They'd all shed a few tears over the story and shuddered at the dangers she and Blair had experienced, Devon seemed especially moved.

"Yes, yes. I got misty eyed for a moment. Everything is

fine."

She didn't meet any of her friends' gazes, and Kate resolved to speak to her privately before the visit was over.

They all helped clean up after supper regaling each other with stories from camp. Devon was the only one who didn't laugh uproariously with the others. Something was clearly bothering her.

They settled in front of the fireplace in the living room, each with her signature drink. Addie drank Sauvignon Blanc, Kim drank her cab, and Kate her merlot, but Devon again skipped her regular champagne and instead sipped the same wine Addie drank.

"So are you going to marry Jim, Kate, or will y'all live together?" Kim asked

"You know how conventional she is. She'd never agree to that, though she might be better off without all the legal entanglements of marriage." Devon tossed back her wine, refilled her glass, and crossed to stare into the fire.

Kate glanced at her other friends. They all had matching raised eyebrows. What was going on with Devon? She was normally the romantic of the group. This was unlike her.

"Well, where are you going to live? Have you decided that?" Kim must've thought it was best to ignore Devon's outburst. And so they did.

"I've wavered back and forth, but I think we'll have to

live in Maine in Jim's home which had been his grandparents' house. I'll hate not being here near y'all, but—"

"Oh, my gosh." Devon whirled from the fire. "You're not going to be here? I hate that. Maine is halfway across the country. I'll never be able to see you!"

Kate rose and crossed to her friend. "Of course, you'll see me. I want you all to come for the wedding. I can't get married without you. I felt like it would be easier for all of you" Kate gestured to her friends "and my work friends to make the trip than for many of Jim's friends to come here. They're not particularly affluent, but the salt of the earth types. They work hard and help others."

Starting with Addie, Kate's gaze met each of her friend's, "Will you and Mike come?"

"I'll be there. My artistic director and technical director can handle rehearsals and business so I can escape for a couple of days." She hugged Kate.

"What about you, Kim? Will you and Caine be able to make it?"

"I'll certainly be there. Don't want to speak for Caine. Besides, you haven't told us when."

"No, we can't decide. Maybe over the Thanksgiving holiday."

"What? That's less than a month off!" Addie shrieked.

"The airplane tickets will be exorbitant getting them this

close to leaving!" Devon set down her wine glass.

"We'll put you all up at our expense, Devon. You'll just need to buy the plane ticket." She'd balked at a plane ticket when Kate had asked her to visit earlier. Hmm. Something was certainly going on.

"That's the latest we can push it and even that's risky because of the weather. If we don't do it then, we'll have to push it into May or June."

"Why don't you do that then?" Devon asked.

"Probably because they're in love and want to make it official." Addie laughed. "Don't you remember what it was like when you and Franklin were first in love? You and Kim have been married for a long time and you've forgotten that first rush of wanting to be with your husband all the time. Kate and I've gotten a second chance at that feeling. It's remarkable!" Addie sipped her wine, a smile spread across her face.

Devon met Kim's gaze and then back to Addie and Kate. "Yeah. Well, maybe we have." She refilled her glass. "Listen, I'm going to turn in. Happy for you, Kate." She raised her glass and then turned and walked from the room. One hand clenched into a tight fist at her side.

"Do either of you know what's going on with Devon?" Kate asked.

"Not a clue." Kim shook her head. "She's been touchy ever since she arrived. It's like she's holding a lid on something that's about ready to explode."

"We were hoping she'd be able to keep it together and not spoil your homecoming." Addie slipped her arm around Kate's shoulder.

"Oh nothing could spoil the joy that flooded my heart on seeing all three of you together when I got off the train. That was...well, perfect."

"What about your job?" Kim asked. "Don't want to be a Debby Downer, but what would you do if something happened between you and Jim?"

"Ever practical Kim. Well, my plan is to study for the Maine real estate license and practice there."

"Good, good. Glad to hear that. Best to be prepared for all contingencies and count on yourself."

"Gosh, Kim, has whatever's bothering Devon rubbed off on you?" Addie shook her head. "This is supposed to be a celebration."

"Well, it is." Kate rose and hugged Kim then gestured for Addie to join them. "We're missing Devon, but only for a moment. I'll talk with her, and she'll be fine tomorrow."

* * * *

Saturday, November 2

Despite being home in her own bed, Kate didn't sleep well. She'd talked with both Blair and Jim before turning in, assuring them she was fine. In reality, she was worried about both Devon and Kim. They didn't have a positive attitude toward marriage. She and Addie seemed to be the glass half-filled gals in the group.

When she got downstairs to make the coffee, she found that Devon had already left. Guess she didn't want to talk about whatever was troubling her.

Her other two friends joined her and they fixed a full breakfast.

"Where'd you say Devon went?" Addie threw the question over her shoulder as she whipped the eggs with a whisk.

"Back to Dallas." Kate flipped the bacon in the skillet.

"Your scrambled eggs are the best, Addie. You ever going to share your secret?"

"No." Addie snapped a towel at Kim who sliced melon. "Be careful. I'm holding a knife."

Everyone laughed but became serious when Kim continued. "Devon has been acting unusual for a while. I asked her to come up to Wichita Falls for a fundraiser for one of my organizations. She's come often. It's the one for the pet shelter, a favorite of hers. She turned me down flat and didn't offer to send money."

Time to talk about something more positive. "I spoke with Jim this morning, and we've decided on the Saturday after Thanksgiving. That way folks can still do the holiday with their families, but have time to come up. I've been checking airplane schedules, and the tickets will cost more over the holidays, but there are still seats left." Kate handed a print out of info to Kim and Addie. "This shows times."

"Sounds like a good plan, Kate. I'll check with Mike today, so he can make arrangements to get off. Even if he can't make it, I'll be there for sure."

"Me, too. Kate. I won't speak for Cain, but I'll be there. I hate to flake off, but I need to get back to Wichita Falls. One of those fundraisers tonight." She rose, hugged Kate and Addie, and then left the dining room.

Both of them were silent for a while then Addie spoke. "Neither Kim nor Devon seem as upbeat as usual."

"Hopefully, they'll be able to work out whatever's bothering them." Kate sipped her coffee.

"Don't mean to bum out on you, but I should get home." Addie rose and carried the plates to the sink. "I have a stack of scripts my new Artistic Director wants me to check out. He's looking ahead to next season and we need to decide which shows we want to try to bring in."

"Thanks for helping, Addie." Kate opened the dishwasher and set the dishes in after Addie rinsed them. "I've got lots of cleaning out ahead of me. Figuring what goes in storage, what to sell, what to give away. Blair's already asked for a couple things that were her grandmother's. I'll only ship a few furniture pieces because Jim already has a perfectly good house."

"Won't you want to make a few changes?" Addie ran hot water in the skillet.

"Yes." She smiled. "Jim's been sweet. Says anything I want to change I can except for the large desk that was his grandfather's. He wants to keep that."

"How are you going to do all this with your house and plan the wedding?" Addie wiped off the kitchen table.

"Well, the wedding will be small." Kate put the remaining butter and jelly back in the refrigerator. "Just a few of his best friends from town and y'all and Blair. We'll have a reception at his friend Tom's restaurant, The Lobster Pot. Tom's feelings would've been hurt if we'd done anything else."

"You be sure to let me know if you need any help. Or if you need muscle, I'll get Mike to bring over a few of his police buddies to help with moving stuff."

"Thanks, Addie." With arms around each other's waists, they left the kitchen. Knowing deep down in their bones, they could always trust each other.

CHAPTER FIFTEEN

Saturday, November 24

Being married in Aunt Liddy's church by her minister made Kate feel like she'd come full circle. She'd have never met Jim, her wonderful new husband, if it hadn't been for Liddy. She glanced at the wide gold band on the ring finger of her left hand. She hadn't wanted diamonds. Shiny stuff attracted thieves.

It had been a simple ceremony. She wore a pumpkin colored, street length dress and carried a small bouquet of mums. Blair, dressed in a dark shade of peach had been by Kate's side. Tom stood with Jim; both wore suits. Blair brought JT. Looked like there might be another wedding in the family's future.

Two of Kate's three best friends had come. It was fun to see Addie with her husband Mike. They were still in that honeymoon phase themselves. Maybe because of all they'd gone through to reach their happily ever after. Kim came by herself without Cain, and she made no explanation about his absence.

Devon hadn't come. She'd called to say she couldn't get away from work. Kate hadn't pushed for details about what was troubling her. Devon wished Kate and Jim well. Whenever the problems bothering Devon and Kim got resolved, Kate would be completely happy.

She walked along the serving line. Tom had gone out of his way to put out a super spread for them. Including, of course, lobsters, but lobster rolls for her. He smiled and nodded to her from across the room, holding up one of his giant bugs. She laughed, waved, and turned her back.

"Is he teasing my bride?" Jim stepped up behind her, slipped his arms around her waist, and pulled her back against him.

She raised a hand to his cheek, since she couldn't quite turn her head enough for a kiss. "I do believe he is, but it's okay. He's laid out this awesome buffet for us. So if he wants to tease me with his lobsters, I'm okay with that."

"He's a good friend."

Jim spun her into his arms, and they danced to a love song played by a small combo. Then people cut in. Women wanted to dance with Jim, and men wanted to dance with her. A fun custom. They went on this way for three long dances. Kate was gasping when the fast music ended, and she found herself back with her husband.

"Wow, fun, but exhausting."

"Only fun because I ended up with you." Jim kissed her on the mouth. A sweet and tender touch filled with the promise of more. He led her to the bar. "You want to sit a minute?"

"Yes, thanks. How nice everyone wanted to celebrate with us." She perched on a barstool, holding Jim's hand in hers.

"Most of your friends came."

She nodded. "I'm lucky to have had them in my life for so many years."

"How about a beer and a wine?" Tom set an empty glass in front of her.

They both nodded. "Where're you taking her for a honeymoon?" Tom leaned across the bar and filled Kate's glass with her usual Merlot and set a frosted mug in front of Jim.

"We're driving to a bed and breakfast on Moosehead Lake. Beautiful views and not much to do there in the winter but snowshoe and make love."

Tom laughed and walked off to visit with the other guests.

A blush crawled up Kate's neck, but it wasn't her victim's blush this time, more from anticipation of being with Jim. Any place with Jim worked for her.

Blair and she had decided to continue to rent the

cottage after it was rebuilt, giving the Conservancy Trust all of the land except for where the cottage sat, and access to it by the road.

"Don't know how you were able to pull this off so fast, but I wasn't about to argue with you over a quick wedding." Jim sipped from the frosty mug. His lips were cold from the beer when he kissed the back of her hand. "God, I'm a lucky man."

A swell of warmth and longing started at her toes and moved up through her being. She trembled with the love she felt for this good man. She was the lucky one.

After 9/11, she'd never trusted anyone or anything, certainly not with her heart. Jim, his friends, and her friends provided safety and protection and love. Her act of trust in him allowing him to bring her to Maine had been her best decision ever.

The End

If you'd like to read more about the four friends, here's the blurb for ACT OF BETRAYAL, releasing in 2016.

Blurb for ACT OF BETRAYAL
Book 3 in the Second Chances Series

A self-employed cosmetics company owner in Dallas, **Devon Moore**, wants to save her company from bankruptcy, but her husband's embezzlement sends her into dangerous waters trying to pay back his clients, replace the money he stole from her company and keep her daughter and her parents safe.

Private Investigator, **Mark Townsend**, wants to find who is threatening his new client and locate the missing money. He suspects the beautiful Devon hasn't been completely honest with him. A wife has to know, doesn't she? When someone runs them off the road in the first of several attempts on her life, he has to adjust his thinking.

Despite Mark's initial doubts about whether Devon really knew about the money her husband stole, still he's attracted to the redheaded beauty and admires her love of her daughter for whom she will do anything. Their attraction for each other sizzles under the surface of all they do.

Will they reclaim the hidden money and find the bad guys in time to save her business and the lives of her daughter, parents, and Devon herself?

ABOUT THE AUTHOR

Marsha R. West, a retired elementary school principal, is also a former school board member and theatre arts teacher. She writes Romance, Suspense, and Second Chances. Experience Required. Marsha lives in Texas with her supportive lawyer husband. Their two daughters presented them with three delightful grandchildren who live nearby. Charley, a Chihuahua/Jack Russell Terrier mix recently adopted them.

MuseItUp Publishing e-released her first book, VERMONT ESCAPE, in July 2013, and her second book, TRUTH BE TOLD, in May 2014. In the fall of 2014, Marsha formed MRW Press LLC to provide a print version of her books. VERMONT ESCAPE and SECOND ACT are both available in print from Amazon.

SECOND ACT, The Second Chances Series, Book 1, is available in e-format and print from all vendors. It follows up with a supporting character from VERMONT ESCAPE and begins a four-part series.

ACT OF TRUST, The Second Chances Series, Book 2, with an expected release in January 2016, will be followed by ACT OF BETRAYAL and ACT OF SURVIVAL.

SNIPPETS OF SUSPENSE, Anthology #1 by the Sisters of Suspense, published in November 2015, contains the first chapter of SECOND ACT as well as nine first chapters by other romantic suspense authors. It's **FREE** on Amazon, KOBO, and Barnes & Noble. Great way to find new authors.

You can contact Marsha at marsha@marsharwest.com and find her at her web site http://www.authormarsharwest.com and www.sistersofsuspense.com

Sign up for her NEWSLETTER at http://eepurl.com/bBcimz https://www.facebook.com/#!/marsha.r.west @marsha.r.west http://www.twitter.com/Marsharwest @Marsharwest https://www.pinterest.com/marsharwest/

She'd appreciate a review and love to hear from you.

www.ingramcontent.com/pod-product-compliance
Lightning Source LLC
Chambersburg PA
CBHW062018170626
46813CB00001B/209